Miles and Sammie haven't seen each other since high school, and while they're able to reconnect and pick up right where they left off, their happy reunion is short-lived when Miles is bitten and turned by a werewolf. They find themselves working through budding feelings as the supernatural world sinks its claws further into their fragile lives.

With the help of an Alpha who takes Miles in to help him learn his new powers, they uncover a winding plot to start a war between their two worlds. They find a few friends and even more enemies along the way as they go from one near death experience to the next. They just hope they can survive long enough to figure out their fragile newfound love.

ALMOST HUMAN

Jo M. Aring

A NineStar Press Publication
www.ninestarpress.com

Almost Human

First Edition, June 2025

ISBN: 978-1-64890-874-3
Also available in eBook, ISBN: 978-1-64890-873-6

CONTENT WARNING:
This book contains graphic violence, gore, and the death of a secondary character.

Chapter One

"Miles!" The shout was drowned out by the sound of splintering wood, rumbling growls, and the feeling of his arm bending the wrong way as he landed on the old wood floor. Awesome. Really. This was just...the absolute best.

He groaned, wincing as he tried to get up, only for his arm to flare with pain from fingers to shoulder as soon as he moved it. "Dammit..." He looked up as footsteps approached, the hair on the back of his neck standing up. Crap. He was going to die. There'd been a lot of close calls, but this was it. Was he a little relieved? Maybe, if he was being honest with himself...

"Are you dead?" a familiar voice called, and he relaxed as a woman crouched through the hole he'd left in the cabin wall. She looked pretty battered from the fighting outside, black hair matted with blood by her temple, claw marks on her forearms and sides, one of her boots half bitten off, even. "Ooh, looks like you might be wishing you were—" She knelt beside him and blanched. "God, Miles. Your arm…"

He rolled his eyes. "Oh yeah, I didn't notice something was wrong with it. What's the verdict, doc? Mild sprai—*ah!*" He yelped as she reset his arm, with little more warning than grabbing his bicep and forearm and twisting. He let out a strained breath through his teeth and glared up at her. "Your bedside manner sucks."

She grinned. "Glad to know your sense of humor is still intact." She looked away, and through his ringing ears Miles could hear the fighting outside getting worse, another voice yelling for help. She looked back down at him. "Listen, it's getting rough out here. As soon as you heal up, you need to grab Sammie and get out of here."

Miles shook his head. "What, but…no, I can help." He grimaced as he got to his feet, cradling his arm against his stomach. "Just gimme five minutes, I'll be good to go. You seriously can't expect me to leave you alone out there."

She shook her head. "I don't, but you have to." She gently pushed him back to the floor and settled him with a look, one he'd been on the receiving end of many, many times. "Miles, this is my mess. I don't want either of you getting killed because of this. Now please, for once, just listen to me."

He wanted to argue, but… "I… Fine." He looked up at her as

she started back out through the hole. "But don't you get yourself killed, either. You better come back alive, all right!"

She glanced back over her shoulder at him one last time before Miles couldn't see her anymore through the wall. He slumped back and looked down at his arm.

Pins and needles filled his fingertips before red-hot pain seared along his arm. Before his eyes, the bruising and lacerations melted away, the numb feeling in his fingertips fading with them. He clenched his fist a couple of times, just to make sure everything worked properly, before he got to his feet.

She had to be okay...right? She'd been at this for longer than he had; she knew how to handle herself in a fight.

Miles's jaw clenched as he peered out of the cabin window to see at least a good couple of hundred hulking monsters outside, tearing through trees and one another, completely mindless, just thirsty for violence...

They weren't going to make it, not like this. It was going to end here.

Miles looked down before he huffed out a breath. "At least I'll have died fighting, right?" He stepped out and jolted as his foot passed through the Earth and kept going, and going and—

"*Wake up!*"

Miles jumped, then yelped as he rolled out of bed and slammed into the ground with a loud thud, earning a yell from his neighbor downstairs.

Where...what was...?

Oh.

"*Wake up!*"

"Shut up." Miles untangled himself from his sheets and patted over his nightstand until he found his phone. He tapped the screen until it went quiet and slumped back to the floor. He really needed to change that.

"—les?"

Miles blinked an eye open and glanced about. He didn't even know what time it was, or the day. Did he have something planned today? He could look at his phone to check but...sleep.

"Miles, yo, you up?"

"No," Miles mumbled into the floor. Then the voice finally clicked in his tired brain. Sammie? But Sammie was halfway across the country.

"Miles, I swear, if you are still asleep, I'm gonna just leave. Pretty sure I can hang out with your roommate if you—"

"Ah!" Miles yelled, jumping from the floor and immediately slipping on the sheet and catching himself with a loud bang against the wall. "Dude, one sec! What the hell are you doing here?" He threw open his door and rushed out to see, waiting in his living room and looking just a little bit jet-lagged... "Sammie."

Sammie laughed, standing from the couch and holding his arms out. "How am I doing here, huh?"

Miles shook his head and ran across the apartment to hug his best friend. It'd been years, it felt like, since he'd seen him. "Shut up, you're so annoying." He sighed as Sammie snickered.

Sammie squeezed Miles back before pushing him away and straightening his glasses as he looked around Miles's apartment. "Seriously, what are you doing here? I thought you were in college?"

"Dropped out," Sammie answered nonchalantly, then let out an interested sound as he started toward the kitchen. "You mind if I make some coffee? The shop at the airport was closed because of some cleanup thing they needed to do so I'm desperate for some caffeine."

Miles started to answer when Sammie opened the cupboard to find an empty coffee container and the words died in his throat. "Oh. I guess not. Pete must've used the last this morning."

Sammie snarled. "I knew he was a dick. I could sense it." He threw the container on the counter. "Who the hell puts back an empty one like that? That's just pure evil, dude. Seriously."

"And who the hell raised you where you don't put trash in the trash can?" Miles quipped, grabbing the container and wiping up the spilled leftover grounds into the bin. "In that case, if you can wait long enough for me to get dressed, you wanna head out? I know a place that has some pretty good drinks."

Sammie smirked. "Are you asking me out?"

Miles rolled his eyes. "You wish. Gimme a sec."

"Wear something blue. It'll compliment your eyes."

Miles ignored him, shaking his head as he grinned. He missed Sammie, really, even with all the comments. It's how they'd always been, back and forth like this. He honestly thought for a while that he wasn't going to see Sammie ever again, considering how he'd looked in all the pictures Miles had seen online.

He plucked a shirt from his closet and pulled on some jeans before he pocketed his phone and wallet and headed back out. He looked Sammie's way. "You ready? It's a bit of a walk."

Sammie snorted. "Of course it is. It's been so long I forgot you were being all active and shit now." He started following Miles then paused, leveling him with a suspicious glare. "Wait, is this all a ploy? Are you going to induct me into your gym like some cult? First, it's a walk to a coffee shop, next I'm gonna be like that Cross-Fit guy with all the bands and stuff."

"Has anyone told you you talk too much?" Miles pulled Sammie out after him. He locked his door and walked ahead down the stairs as Sammie followed.

"Oh, dude, like, all the time. Constantly, every minute of every day, my guy. I could go on, you know, if that's your thing, hearing about how much I annoyed everyone in your absence."

Miles snorted. "Maybe after coffee."

They got out onto the street and Sammie immediately started filling the silence, just as he always did. Miles was content to listen to Sammie babble on about everything and nothing all at once. He did notice Sammie strayed away from actually talking about anything like how the last three years of his life had been since he left town to attend college in New York, or about how his relationship with whatever her name was had gone. Miles did feel bad that he couldn't remember Sammie's girlfriend's name, but considering Sammie had shown up out of the blue, freshly dropped out of college and talking about everything but himself, he could only guess how that relationship went.

"How were classes?" Miles asked, eyeing the shop down the road as they walked. "Last I knew you were majoring in...theater?"

"No, pretty sure I told you I had switched to music theory. But before that, yeah, theater, then before that...engineering, I think. Too many eggs in too many baskets, my dude. I couldn't decide."

"You were never very good at that whole decisions thing. Took you twenty minutes to decide what to order every time we got pizza."

"There's too many options nowadays. Should I get all meat, veggies, all of the above? Should I be a monster and order pineapple just so the cook has to cry himself to sleep knowing there's another member on the pineapple belongs on pizza side?"

"You should probably get that checked out. I heard anyone who likes that is a psychopath."

"You know, I missed our talks, bud. Everyone back there never called me a psychopath with that much love in their voice."

Miles laughed. "Glad to know I was missed." He gestured toward the shop. "Here it is, I'll order first so I don't have to wait a century for you."

They finally settled in at a table near the window. People bundled up from the weather walked by as fall leaves blew around them. The skies were clear, for once. *Ironic, the one day it doesn't rain in Seattle, Sammie comes back into town.*

"How have you been, man? After...your mom..." Sammie asked, the first time he'd addressed anything remotely close to *that*. He looked sad, but not like everyone else when they asked.

Miles cringed, choking down his usual lie. This was Sammie, yeah, they hadn't been talking in the last couple of years, but they grew up together. Sammie was there when Miles lost his dad when he was younger, held him up whenever Miles was down about anything. If he could tell the truth to anyone, it was him. "I... Well... Not good. I mean... It's been hard, you know."

Sammie reached across the table to squeeze Miles's arm. "Yeah, I get it. I was gonna come out when I heard but...there was stuff that came up." He winced. "Sorry, I'm a bad friend. That's not an excuse, I know."

"Nah." Miles smiled. "I haven't felt like myself in weeks, so this is the first time I've left home for something other than work, you know. I get to feel like living again, not everyone can pull that off after a funeral."

Sammie let out a breath, sounding relieved. "I'm glad I can help." He perked up. "Hey, how about we just stay out all day? You don't have work today, right?"

"What did you have in mind?" Miles took a sip of his drink. "We're not sixteen anymore, you know. Kinda weird for us to hang out at the game store all day like we used to."

Sammie bobbed his head back and forth in indecision before he answered. "We'll wander around until we find something that jumps out at us. It'll be fun. I'll buy us a round to go, come on."

"Sure." He killed off his drink and followed Sammie as he went back up to the counter. *It'll be fun. Honestly, Sammie could probably make watching paint dry entertaining.* Anything that got his mind off everything.

They stepped out of the café. Sammie immediately tugged Miles down the alleyway next to it with a manic look on his face. "Let's just get a little lost, see where we end up."

Miles shook his head. "Not one of your brightest ideas but...whatever. If we get killed, I can taunt you about it for eternity."

"Sounds like a plan."

Sammie continued leading Miles along, turning when he felt they'd been going in the same direction for too long. Occasionally they got back to a familiar street, only for Sammie to pull them away again. He couldn't tell exactly how much time had gone by. Buildings made the alleyways darker than they should be, throwing off his ability to work out how much daylight they had left.

"How about this way—oh!" Sammie backpedaled as he bumped into a girl, shorter than him with choppy black hair and gray eyes. She looked surprised for a moment before she glanced away. She seemed familiar, somehow. "Sorry."

She glanced Sammie's way again before something drew her attention away and she sprinted off. Sammie blinked, then looked at Miles. "Did I say something?"

He made a non-committal grunt, glancing back after her for

a moment before Sammie started off again.

Just...where had he seen her?

"Huh..." Sammie brought them to a stop. They stood at the mouth of a darker than usual alley, a dead end revealing a couple of trash bins and rats running about. "I don't remember any there being any dead ends like this before. Must've put a new building in or something."

Miles opened his mouth to answer when he stopped, a sudden chill racing along his spine. He felt like they were being watched.

"Hey, does it seem like it got darker all the sudden?" Sammie asked, then jumped back as the rats in the alley all started sprinting out of it, scared squeaks filling the air. There was a beat before Miles heard it.

A low, rumbling growl, almost like a bear, more like something out of a horror movie. Miles glanced up and his body went cold.

Red eyes, glaring down at them from the building above, a giant black-haired creature panting with bared teeth, lethal-looking hands curling into the stone.

Miles didn't think. He ran, grabbing Sammie's arm and tugging him after him as he went. The ground rumbled, making him stumble as his feet left the ground with the impact of that giant thing. He didn't stop, he ran, hoping for an exit, there had to be an exit, why couldn't he find a way out?

"Miles, stop!"

Miles looked ahead, gasping as he skidded to a stop as they nearly ran into another dead-end alley. *But that shouldn't be possible. I looked up just a second before that and didn't see it. How…*

A growl rumbled through his chest and Miles anxiously looked back to see that monster blocking the only way out and advancing toward them.

They were going to die. Or…maybe he could distract it so Sammie could get away…

"Miles." He could hear the tone in Sammie's voice: worry, disapproval, fear. He knew, but Miles wasn't about to let him die if he could help it. "Don't."

He moved without much more thought than that. He pushed Sammie behind him and started sprinting toward the thing, hoping he could get it to move or chase him if he could get past it. He swung his arm back and yelled as he punched its muzzle.

He heard a crack, his fingers losing feeling and a pain that made his vision blur flaring up his arm. The thing growled before it simply shoved him to the side with a massive paw the size of his torso and moved past. *No. No, no, no, no.*

Miles grit his teeth as Sammie backed against the wall, and picked up the closest thing he could find for self-defense. Something that might get the thing to go for him instead. He just had to buy Sammie time to get out and maybe he could get help before it was too late.

Broken bottle in hand, Miles ran toward it, yelling again

before he stabbed at its flank. The monster yelped, then rounded on him with a snarl.

"Miles, just r—"

The thing lunged, and Miles couldn't react. Teeth sank into his side, and his world condensed down to the blooming pain radiating from it. They pulled out, and something wet poured down his body as his hands went numb. He fell to the ground in a heap as the monster pulled away. His ears were ringing, his vision swimming; he could taste rust on his suddenly heavy tongue.

Was this how death felt? Everything thick and viscous like moving through honey? He felt pressure on his side, then a searing pain that had him screaming as it increased.

Gray eyes swam into sight for a moment, a flash of red for a split second before everything went black.

*

"—be okay?"

"Yes, just give him time to rest. He's going through a lot right now."

Miles swam back to consciousness slowly, quiet conversation lulling him back to the waking world first, then the realization that something was off.

It felt like a wall of sensation had hit him as multiple scents filled his brain like cotton candy. Coffee, vanilla, caramel, grass, mud, rust, spices, cinnamon, electricity. He could hear the buzz of electrical wires in the walls, coins dropping into the machines in the laundromat twelve stories down...

He felt different, somehow, other than the senses, something inside him. A pressure filled his head until it felt fit to burst.

"He's awake." A female voice spoke, and Miles opened his eyes to see that woman from earlier for a brief second before sandy-brown hair filled his vision.

Sammie squeezed himself against Miles's chest like he was trying to crawl inside him. "I thought you were dead." His hands were shaking against Miles's back, and his breaths were ragged and rough. A sour scent filled Miles's sinuses; his head felt clogged with cotton as the scent saturated him. "I—I couldn't get you to look at me, or respond, and...I couldn't get the bleeding to stop. There was so much, and then Naomi, she said she could help but how can you help someone bleeding to death like that but—"

"I think I should explain it, Sammie," the woman, Naomi, gently interjected, walking up to the bed and settling herself at the foot of it. "It'll be easier that way."

"I—" Miles winced as he tried to speak, his throat rough and his tongue heavy. Naomi stood to retrieve something from the ground. Maybe from an ice chest?

"Drink," she ordered, handing Sammie a bottle to give to him. "Your throat is gonna be sore for a bit." She grimaced, almost wincing as she spoke. "You probably don't remember it, hopefully you don't, but you were screaming for a while."

He remembered at least a little bit of that, right before he passed out. He took a couple of sips of water before trying again.

"I don't understand what's going on. Who are you? And what happened to that...thing?" He looked down at his body then, a sense of relief and even more confusion washing over him as he saw no sign of the massive wound on his stomach. "How am I alive?"

Naomi nodded. "I'll get to everything, just be patient. We'll start with introductions, I suppose. I'm Naomi Chae, we've accidentally bumped into each other before the attack. I...well—" She paused, tapping her chin for a moment. "This is going to be difficult to explain without just coming out with it. That thing you found in the alleyway yesterday was a werewolf."

Miles's stomach sank, his mind going a hundred miles an hour. *That's impossible.* But, then again, what else could it really be? As far as he knew, no regular animal looked anything like whatever had attacked him. But then, if that were true, what did that mean for him? If all the myths about werewolves were correct, that meant bites were contagious. Was he going to turn into something like that? Oh god, he'd rather he'd died in that alley. He didn't want to become a monster. He—

"Miles." Naomi's voice cut through his spiraling thoughts like a knife, bringing him back to the room. She scowled, and a hand settled on his ankle. "I get it, you're scared. I know exactly every thought going through your head right now, because I've been there, just like you." She continued with a small pause when Miles looked at her quizzically. "I'm a werewolf, just like him, and just like you. The only difference between us and that one from yesterday is we still have our wits and minds intact. So, as crazy as this all is, please know that you're not going to turn into a monster like him. I'm here to help you, so any fears of hurting anyone, you don't have to worry about them, all right?"

Miles nodded, his heart slowly getting back down to a normal rate. Naomi hesitated a moment before pressing on. "Right, so, there's a reason I was there yesterday; to find that werewolf specifically. He'd been terrorizing the city and the whole of the northwest for the last several months, and I'd never had the chance to catch him until now. I was there to try to subdue him but once you were injured, I was more concerned making sure you made it through all right."

"T-thank you," Sammie muttered, still holding tightly on to Miles's arm. Like he thought if he let go Miles would disappear.

He looked up at Sammie and his chest ached at his expression. He looked completely devastated, face red and wet, eyes bloodshot and puffy, like he hadn't slept in weeks...

"Miles?" Naomi called his attention again, and when he focused back on her she was wearing a serious expression, her gray eyes settled on him firmly. "This next part is important, okay?" She waited for him to show he was paying attention before she continued. "There's something very important about how we work. There's a hierarchy of command, basically. It's something instinctive to us, especially as you're brand new to all of this. If I hadn't intervened to help you, he would've been able to command you to do whatever he wanted. He'd be your creator; we call them alphas. There's not much of a way to break out from an alpha's control without some serious willpower, and even then, it's years and years of breaking down the wall of power they have over you. The only way to change that control easily is to have another alpha step in, overtake the bite, and hope it takes."

Miles swallowed heavily. "So, I might be...what, mind controlled by that monster?" His heart rate started to skyrocket again. He needed to get out of here, away from Sammie, away from people.

Naomi raised her hands. "Calm down." Her voice had an air of command there, and the panic thumping through his body dimmed, much like he'd been covered by a thick blanket of calm. "Like I said before, if I hadn't intervened, that's what would've happened. I cleansed his bite, then replaced the claim with my own. I stayed until I made sure it took." She frowned. "I should've been able to stop it happening in the first place. I wasn't about to let you suffer because I messed up."

Sammie sniffled, then looked up at Naomi. "You said that before. What do you mean?"

Naomi winced again, rubbing the back of her neck. "I was there to catch him, and because I didn't realize you all were there with him, I trapped you all along with him."

Miles remembered the impossible dead end they ran into, his brow furrowing. "So that's why I couldn't find a way out."

Naomi clenched her jaw. "Yeah. By the time I realized, it was too late. I thought I might've had some time if you did get trapped but..." She shook her head. "I miscalculated."

"But if you hadn't shown up then I would've been in the same boat as Miles," Sammie commented, his voice still strained but a sense of relief coloring his tone.

"Wait." Miles frowned. "How, though? Werewolves can change the geography of cities now? I looked ahead and there was a way through, then the next time I looked there wasn't."

"Well..." Naomi drawled. "Not exactly. I didn't do it directly, more so communicated what I needed to someone who could." She seemed to go back and forth on whether she wanted to continue. "So, this is going to be a little unbelievable probably, but... there's a society of beings like us in the world. All hiding in the shadows keeping the waking world safe from nuisances only we know about. Some of us actively go about stopping them, like myself, and others support the rest through means of magic, in most cases anyway."

So, there's a secret society of werewolves and other things?
"Okay, so beings like us? What does that include? Vampires? Uh, wizards? Witches? I guess that's the same thing basically...oh, Fae?"

Naomi kept answering affirmatively as Miles listed off all the mythical and fairy tale creatures he could think of. After a couple more she let out a laugh and raised her hand. "Okay, okay, basically, if you've heard or seen it in fiction, it's probably there."

Neat.

"Um, can we get back onto what's gonna happen with Miles?" He perked up, settling his gaze on Naomi.

"Right, so, since you're freshly turned, you have to go through the process of your body changing. I believe you're past the hardest part, but there's still going to be a good amount of discomfort ahead, unfortunately. Probably another day or two for the process to finish completely, so it'd be a good idea to stay in bed and rest until then, conserve your energy and all that. Then, once that's done, we'll have to get started on training you for control. Don't worry about that at all. It's easy, and you have the advantage of a decent mentor where most don't. Probably a couple weeks or so, then I can be out of your hair."

A modicum of relief flooded Miles at her words. At least it wasn't going to take him that long to figure this all out, and he had help. Maybe his life could get to some point of normal after this. As normal as it could be, anyway.

Naomi glanced between the two of them, then looked down as a vibrating sound filled the air. "Ah, well. I have some business I gotta take care of real quick." She leveled Miles with a caring smile. "Get some rest, all right?"

With that, Naomi stood up and left, pulling a phone from her pocket and tapping out a message before she was fully out of the door. Sammie let out a shaky breath, drawing Miles's attention back to him. "Hey, how are you holding up?"

Miles took stock of himself for a moment before he answered. "I feel...heavy, and I dunno if I can believe everything she just said, though after what we saw I guess I kinda have to." He looked at his best friend, reaching over to squeeze his hand. "How about you? You've barely said a word since I woke up, which is unusual for you."

Sammie let out a wet laugh. "I thought you were dying, Miles." He shook his head harshly. "I'm never going to get that out of my head, seeing you fall to the ground, seeing all the blood..." He grimaced. "I scrubbed at my hands so hard I lost feeling in my fingers once we got back. I can still feel it on my hands." He clenched his hands into fists, shuddering, and Miles could smell that same sour scent from before filling his head, tinged with something incredibly bitter that nearly had him gagging. "And it's because of me that happened. I had the brilliant idea to go wandering through there. You're like this because of me."

"Hey, Sammie, no." Miles sat up fully and grabbed Sammie's hand. "Don't blame yourself. You didn't know that was going to happen. There's no way you could've. If anyone can be blamed for this happening to me, it's me. I decided to get up close to it, to attack it. Of course it was going to retaliate. I just wanted to make sure you didn't get hurt. As long as that didn't happen, I couldn't care less what happens to me."

Sammie choked out a hysterical chuckle, sniffling as he shook his head. "You're so dumb." He shoved Miles back down into bed. "Go to sleep, already."

Miles huffed. "Only if you do, too." He got up stubbornly, pushing back against Sammie's hands. "You look like you haven't slept in weeks. I'm not going to sleep until you do."

Sammie's blue eyes glared at him before he relaxed finally

and agreed. "Fine. I'll go out on the couch. Just—" Another, more mellow scent clogged Miles's senses, and he blinked as it filtered through his brains like fog. His eyes went heavy for a moment before it disappeared, something like overheating electronics taking its place. "Never mind. I'll see you when you wake up."

With that, Miles was alone. He shuddered lightly before he settled down into the bed, closing his eyes to force himself to go to sleep, as much as his brain wanted to keep running over just what the hell had happened in the last day.

He tossed for a couple of minutes, then that same heaviness he'd felt since he'd woken up dragged him back under.

Chapter Two

"*H*elp!" Sammie's voice, full of pain and panic, rattled in Miles's head. "Someone! Anyone! *Please help!*"

Miles tried to speak, reassure Sammie whatever was going on, it was going to be okay. But he couldn't—his tongue felt swollen in his mouth as wet warmth spread over his chest.

Sammie cursed, and he felt a pressure on his stomach, a flare of pain rocketing up his spine. "D-don't don't move. God, Miles, don't move, please, please don't...don't..." Sammie's words faded, and a ringing filled his head.

"—kay. You're okay." Another voice swam into Miles's head. There was an agonizing pressure in his side, like someone was searing his skin off. He screamed, his throat burning, a horrid scent like burning flesh making him gag for a moment before he lost all ability to keep awake.

The two voices swirled through his head, lazily spinning circles through his limited consciousness, sending him spiraling further into the dark of pain-free unconsciousness.

Everything is changing. Everything is gone. Everything is here. Everything is there. Where...where is there? Where am I? What's happening?

A hand gripped into his hair, shoving him down, down, down. He opened his eyes and gasped as he saw a maw of teeth opening for him, snarling, hot wet breath sticking to his skin.

"No, no, get away. Let go of me."

Can't, won't, can't, won't, stay stay stay stay stay.

The words filled Miles's head faster than he could think. He tried to swim away, tried to climb, find some semblance of an escape from this.

"Listen to me."

The voice rattled his bones, knocking the air from Miles's lungs. He squeezed his eyes shut as he got closer before the hand left his head, another taking his and pulling him up and away from his death.

"Miles."

The voice seemed to scare off everything around them. Only the dark stayed. All sound left at once, making his ears ache.

"You're okay," the voice repeated, and dots of light started swimming back into his vision. Gray eyes locking onto his, red splashed on tan skin... "You're okay. Stay with me. You're okay."

The voice kept repeating the same words, over and over.

Miles's adrenaline drained from him before he drifted back under, the words fading as he slipped into the black again.

*

"Miles?"

He blinked awake, coming to slowly, but much faster than before. He felt...better. Amazing, actually. He hadn't felt this good in years. He sat up and glanced around to find Sammie seated beside the bed, just like before. "Did you sleep at all?" Miles questioned, leveling him with a suspicious look.

Sammie replied halfheartedly. "Kinda. I tried." He grimaced. "A little hard to sleep when every time I close my eyes I go back to that alley."

Yeah, that's fair. Miles was at least out for most of it; Sammie had to be awake to see everything, all while worrying that Miles wasn't going to make it out. He frowned, sitting up then. "Hey, how about we get something to eat? I don't have coffee here, but we should have some stuff left I can make."

Sammie made a choked-off noise as Miles started standing up, pressing him back down. "You're supposed to be resting!"

Miles waved him off. "I feel fine, I think a few minutes out of bed isn't going to hurt." He tried again, and Sammie paused, a small gasp falling from his mouth before he backed out of the way. He was staring at Miles's stomach. *Oh.*

Miles looked down, expecting the worst, only to find the lightest bit of a scar where the first werewolf bit into him. He could see why Sammie was so afraid of Miles dying there now, but it looked to be years old now, not two days. *Actually, thinking back...* Miles examined his left hand, finding no sign of the break he knew he had two days prior. "Whoa." He wiggled his fingers, without a hint of pain. "I can heal. Cool."

"You're not freaking out about this?" Sammie squeaked.

"Why?" Miles ran his hand over the scar. "I'm alive, and I technically have superpowers now."

Sammie's face went red before he shoved Miles, a small glint of happiness on his face for the first time since that morning. "Shut up, you're so annoying."

"Seriously, I'm fine. No freak out or anything. Now come on, lemme make something." He pulled himself up again. "I feel like I could eat a horse."

"I mean—" Sammie followed Miles as he padded out toward the kitchen. "I hope you're joking. You know, all things considered."

He rolled his eyes, pulling over a stool with his foot and tugging Sammie down onto it. "Sit. Talk to me, but not about, you know, that stuff." He glanced up. "Like, where's Pete at?"

"He was gone when we first got back, came back for a little bit after you went back to sleep but he's mostly been out. I think he said he was working two doubles in a row."

That sounded about right. Pete usually tried to spend every waking hour working so he could save up to get out on his own. He was a decent enough roommate, but Miles got it, living with other people sucked. He checked the fridge, looking over every-thing before he pulled out some leftover rice, eggs, peppers, scal-lions, and soy sauce to make something quick. "So, he probably doesn't know anything. Good. Probably a good idea to keep it that way."

"Mmm, probably." Sammie drummed his fingers on the countertop. "Naomi's still been out, too. No idea what's going on there, I can only assume it's important supernatural world stuff." He shifted in place then. "I know you said not to talk about the stuff but...is anything different?"

"Oh, now you're curious? First my superpowers are annoy-ing, now you want to know more." He dropped the peppers and scallions in the eggs and carefully folded over the edges of the omelet. "Hmm, I'm not sure if I should say. I think my feelings are hurt."

Sammie scoffed. "Come on, dude, I was kidding. Well, mostly." He rocked the stool back and forth with a smug smirk on his face. "*You* are annoying. Just your 'superpowers' are cool."

"I can tell you just did the finger quotes thing." Miles finished assembling everything before he joined Sammie at the counter, standing up to start shoveling bites into his mouth. He felt like he hadn't eaten in months.

"Gross eating habits, huh. That's not a very cool super-power."

Miles glared at him as he finished his mouthful. "Ah, so, I'm not sure exactly. It all seems to like, come and go. But I think my senses are better, my hearing and my sense of smell, I dunno about my vision or anything else. And I feel like I could run a marathon right now, easy." He scooped another bite up and continued. "Otherwise, I dunno. I feel pretty normal."

"Huh." Sammie leaned forward. "'Kay, in that case, what do you smell now?"

"Egg," Miles answered without skipping a beat. Sammie let out a frustrated yelp before Miles shook his head. "I dunno, like I said, it comes and goes. I guess I could try and see if I can focus on something."

Sammie bounced in place with excitement and Miles exhaled slowly, closing his eyes and straining his ears. He tried to listen to something specific, the muttered conversations through various floors blurring, a car with squeaking brakes turning at the street nearby, but nothing specific. He shifted, a consistent thump filling his head, like a heartbeat.

"I think...I can hear your heart beating." An uptick in the rhythm, just for a moment. "I'm not sure." He opened his eyes to find Sammie staring at him, excitement dimmed for a little surprise to shine through. "Can you...I dunno, I guess...tell me two truths and a lie."

Sammie barked out a laugh. "Okay, I guess, lemme think..." He scratched his chin, then started with a sly expression. "I still can't drive, I still have a crush on Spider-Man, and I might be a little jealous of your newfound possible lie detector powers."

Steady, steady, then another uptick. "Last is a lie." Sammie blinked, then gave a halfhearted nod. "So, you're not jelly?"

"Lucky guess," he grumbled. "I've always sucked at that game anyway." He pushed up to his feet and leaned past Miles to peer into the fridge. He grabbed an apple and spun on his heel to walk into the living room. "So, you ready to rest up some more?"

Miles paused, thinking it over. He really felt better; the thought of crawling back into bed had him groaning.

"I want to do something. I feel like I'm gonna burst if I don't get this energy out."

Sammie watched him with an almost suspicious look. "Right, and you're not planning on jogging inside, are you?"

"I...can't go out?"

"Nope," Sammie blurted. "Naomi specifically told me before you woke up that you needed to stay in until she got back. And I agree with her, considering we don't know everything you're going to be able to do. What if you turn into something like that feral one and hurt someone?"

He had a point. Miles groaned, following as Sammie flopped onto the couch. "But I have so much energy. I gotta do something."

"You're asking the wrong person about that stuff. You're the gym buff, figure something out." He fished the remote out of the couch cushions. "Do some sit-ups or something."

Miles grumbled, falling over the back of the couch and knocking the remote out of Sammie's hand as he spread out over the cushions. "Entertain me."

"Dude." Sammie laughed, pushing Miles off him. "You're a

grown ass man; you can figure something out."

Miles whined, slumping to the other side of the couch with a pout. He could probably beat Sammie to the door if he ran, but they were right about it not being a good idea. Still, he felt like he was vibrating in place; he needed to get this energy out of himself. Just let Sammie get distracted, then he could...

A spicy scent filled Miles's head, throwing off any thoughts he had before. He remembered it, kind of, it was a little familiar. Cinnamon, cayenne, spices, dirt...fresh rainwater?

There was a knock on the door. Sammie hollered that it was open, and Naomi came through, soaked from head to toe. She huffed, pulling the soaked headband from her hair. "Oh." She glanced between the two of them. "Am I interrupting something?"

"Miles is going stir crazy," Sammie mumbled.

Naomi's lips curled. She appeared almost feral with her teeth bared, her abnormally sharp canines on display. "In that case, I guess you'd be up for some training, then?"

"Uh..." Suddenly, going back to bed and resting didn't seem like such a bad idea. "What exactly does that involve?"

Naomi walked fully into the room. "Depends on how much your changes have developed."

Miles gulped nervously. "Um, I can sometimes smell better and hear better, otherwise I don't notice anything that much different."

She clicked her tongue, looking over him. "Interesting, lemme just test something."

That was the only warning Miles got before a suddenly clawed human hand was flying straight at his face. He tensed before he moved on instinct, his own hands rushing up and catching Naomi's. He heard Sammie let out a sound of surprise and felt a dull pain in his fingertips and his jaw.

"Huh." Naomi pulled back, looking impressed. "You don't sense something else new with you? Like...for better lack of a description, another being in your head?"

Miles blinked owlishly, all the aches fading all at once. "No, not that I notice."

"Huh," she chirped again, scratching her jaw. "That's really interesting."

"What?" Miles sat up. "Is something wrong?"

"No, the opposite, actually." She tugged Miles up. "Come on, let's go somewhere that won't get too damaged."

"Can I come?" Sammie called after them, and Naomi made a small, uncomfortable face.

"That's probably not the best idea. I need to make sure that Miles has full control before he comes around you. Sorry."

Sammie pouted, but agreed, seeming to turn his attention fully back to the TV, but Miles could hear him mutter something about not wanting to be left alone, and smelled a sharp scent that felt like a blow to his sinuses.

"We'll be back soon," Naomi added, "I promise."

They left the apartment, and Miles rubbed his nose, the strong, sharp scent sticking in his head. He felt anxious, for some reason, his chest clenching as they went further away. "He'll be okay, right?"

"Yes," Naomi answered easily. "I have connections, they've been keeping an eye on the building since I left. He's safer in here than where we're going."

Miles chewed his lip. He hoped she was right. Now that Miles was out here, and moving away from the apartment, he felt less sure of everything, a ball of nervous energy growing in his chest.

Naomi knew what she was doing. He just had to trust her.

"Okay, so just breathe. Try to focus. Find your center."

Miles let out a harsh exhale, his chest still tight and his mind running a million miles an hour. *What if Sammie's not okay? What if something happened? What if I can't get control and something happens to Sammie because of me? What can I do to protect him?* He didn't need to be dragged into anything more with that monster. Miles would protect him however he possibly could, even if it meant his life.

"Miles." Naomi's stern voice broke through Miles's thoughts. "You need to be calm, relax your hands."

He did so, wincing when he felt a sharp pinching feeling in his palms and looked down to find... Oh.

His skin was covered in blood, his nails somehow replaced with lethal-looking claws, a row of wounds in his hand where they dug in. "O-oh, sorry. I..."

Naomi's fingers gingerly tapped along his jaw, her voice gentle now. "It's okay, just breathe. Your jaw is going to hurt, and your head will ache, but just stay calm."

He tried to follow her advice, steadying his breaths. He grimaced as his head throbbed and his jaw seemed to shrink, a pinch making him jump. Naomi settled her hands on his shoulders and cooed softly at him. "You're fine. The first time coming out of it is scary, but I'm here. You're all good."

Miles swallowed, tasting rust on his tongue, and shook his head. "Could... I want to go back. Is that...? I mean..." His head felt clouded, those thoughts about Sammie's safety filling his brain, along with a sensation like coming out of anesthesia. His tongue was heavy in his mouth, making talking a strain all the way around.

Naomi, thankfully, seemed to understand. "Yeah, that's fine. We'll go back once you get your bearings back." She squeezed his shoulder, gray eyes boring into him. "It's better to let yourself come back fully before you get around other people, or you can get overwhelmed with everything."

He closed his eyes. Everything already felt like too much here.

Naomi took them to a nature preserve, away from people, where they could be undisturbed were anything to happen.

The scent of pine, stagnant rainwater, various wildlife, blood from his fingertips, his palms tingling and burning in cycles, his fingertips aching, his jaw hurting as something stabbed into his gums—

"Hey, Miles, focus on me," Naomi called again, worry clear

on her face when he drew his attention back to her. She moved a hand to the back of his neck, and he felt much like a kitten at that moment, being picked up by his scruff and his instinct to move and run and lash out draining out of his body. "You're good, remember? Just listen to my voice, you are perfectly fine. Relax your jaw, let yourself just relax, okay?"

Miles focused, setting his jaw for a second before his entire body seemed to reset. It was odd, really odd, feeling himself almost shrink, but not being able to actually tell what changed, how he changed. He'd seen his hands, but what about the rest of him? What happened to him every time Naomi had to pull him back?

A hand grasped his neck, and his quickening breath caught in his chest. Miles grimaced, shaking his head and squeezing his eyes closed tight. "Sorry, I...sorry."

"Don't apologize. You're doing fine. It's always hard the first time. You're not used to any of this, it makes sense." Naomi pulled her hand away slowly. "We're gonna try to go back home, all right? Just focus on me, no one else, 'kay?"

Miles relaxed slightly. *Home, yeah, that's...that's a good idea.* He needed to be somewhere familiar right now, somewhere his senses weren't telling him about every little thing that could be a threat hiding out there. Where he didn't have to worry that Sammie might be unprotected.

A warm hand clasped his and he looked down to find Naomi squeezing his hand tight, red smearing slightly against her fingers. She tugged him gently and grinned. "Come on, just stay close by and breathe if you feel anything like before."

"R-right." Miles followed her as they started out of the preserve. Shockingly enough, the walk back wasn't bad. Miles timed his breaths with their steps, the promise of safety and familiar grounds making it easier to keep his head. As they entered the empty elevator up to Miles's apartment, he finally relaxed fully. Coffee, vanilla, burnt sugar, lavender all filled his head with a sweet, scented fog, so distinct he could almost taste it on his tongue.

Naomi's hand untangled from his, and Miles walked into his apartment and felt himself wholly melt, all the tension from before bleeding out of every muscle and sinew in his body.

Sammie looked up from where he was lounging on the couch, scrolling aimlessly on his phone.

He let out a small gasp before scrambling up, his phone clattering to the floor in his hurry. "So, how'd it go? Everything okay? No surprises or anything?"

Miles opened his mouth to answer only for Naomi to beat him to it. "Considering everything, he did good. We weren't disturbed by anyone or anything, and he was able to get himself back under control fairly easily."

Sammie's brow furrowed. "Back? So, like..." His blue eyes met Miles's brown ones, and Miles's chest tightened as those scents from earlier sharpened, a sour tinge he couldn't place making his nose itch. "You actually...like, changed? How much? It didn't hurt, did it?"

"Uh." Miles shivered slightly, a sort of nervous energy thrumming through his body. "No, no, not at all. Well, a little, maybe."

"That's normal, though." Naomi sounded reassuring. "Your body has never done this before, so getting used to it changing and shifting like that is going to take time. The pain won't be noticeable once you're used to it and your body adjusts." She looked at Sammie. "And the change isn't terribly drastic, at least not yet. It takes a while to be able to shapeshift fully, and most of the time the forms we take aren't anything like the one you met. The majority of the time, once we're able to fully shift, we could blend in with actual wolves. But it does take time and practice to be able to do it and hold it." She patted Miles's shoulder and squeezed. "But, for a first time, Miles did pretty well."

Sammie relaxed slightly and exhaled, his breath catching as he released it. That nervous energy built in Miles, becoming unbearable. "You probably want to rest, huh?" he asked, taking in Miles for a moment. "You look a bit tired."

He certainly didn't feel it, but the thought of running off his energy wasn't as tempting as it was before, especially if it meant leaving the safety of his home and his friends. "Y-yeah, I could sleep." He looked to Naomi. "Is that okay?"

"Yeah, get some rest. I should probably check into some things anyway." She dropped her hand from his shoulder and did a mock salute as she started toward the door. "I'll check in with you tomorrow."

The door clicked shut behind her, and Miles's skin buzzed. He glanced at Sammie, then pointed to his bedroom wordlessly. Sammie relaxed back against the couch. "Sleep well, Miles."

The nervousness drained from Miles's body. "Yeah, I'll see you tomorrow."

Sammie grinned in response. It didn't quite meet his eyes fully, and Miles paused for a moment, a thick sourness filling his head as Sammie turned to the TV and flicked it on to something random. Miles stepped back, frowning as Sammie blinked. "Everything okay?"

"I could ask you the same thing." Miles leaned on the back of the couch, Sammie staring up at him with a confused look. "What's wrong?"

"Nothing." Sammie laughed lightly. "Why would something be wrong?"

Miles glanced at the TV then gasped out a laugh. "You're *watching* sports."

Sammie followed his eyes to the screen and back, narrowing his eyes. "I'm fine with sports; you don't know my life. I love sports." He cleared his throat, turning his attention back to the TV. "Go Bears."

Miles laughed. "Sammie, come on." He reached down, clicking off the screen with the remote and tossing it away to earn Sammie's full attention. "What's going on in that head of yours?" He got a sharp spike, spicy and sweet like cinnamon, before Sammie shook his head and pushed up to sit. "Nothing! I am acting perfectly normal. Everything is good, and you should stop worrying about me and go get some rest."

Miles stared at him for a couple of moments, a steadily increasing thumping filling his head, that cinnamon scent getting stronger and stronger. He licked his lips and pulled back before heaving himself over the back of the couch to plop beside Sammie. He ruffled his sandy-brown hair as Sammie blinked owlishly at him. "I'll rest out here, and if you happen to feel like talking about it, I'll be all ears."

"Oh." Sammie's voice wavered. "Okay, I mean... If you're sure, I guess." He furrowed his brow. "I...dammit." He sighed heavily, twisting to face Miles. "I'm just worried. For you, and about you. I wanted to be there with you two to make sure nothing went wrong. I mean, I'm glad it went okay but..." He inhaled through his clenched teeth. "I dunno. I know it's dangerous, or it could be, but since...*that*... I just... I don't like you not being by me. Like I'm afraid if you're not right there that everything after that was a dream, and you're..."

Sammie's voice broke, and Miles's chest ached, salt and sourness like vinegar filling his sinuses. "Sammie..." Miles pulled him in, squeezing him to his chest. "Hey, it's fine, everything is fine, all right?" He patted Sammie's back, pulling him back. "See, I'm all right."

A hiccup, a teary-eyed, half-hearted smile. Miles felt that nervous tension in his chest again and gulped down the sudden lump in his throat. A beat, then another. Miles could hear the ticking of a clock, footsteps outside his apartment door, the squeal of tires several stories down. A steady heartbeat, increasing in pace with every second of silence. A key scraping on the lock, the shifting of cloth on cloth as Sammie looked over his face.

Ba-bum, ba-bum, ba-bum.

It drowned out every other sound, thumping in his head, louder than anything else. The tension grew and grew, the air felt electrified, the hair on the back of his neck stood on end. Sammie's eyes flickered downward and met his again.

The air filled with that cinnamon spice scent, so thick Miles could almost taste it. Another beat, then another, and was Sammie closer than before? Miles couldn't tell, he could barely think, that cinnamon and that constant thump, thump, thumping making it nearly impossible.

A *click*, and Sammie was suddenly far, far away, his blue eyes widening in surprise, and Miles was brought back to the present.

"Oh." Pete's teasing voice broke all the tension in the room. The nervous energy melted from Miles's bones. "Am I interrupting?"

"No." Sammie cleared his throat, reaching to the floor to pick up the remote. "No, no, not at all. We're trying to, uh, figure out what to do for food."

"Uh huh." Pete chuckled, then stopped behind the couch, leaning forward into Miles's vision, blocking Sammie's red face. "Hey, you feeling better finally? I was getting worried we'd have to call someone for you."

Miles blinked, his brain still trying to catch up from whatever that was. "Yeah, yeah, I'm better, um..." He stood up, brow furrowing. "I uh, I'll look at ordering something, if that's fine."

Sammie chewed on his thumbnail and stared a hole into the wall behind the TV. Pete grumbled, taking Miles's vacated spot. "Sure, I had to skip lunch so whatever you get is fine with me."

Great. Great great great. Miles rushed to his bedroom and closed the door, sagging against it and giving his reflection in the mirror across from him a look. "What the hell was that?" he muttered, pushing off the door and pacing for a moment before he spun on his heel mid turn and shifted into his bathroom. He splashed cold water on his face and stared at his reflection once more. "What was that?" he asked again, as if this time it would have an answer for him.

Whatever it was, Miles needed to bury it, deep down. Sammie was already scared enough, and he was traumatized. The last thing he needed was whatever that was.

Did Miles like Sammie? Well, yeah, he'd always liked Sammie, Sammie was his best friend. But did Miles *like* Sammie?

"Oh my god." Miles groaned, dropping his head against the wall. "I'm not sixteen. I can't be doing this anymore." He glanced back to his reflection and paused. For a split second, it looked like his dark-brown eyes had been gold but...*no, I'm stressed. That's all any of this is, is stress. And stress and traumatic experiences are the worst way to start a relationship.*

Not that he wanted a relationship with Sammie.

"Dammit." Miles slammed his hand against the light switch, and flinched when he heard the plastic splintering, the light flickering for a second before turning off, the switch completely broken under his fist. "Great." Miles deflated and walked out of the bathroom. He flopped onto his bed face first.

He should've just stayed in bed.

Chapter Three

Miles awoke with a start, the light outside still dim, little trickles of early morning beaming through his curtains. He groaned, sitting up and grimacing as the sheets shifted uncomfortably underneath him.

He listened, holding his breath for a moment as he heard footsteps creaking through the hallway and a set of steady beats. *Okay, so both Pete and Sammie are okay, good...*

"Miles still hasn't woken up, right?" Pete's voice carried up through the door, and Miles paused.

"No, not as far as I know," Sammie muttered, sounding tired. "You'd think he'd be up first considering he was out first."

Pete snorted. "Right? Promised food then bailed, like a jerk."

Sammie laughed lightly, and Miles was up on his feet before he knew it. He opened the door and peered out. Sammie and Pete were settled at the kitchen counter, eating cold pizza out of a box they must've gotten last night. Sammie looked even more exhausted than he had before, eyes bruised and swollen and reddened from lack of sleep. Miles frowned before he left his room fully. The two of them turned to face him.

"Ah, finally," Pete drawled. "You sure you're doing okay? I think that must've been fourteen hours you just slept."

Miles stared at Sammie, who was resolutely not looking at Miles. That cinnamon scent filled his senses again, seeming to get stronger the closer he got to his friend. *Huh. So that's coming from Sammie...?*

"I guess I'm sleeping enough for the both of us," Miles muttered, clapping Sammie on the back as he settled beside him. "You look horrible."

Sammie cleared his throat. "Yeah, didn't sleep well," he mumbled. "Still not used to the time change, I guess." He dragged the box over to Miles. "Breakfast, all meat."

Miles narrowed his eyes, squeezing Sammie's shoulder to let him know he was going to ask about it later. For now, though, he was starving. "Thanks." He looked up to Pete, who was watching them both with a curious look on his face. "What?"

"Hm? Oh, nothing." Pete stretched and grimaced. "Well, I gotta get back into the shop today. Had another two call-offs today so...I'm it, I guess. But it's overtime, so, whatever. Don't wait up for me." With that, Pete was walking into his room to get ready for work, leaving Sammie and Miles alone, again.

Miles chewed thoughtfully, watching Sammie as he squirmed slightly under his gaze. "So...can't sleep, huh?"

Sammie hissed in annoyance. "Yeah. I already told you that." He glanced toward Pete's door. "We probably shouldn't talk about that now."

"You need to sleep, though. You'll get sick."

Sammie's attention snapped back to Miles, and he heated through again, face going pink and that cinnamon scent getting stronger before it shifted to a smell similar to overworked electronics. "Right, so let's talk about something else, then. What was that last night? And, for that matter, this right now?"

Miles blinked. "What do you mean?"

"That!" Sammie pointed accusingly at him. "That look! You look like you shifted into something else. You go from Miles to...this hungry look."

Sammie flushed further, and Miles gulped. *Oh, so it's obvious.* "I, uh, I dunno. I just... Um." He couldn't speak, why couldn't he speak? Sammie stared at him expectantly. "Dude, I dunno! I can just hear and smell stuff and...I don't notice when it happens! I don't have control over this stuff! I got overwhelmed last night and if whatever I did upset you, I'm sorry."

Sammie stared for a few moments before he relaxed a bit. "So, do you remember what happened?"

Now he wasn't sure if he did or not. "Uh, I remember we were on the couch and then Pete came in and you moved away after you were much closer than you were before."

"Huh, okay," Sammie muttered slowly. "So, that's it?"

Yes? "Yes, I think. I mean, I don't know. I'm not sure anymore."

There was a knock on the door, making both of them jump, and Sammie looked up at him when Naomi's voice carried through the door. "Guys? It's me. Let me in."

"Just a minute," Sammie called, mouthing to Miles that they were going to continue this later.

He headed to the door to let Naomi in, and the second the door opened her eyes snapped to Miles, a flash of confusion then understanding as she rubbed her nose. *Oh. I don't like that look.*

"Did I interrupt something?"

"Not at all!" Miles answered before she even finished her sentence, spinning on his stool and trying his best to look neutral. "What's up? Anything happening?"

Naomi stared blankly at him. She wandered over to the breakfast bar, Sammie following with a pointed look in his direction. "No, not really?" She tilted her head. "Are you all right? You look a little flushed." She glanced in the direction of Pete's room, where Miles could hear him showering if he focused. "You're still not having any pains or weird mood swings, are you? Anything like that?"

Miles shook his head, tensing as Sammie sat next to him. Her eyes snapped from Miles, to Sammie, then back, and Miles tried to come off as nonchalant as he could. The last thing he wanted was to hash out these feelings in front of anyone. He prayed that she wasn't going to ask him about it. He wondered if she could sense the tension in the air, somehow.

"Okay, well, after yesterday I want you to take it easy. I still gotta find that one, and I have the feeling you're still developing." She gazed at him fondly, squeezing his shoulder. "I wanted to make sure you were all right after all that. I was a little worried leaving you to fend for yourself after, I'm not going to lie."

Miles blinked. "Like, that I would've...lost it, or something?"

"Kinda. Sometimes there's some heavy mental toll from the change. I was hoping you didn't have to deal with that." She paused, tapping her hip as a small buzzing filled Miles's head. "Shit, well, that's my cue." She started to the door. "Try to relax today, okay? Hopefully I can get this cleaned up sooner rather than later, and then we can focus on you."

"Sounds good," Miles responded, the hair on the back of his neck rising as Sammie huffed. "I'll see you later, Naomi."

The alpha gave a small wave before she headed out of the door, and Sammie grabbed his shoulder to spin him around, eyebrows raised as he turned Miles to face him. "Uh—"

"'Kay, so, you really don't remember anything else happening last night? Wolfy or otherwise."

Miles heard the door of Pete's room open, and he sagged in relief, looking up as his roommate walked into the room, interrupting this dreaded conversation all over again. "Hey, you getting ready to go?"

"Yeah, I got a message in the shower about heading in ASAP

so I gotta." Pete yawned. "Any chance I could convince you to come by with as many energy drinks as you deem safe for me?"

Miles laughed. It wouldn't be the first time he had come by to feed Pete's caffeine addiction. "Sure, I'll message when I'm on the way."

"I love you." Pete groaned. "You're the best roommate." He spun around on his heel and walked toward the door. He gave them both a little wave before he left, leaving Miles alone with Sammie.

Sammie clicked his tongue, staring through Miles's very soul with those piercing blue eyes.

"Well?"

Miles threw up his hands. "Dude, I dunno what you want me to say. I remember what I remember. If I changed or something on you, I'm sorry, but I honestly don't remember anything else."

Sammie looked him over before he backed off. "Fine. I'll drop it." He gently nudged the cold pizza box in Miles's direction. "Eat. I'm gonna go shower."

"And then take a nap, right?" Miles called after Sammie, who wandered off in the direction of Miles's room. He chuckled as Sammie flipped him off over his shoulder and tucked into more of the offered food.

He did notice at least a few things from this whole change he was going through; he seemed like he was always hungry, he was oddly more comfortable in his skin, and he had more energy than he ever remembered having. He felt confident in a way he never had, and from what he could see, nothing had really changed outwardly. He still looked the same; still the same too fluffy and un-cooperative black hair, stubble that never grew into anything more, semi-tired dark eyes, and skinny string bean limbs. He just felt...better.

Chewing slowly, Miles pulled out his phone to scroll through something, whatever, to keep him occupied until Sammie got done, when a text lit up his screen, then another.

From Pete.

Miles frowned, tapping the notification to open it, and immediately choked with what he saw. Pete had sent a text, a garbled mix of letters and some numbers, and a short video that had Miles's heart soaring into his throat.

Right on the street in front of Pete's work, that same wolf from before, snarling and snapping at him before the video went black. *Oh god, what should I do?* He needed to help, somehow, stop Pete from going through that same pain he did. But how? He should get hold of Naomi, but did he even have her number?

"*Sammie!*" Miles yelled, hearing a loud *thump* from his bedroom.

"Y-yeah?"

"Tell Naomi to head to the store in downtown, if you have her number, please tell me you have it, 'cause I don't think I do and I don't know—"

"Miles," Sammie interrupted, opening the door to peer at Miles in concern, hair wet and his dirty clothes thrown over his body haphazardly. "What's going on?"

"Pete's in trouble," Miles explained, then paused, his anxiety bleeding through his fingertips and settling in his jaw in a dull pain, the gears in his head turning. "I don't know if she can get there in time, so just tell her! I'm gonna try to help!"

"Miles—wait, *Miles!*" Sammie's yelling faded as Miles sprinted out of the door and leaped down the stairs in his hurry to get outside.

He slipped and skidded on the sidewalk, shoving his way through groups and crowds to get there as fast as he could. If he could just get Pete in and out, then maybe Naomi could get there in time to stop the beast from hurting anyone else.

He heard screaming and upped his pace, moving against the sudden wave of people running toward him. He finally broke through the congested crowd to find the same massive werewolf from before, a light wound on its flank where he'd stabbed it...

He scanned the area for Pete. *He's not there, shit, please, let him be okay. If nothing else...* "Hey!" Miles shouted. The thick fur on the nape of the monster's neck rose. It bared its teeth in his direction and snarled. The sound made Miles's ribs rattle. "Yeah, you wanna finish the job? Come on, you don't want any of them. You want me."

Miles continued talking, trying to keep the thing's attention. He walked around it, slowly, his heart racing as its red eyes stayed on him. The snarling got louder and louder. As long as it kept its attention on him, that was fine—he just hoped it didn't try to attack him. He still had no idea what he was doing and had no chance of protecting himself if it did.

Its maw split open, sticky saliva dripping onto the concrete. The snarling turned into full-on roaring as it charged.

"No, no, no, no, no—!" Miles stepped back a couple of steps as it charged him, then held up his hands, the tips of his fingers tingling. Time seemed to slow as Miles realized his plain blunt nails had shifted to wicked-looking claws, and he didn't think, reeling back another step and slashing his hand over the monstrous werewolf's muzzle.

Spittle hit his chest, and he heard a yelp as his hand connected. He slashed across its right eye; blood hit the cement with a splatter that sounded deafening somehow. Miles sputtered as he stumbled back, flailing to keep his balance as the werewolf shook its head before taking off down the street.

Miles started after it, when he felt a hand slap onto the nape of his neck. "Don't you dare." Naomi's voice sounded like venom, and Miles froze in place, shrinking under his sudden anxiety. "You leave him alone. Let us take care of him. Miles." Naomi shifted in front of him, her jaw set, her usually gray eyes dark and stormy. "You could have been killed. What the hell were you doing?"

"U-uh," Miles stuttered, glancing at the shop behind her. "I...I was trying to help my roommate. He sent a video of the werewolf here and I didn't want him to get hurt or killed or anything and I didn't know if you could get there in time, so I went and tried to distract it and—"

Naomi cut off his rambling with a snarl, pinching the bridge of her nose. "Look, Miles, I understand why you did it, but it's dangerous. For more than if you get hurt." She glanced around the group, and Miles finally noticed everyone nearby acting like there hadn't been a giant monster roaming the street just a few minutes ago. His brow furrowed. "There's a very good reason you hadn't ever heard of anything like this happening before. Keeping our world secret is for *everyone's* sake, human or not. You can't just go running into broad daylight by yourself to go fighting things half shifted." She gave his nape one last rough squeeze before she let him go. "I'll talk to you later, explain everything, and *apparently* set some ground rules. I have a mess to clean up." She gestured to the store. "Go check on your friend."

With that, Naomi stalked away, heading for a group of people who appeared to have a weird haze over them. The edges of Miles's vision blurred when he made direct eye contact with them. He blinked hard and shook his head, huffing, as he walked into the store.

It was a little wrecked, not as bad as Miles expected it to be, but still rather messy; broken glass littered the floor, and several of the displays were ripped apart. Jewel cases and compact discs joined the shards of the window on the carpet. Pete was leaning against the counter, holding a towel over his hip, grimacing but not seeming to be in as much pain as Miles had been.

"P-Pete?"

He glanced up, then slumped in relief, waving Miles over.

"Dude. I knew I never should've gotten out of bed. A freakin' bear came into the store and tore everything up." He pulled the towel back slightly, and Miles felt a tiny bit of relief wash through him when he saw no sign of a bite. "Got me pretty good when I tried to get it out of the store."

A bear? Miles frowned slightly, glancing back to the street. Sure, the thing probably could've been mistaken for a bear from a distance, but up close it was clearly something entirely different. *Is this part of keeping them a secret? Why didn't they just wipe Sammie's mind then?* It made some sense for Miles, considering his condition, but...

His thoughts were interrupted by paramedics coming into the store, and Pete was looked over for any other outstanding injuries as they brought in a stretcher. Miles tried to stay out of their way, watching Pete get loaded into the ambulance before he left the destroyed store.

The walk back was...different. Walking through people he recognized from the crowd running away, finding them acting as if nothing had happened. He'd occasionally hear snippets of conversation about a giant bear tearing apart a store, noticing every single time he did the story seemed eerily the same. Like they were each reciting a line.

Miles walked back into his apartment, only to have a towel hurled at his head the first step he took inside. He sputtered, looking further inside to see Sammie, face red and jaw set, his fingers tapping a nervous rhythm on his hip. All at once, Miles was hit with an amalgamation of scents: fried electronics, fresh rain, sea salt, citric acid, and a dim underlying bit of cinnamon.

"Please tell me you aren't hurt, because I swear to god, I will murder you if you are."

"N-No." Miles held up his hands. "I'm fine. I—"

The rest of his sentence was cut off when Sammie sprinted across the apartment to slam into Miles. He squeezed him into a tight hug. "You are such an asshole," Sammie muttered, hands clutching the back of Miles's shirt as he hiccupped.

Miles frowned, gently wrapping his arms around Sammie. "I'm sorry," he apologized automatically, chewing his lip. "I just...I couldn't risk him getting hurt, too."

Sammie sniffled, rubbing his wet face against Miles's shirt, unwilling to pull away enough to look up at Miles as he talked. "Y-you don't think you getting hurt is just as bad?" he mumbled. "I had to worry about you dying once already this week."

Oh. When it was put like that... "I'm sorry," Miles repeated, squeezing Sammie a little tighter. He managed to get them over onto the couch; Sammie did not want to let go of him for anything. If it helped him feel better, that was fine. He could explain what happened later, when Sammie was better. For now, Miles was content to let Sammie cling to him, his chest warming with the proximity.

It was several moments before Sammie settled, and by that point Miles had maneuvered them both onto the couch and tucked a blanket around Sammie's shoulders. He panted, wriggling out of

Miles's hold and pulling the heavy fleece from his back. "Ugh, you feel like a furnace."

Miles blinked. "Oh, I don't feel any hotter. Must have something to do with the whole werewolf thing. Maybe my metabolism and everything else got more efficient. Would explain why I'm starving all the time."

"Is that your way of saying you want food right now?"

"I mean," Miles drawled teasingly, "I wouldn't say no."

Sammie shook his head, pulling out his phone. "Chinese okay?"

"It's perfect," Miles whispered, draping his hand over Sammie's nape and giving a light squeeze. "I love you."

Miles heard Sammie's heart rate spike. The cinnamon scent was so strong it almost felt like a sucker punch to his senses. He tasted the spice on his tongue and watched as Sammie stuttered, just for a moment, before focusing again on the task at hand.

Huh.

Did I say something wrong?

He'd always been very vocal with his love of Sammie before, though never explicitly. Miles had always thought of them as soulmates. Granted, before all this, he'd always believed their relationship would stay platonic for the rest of his life, since Sammie had a type that was very much not Miles.

Now that he could sense Sammie's reactions to things, he was unsure. Did Sammie not like it? Did he want Miles to stop expressing his kinda-sorta platonic love for him?

He can't possibly like it, right?

"And done..." Sammie leaned back, dropping his phone on the blanket in his lap. "Should be here in about fifteen." He glanced at Miles, the noticeably dimmed cinnamon surging for a split second before it was gone. "Wanna find something to watch in the meantime?"

"Sure." Miles sunk further into the couch, his head clouding as Sammie reached forward for the remote and tucked back into his side comfortably, murmuring about being cold again.

Yeah, there was no way. Miles was just projecting.

Chapter Four

"How are you feeling?"

"Like I got mauled by a bear." Pete settled in his hospital bed. "At least I don't have to stay for long; they mostly just wanna monitor me and make sure it didn't get infected or anything." He paused to catch his breath, sounding defeated as he continued. "I do have to take a couple weeks off work, since they gotta get repairs done and everything. Which sucks, but hey, at least I'm getting paid for a little bit of the time."

"I mean, gives you time to heal up fully at least," Miles answered, chewing on his lip.

He did have to wonder exactly how much Pete remembered. It was clear that those people Naomi went to talk with after him had something to do with everyone telling a story about a bear that so very clearly was not a bear. "So, uh, I hate to drag this up again, but anything else you remember from the, uh, attack?"

Pete frowned. "Why are you so interested in that? I think that's the third time you've asked about it."

Miles scratched the back of his neck. "No reason." He glanced back at his roommate, deciding to just drop the subject. Pete didn't need to be agitated while he was trying to heal up, after all. "So, uh, did they give you an ETA on when you get to leave? Your phone should be fully charged now so if you get released early just message me and I can meet you with a ride."

"I think they said tomorrow, as long as there's no complications." He glanced toward the door, then leaned forward. "Think you can sneak me in an energy drink? You still owe me from earlier."

"Maybe when I come pick you up." He stood up and patted Pete's leg as he pouted. "Get some rest, man."

He walked out and quietly greeted the nurse who was waiting outside the door. He stuffed his hands in his pockets as he walked, a frown forming on his face as his mind raced. Was it weird that same werewolf went after Pete? Out of all the city, why him? It was probably just a coincidence, but something still didn't sit right with him.

Miles rubbed at his nose. The smell of chemicals and blood and sickness gave him a headache. He always hated hospitals.

"Miles?" He paused, blinking as a soft, feminine voice called his name.

Turning toward the source, Miles found a very kind-faced,

middle-aged nurse, her salt-and-pepper hair pulled back into a low ponytail. She looked vaguely familiar. She wandered closer, then nodded, as if reassuring herself. "My, you do look just like her…" She mused softly, a bit of sadness behind it. A salty scent added to the other offenders assaulting his senses. "Oh, you probably don't remember. You were distracted." She held her hand out. "Anya Carro, I was your mother's nurse. She talked about you all the time when you weren't there."

"O-oh." Miles shook her hand, a little dazed. It felt like months had gone by since…

"Oh, sorry. I'm probably holding you up." She paused a moment, then looked over him. "If you ever need someone to talk to, feel free to visit any time, Miles. Of course, I might be busy, but your mother was one of my favorite patients. She was always so kind and concerned for all of us, even through the worst parts of her treatment." She patted Miles on the arm before she left, and for a split second, he could scent something completely new. Something like that spicy-earthy scent he caught when he first woke up, but also different. Sharper, like fresh rainwater and the snapping of a young plant root.

Miles stared after Ms. Carro for a couple of moments before his phone buzzing in his pocket drew his attention. He pulled the device out to see a message from Sammie, letting him know Naomi was looking for him. *Great.*

"Oh, she's gonna tear my head off," Miles mumbled, slamming out a text back before he jogged down the stairs and out of the hospital. The less he kept her waiting, the better for his health, probably.

*

"Oh good, you're back. Don't take off your jacket." Miles was barely in the door when Naomi grabbed his hood and steered him to the hallway outside.

"Wha—hey, but—"

"Nope." She popped the "'p" as she started dragging him down the stairs again. "We have a serious discussion to have, and we can kill two birds this way." Her gray eyes glanced back his way, and Miles shuddered at the mischievous glint in them. "Since you clearly don't have trouble running in to fight things, you'll need some proper training for it. Hope you're still as gung-ho as you were earlier."

Why didn't he like the sound of that? Miles sagged, finally not fighting her grip as he resigned himself to what sounded like a rough night.

Naomi had gotten them to that same clearing as before, and now that Miles looked, he noticed an odd little glow to the trees surrounding it, almost like those people from before, hazy and jumping from his vision when he made direct eye contact. "Uh, was that here last time?"

Naomi followed his gaze and arched her brows. "Ah, you noticed finally. It's a sign of magic; there's a barrier here so humans don't accidentally stumble in on us. Most large preserves or parks have them." She maneuvered him to one of the stumps at the edge of the clearing. "Now, no interrupting till I'm done, got it? If you do, I'll just go less and less easy on you."

Miles sat back on the stump as Naomi exhaled. "Okay, so I already told you about the society of supernatural creatures. It should go without saying that we can't be discovered." She gave him a very pointed look at that. "The reason being how dangerous that'd be for both parties—humans and us. Before we'd tightened down on our secrecy, there was a lot of unnecessary death. Humans getting killed or changed just to level the playing field, supernaturals being slaughtered by the thousands just for existing. We managed to wipe our existence from history, leaving behind the tales and folklore that we couldn't erase, and we live at the edge of human knowledge, to make sure those massacres don't happen again."

A flicker of something, a mix of anxiety, fear, and shame, crossed her features, before she continued. "Acting like you did, as much as I understand why, it's a danger to our secret." She knelt, hands on Miles's shoulders. "You're good, I know that, and you've shown that you're absolutely selfless when it comes to your friends, as stupid that it is, but I'm not always going to be there to protect you. The only reason why you're not being hunted down like that feral alpha is because I talked them out of doing it."

So, he could be a lot worse off right now than being lectured...

"So, you understand now? No running in to attack something like that again, right?" Naomi gave him a small, lopsided smile. "Leave that type of stuff to us."

"Yeah, I get it." Miles leaned back for a moment, before Naomi pulled him to his feet, that soft look shifting into a full-on smirk. "Uh?"

"Oh, did you forget about our training?" Naomi pulled him to the center of the clearing, then took several paces back from him as she cracked her knuckles. "If you happen to get caught up in something like that again, you need to know how to actually defend yourself, rather than relying on your instincts to save you."

"Okay," Miles started, unsure, given how eager Naomi seemed. "What do you want me to—" He yelped as Naomi punched him, his shoulder immediately aching as he stumbled back. "Wh-what the hell was that for?"

"Hmm." Naomi relaxed, ruffling her hair softly. "Figured you'd, you know, block that."

Miles sputtered. "Block— You didn't tell me anything! You just punched me!"

She leveled him with a blank look. "Miles, really? If you get attacked by someone, they're not exactly going to announce it. You gotta stay on your toes, listen to your instincts."

"I thought you said I shouldn't rely on my instincts."

Naomi gave a frustrated groan. "I mean that more as *only* relying on your instincts. You have to actually know how to protect yourself. Trust your instincts for knowing when there's danger and trust your body for helping you out of it." She held her hands up, eyebrows raised. "Understand?"

"Yeah, I think—" Once again, Miles was cut off as Naomi jumped toward him, leg dropping directly toward his face. He had a split second to leap out of the way, stumbling back and landing hard on the ground.

"I mean, that's better but..." Naomi mumbled, her disappointed face swimming into focus. "You want to not fall."

This was getting ridiculous. Miles tried to pull at her leg to get her on the ground as well, only for Naomi to easily step outside of his reach. "Too slow."

He growled, scrambling up to his feet, only to immediately go on the defensive as she rushed him again with a flurry of punches and kicks that Miles tried and sometimes succeeded in catching. He winced as her boot slammed into his ribs, lurching back and catching a punch flying toward his face. Before she could pull free, in a frustrated fury, Miles pulled her toward him, leveraging his hold to throw her over his head. Impossibly, Naomi managed to land on her feet, softening the blow as she sunk to the ground slowly and looked up at Miles with a hint of pride. "Impressive," she complimented, before yanking his foot out from underneath him.

Miles yelped, groaning as his tail bone slammed into the earth. Naomi's laughter rang through the clearing as he grumbled, the moment of pride at having grounded her gone with it. "You couldn't let me just bask in taking you down?"

"Nope." She popped her lips, gracefully jumping to her feet

and pulling Miles up. "You just happened to succeed once. Now, the question is if you can do it again, without me hitting you?" Her expression was almost feral. "Just so you know, the cockier you get the more I'll be trying to keep your ego in check."

This is going to be a long damn night...

*

By the time Miles got back home, it was well past midnight, and every muscle in his body ached. He'd managed to ground Naomi on about four occasions that entire time, and she'd made sure to pay him back triple-time for each one. He groaned, rolling his shoulders as he walked into the apartment, then stopped when he couldn't hear Sammie.

He glanced around the living room and found no sign of him. His heart rate kicked up several notches. "Sammie?" He walked up into his room, relaxing as the scent of cinnamon, coffee, burnt sugar, and an underlying shock of something else that Miles couldn't quite place washed over him. He sagged in relief as he saw Sammie, finally fully asleep, curled up in Miles's bed, glasses tossed haphazardly onto the pillow beside him, phone playing a video quietly in his loose hand.

Carefully, so as not to wake him, Miles turned off the video, then set his phone and glasses on the nightstand. He laughed to himself when Sammie barely even moved, just wriggled a bit and mumbled nonsensically in his sleep.

Good.

Now the only problem was, Miles needed to sleep, and he wasn't about to kick Sammie out of his bed...

Staring down at the little empty space behind Sammie for a couple of seconds, Miles eventually shook his head, gently lifting the unused pillow from the bed and plopping it on the floor.

He grabbed a blanket from his closet and flopped on the floor next to the bed, grimacing as his back protested. He could probably sleep better on the couch, but...

Something didn't want him to leave the room, and within a few seconds of lying down, Miles was out anyway, drifting into the easiest and best sleep he'd had in weeks.

*

Miles awoke, squinting as light streamed in through his blinds. Surprisingly, his back didn't feel too bad, considering all the training he'd been through. When he sat up, Miles found Sammie still fast asleep, arm dangling off the bed and face scrunched up where he was pressing into the pillow. Miles stared for a few seconds before he realized his starry-eyed expression was making him appear like an idiot watching his best friend sleep. He got up, groaning and ruffling his hair. He was being stupid. So, so stupid. What idiot falls in love with his best friend? Apparently, Miles!

Granted, Miles had always kinda liked Sammie, but still. He was being dumb. Because everything had changed now. *There's no way Sammie would be interested in me, given everything that's happened...*

Miles let out a heavy sigh, scratching through his stubble as he pottered about the kitchen. He needed to get over this crush, or whatever, like he had before. *Just because Sammie came back doesn't mean it needs to, too.*

"Why did you even come back?" Miles wondered aloud, watching his coffee machine slowly come to life. "Why didn't you stay there, where you seemed happy?"

In all the pictures Miles would see online, Sammie was laughing, having the typical fun college life, an actual relationship that seemed like it was going well. Why throw all of that away? Why come back here?

"Smells good."

Miles jumped and paused a beat before he turned to find Sammie shuffling up to the breakfast bar, rubbing his eyes and yawning. "Oh, did I wake you up?"

Sammie shook his head, grumbling sleepily as he sat down. "Nah, I slept long enough anyway." He blinked blearily up at Miles. "I think I knocked out about...like an hour after you left with Naomi."

"Ah." Miles focused back on the coffee maker, debating, before he turned and leaned against the counter as he watched Sammie for his reaction. "Was my bed comfy?"

"Yeah," Sammie replied, then blinked and grimaced. "Oh, sorry. I..." He frowned, looking down at the counter. "I really only meant to take a nap, and the couch was too rough, and I didn't want to use Pete's since I don't really know him that well, so..." He frowned. "You could've just woken me up."

Miles turned back to the finished coffee and pulled down two mugs. "It's no big deal." He poured their drinks, adding the little bit of cinnamon and caramel that he remembered Sammie liked, before turning back to him. "Glad you slept finally. How do you feel about pancakes?"

Sammie blinked, taking the coffee and staring up at Miles for a second. "Yeah, sounds...good. Are you feeling okay?"

"Yeah, why?" Miles lied, trying to keep his mind off the questions he desperately wanted to ask. Why did you come back? What happened in New York? Why leave when you were happy? What was even back here worth coming back to? Did you come back for me?

"You just seem like something is bothering you." Sammie jolted as Miles set the skillet down on the burner with a bit more force than he meant. "Uh—"

"Is there a reason you came back? I've seen all those pictures you posted, and you seemed fine, so why did you come back here?" The questions left his mouth before he could stop himself. Miles froze. When he turned, he found Sammie staring up at him, a sort of lost look on his face. A sourness filled the air, like citric acid, making his sinuses burn.

"I—I mean, those are just pictures, Miles." He mumbled, voice quiet and wandering. "You know, most people try to look happy. It's an act. I usually had to act when I was there, because it wasn't home. Wasn't where I felt like I needed to be." He tapped his mug for a moment before looking away. "I came back because I needed to be back home. Back with the people I cared about. Who cared about me." Sammie sniffled. "Figures my first day back, it hurts them—"

"Hey." Miles crossed the short distance to the counter and fitted his hands over Sammie's warm fingers. Sammie's blue eyes shifted up to meet his. "I'm sorry. I told you before, this is all not your fault." He offered a soft look, trying to be upbeat, as usual. "I'm still alive, still here for you to ramble to and for you to lean on, all right? Just...a little hairier sometimes."

Sammie huffed out a laugh, shaking his head. "You're too optimistic."

"Evens out with you, you pessimist." He rubbed his thumb along the back of Sammie's hand, then he pulled back, grimacing as he turned away. That was probably unnecessary.

The thumping of Sammie's heart slowed slightly, and Miles continued making breakfast as Sammie started mumbling about the shows he watched while Miles went out training, about what they probably needed to buy next time they got a chance, about finding some work while he and Pete were out.

Miles told his stupid, lovesick heart to calm down, and continued about the kitchen, pointedly ignoring the urge to kiss Sammie as he asked for chocolate chips in his pancakes, or when he beamed on the first bite.

Mostly, Miles tried to ignore how utterly and wholly in love he was, when he knew it'd never be returned.

Chapter Five

" . . . **S**eems like he's moved, so I'll be out of town for the next couple days. Hopefully. It might go on longer, depending on whether we can track him down. If you need me though, just call me, I'll be here as fast as I can, got it?" A beat. Miles traced the swirls of the faux granite on the countertop as Naomi cleared her throat, bringing his attention to her. "Miles, did you hear me?"

"Yeah," he mumbled, his face mashed into his other hand. "You'll be gone, but I can call you if I need you." He looked at her fully. "It's not like anything is going to happen, anyway. It's been quiet, aside from that incident at the shop. I haven't had any problems, you're good. The faster you can get him under control the better."

Naomi looked him up and down before she seemed satisfied

with the state of him. "Okay, just please, if you feel the slightest bit off, call me right away."

Miles waved her off. "Will do. Don't worry about me, just make sure you get him."

With that, Naomi was out of the apartment door. Sammie poked his head up from behind the couch with a frown. "Are you sure you're okay?"

"Yeah. I mean, I haven't had any issues, right? I'm not as important as making sure no one else gets attacked like me or Pete." He flopped over the back of the couch and stretched. "Besides, means I can rest after the absolute ass-kicking she gave me last time."

Sammie shot him a mischievous expression. "You told me. Kinda wish I was there to see it. Sounded hilarious."

Miles turned to give him an unimpressed look, setting his jaw and narrowing his eyes at the completely not-innocent smirk on Sammie's face. "You know, you're not funny."

Sammie gasped, dramatically throwing a hand to his chest and reeling back. "How dare! I am a riot, good sir!"

"Oh my god," Miles muttered, standing up and ruffling Sammie's hair as he passed by. "You're a drama queen, is what you are."

"You're not wrong." Sammie turned, watching Miles as he walked toward the front door. "Where're you going?"

"A walk." He shook out his limbs, hopping in place as he answered. "I got this weird like...I dunno, tense feeling. Figure I can jog it out or something."

Sammie stared at him for a couple of seconds before he scrambled up off the couch as Miles reached for the door handle. "Ah, ah, ah! Dude."

"What?"

Sammie raised his eyebrows, throwing his hands up. "You don't get anything off about what you just said? Naomi literally just said if you feel off to call her and you told me you feel off. You don't see a problem with that?"

Miles blinked. "I mean, no? She meant, like, supernatural stuff. This is stress tense. It's not the same."

"Nope." Sammie yanked Miles back by his collar, causing him to yelp. "I don't trust this. You're staying right here until this feeling goes away, and if you act the littlest bit out of the ordinary, I'm calling her."

"Sammie, I—" Miles grunted as Sammie flung him down onto the couch. "What is *wrong* with you?"

"Excuse me for having your best interests in mind." He flung himself into Miles's lap and glared up at him. "I'm not about to let you get yourself in trouble."

Miles let out an exasperated laugh. "I'm not gonna get in trouble! I'm just stressed, and you are not helping!" He shoved at Sammie, earning a kick to his hip as Sammie fell to the floor with a shout. "Seriously, you worry way too much." Miles stood up, shaking his head as Sammie sputtered. "I'll be back in an hour." He turned around to face his friend as he stumbled back up to his feet, a nervous air making his nose itch. "Don't worry about me."

"Miles, I'm telling you, I have a bad feeling about this!" Sammie shouted, letting out a groan as Miles shut the door. He shook his head, pulling his phone out of his pocket to make sure it had enough juice to get through his run, before he was jogging down the stairs.

Seriously, Sammie worried too much for his own good sometimes. Miles had done this hundreds of times, his neighborhood wasn't that bad, and with Naomi and that alpha out of town, he had nothing to worry about.

Everything was going to be fine.

*

Miles panted, legs shaking with every step he ran as he closed in on the preserve where Naomi usually brought him to train. His head felt even more full, his chest tight with anxiety, but he couldn't find a reason. Why? There was nothing here, why would he be feeling like this?

An odd sensation, something like an invisible rope, tugged him forward. His legs automatically moved, and a warning bell sounded through his brains.

Something *was* off.

Miles anchored his feet, grass and dirt causing him to slip slightly. He sucked in a harsh breath and nearly gagged. He could smell blood.

Copper, mud, rain, rot...

Miles shuddered, then jolted as a voice spoke.

"Huh, so, she really did leave, did she?"

Miles looked around frantically, searching for the source of the voice, his heart pounding in his chest. He needed to run, needed to get hold of Naomi, something.

His phone. *That's right! I have Naomi's number; I can just call her!*

His fingers shaking, Miles ripped his phone out of his pocket, trying desperately to calm his hands, when he felt a cold, firm grasp around his bicep. "Ah, trying to call for your false little alpha, boy?"

Miles tried to kick out, but the hold vanished before a palm slammed hard into his back, sending him to the dirt, his phone clattering away. *Shit.* He had to get up.

A sharp pain flared through his stomach, and Miles cried out, the force sending him sprawling over onto his back. He blinked through tears at his attacker.

The man looked normal, for the most part. Long brown hair tied back, tidy beard, brown eyes, well-dressed in a suit. Miles would've thought it was a completely different alpha, if it wasn't for the scar Miles knew he'd put there running over his nose and cheek.

The alpha sneered, leaning down toward Miles. "Ah, so you do recognize me. Good." He stomped down onto Miles's leg, ripping a pained cry from him as the bone snapped. "Now, to get rid of that pesky claim the mutt left on you."

"W-wait, please..."

The man just snarled, and Miles couldn't move. There was a piercing pressure on his stomach, right where his bite was, and the next thing he felt was something like he imagined it'd be burning alive.

He could only remember the pain, the seemingly endless agony, before he was shoved to the back of his own mind, his body acting on its own, and Miles was left to watch as his body rose up, on a broken leg, and he followed the alpha, despite his consciousness screaming at his legs to stop.

He had no control.

*

"Where are you...?" Sammie mumbled, chewing nervously on his thumbnail, his finger hovering over Miles's contact. He should just call, make sure he was all right. Sammie couldn't shake the feeling of dread settled in the pit of his stomach.

Screw it. Sammie tapped the call button and brought the phone up to his ear. One ring, two, three...

"Hey."

"Miles! Oh, thank god, you're—"

"You're talking to Miles's voicemail, leave your message now."

Sammie was going to kill him.

He threw his phone down in a huff and paced, scrubbing a hand over his face, before he snatched the phone back up and called again. "Pick up, you asshole..."

Voicemail.

Again. *Voicemail.*

"Shit." Sammie hung up, his heart beating in his throat now. Something was definitely wrong. He pulled up Naomi's number and dialed it, trying to slow his breathing as the phone rang. "Please, please, please pick up."

"Sammie?"

He sagged in relief. "Naomi, listen, I—I don't know if anything happened, but...I have a bad feeling; I think something did."

"Slow down, where's Miles?"

He stuttered and shook himself, trying to choke down his growing anxiety. "He went out for a jog, and he said he was going to be back in an hour, but it's been past that, and I tried to call him, and I kept getting his voicemail."

Naomi cursed loudly, and Sammie could hear panicked talking in the background. "Dammit, all right. I'm on my way back now. Just stay where you're at. We'll find Miles."

"Okay, can you stay—" The line went dead, and Sammie sucked in a shaky breath, dropping his phone and continuing pacing. So much anxiety buzzed under his skin it felt like it was going to peel off, like electricity buzzing through his veins instead of blood. He wanted to go out and look for Miles, but Naomi was right—it was better for him to just stay where he was and wait for her to take care of it.

Just because she was right didn't mean he felt any better; his heart still felt like it was trying to crawl up his throat. His hands came over with pins and needles and his chest tightened. A lump formed in his throat as he tried to breathe, to focus on the idea that Miles was going to be fine, Naomi was on the way, everything was going to be fine.

Just breathe. Breathe. Everything is fine. It's fine...

Sammie sank to the ground, running his hands over his face, letting out a harsh wheeze. Feeling surged through his fingertips before it went back to numbness.

He was not panicking. Everything was fine. It was going to be fine. He was fine.

Something sparked, just a quick flash of blue, so fast it must've been his frazzled brain making it up.

Breathe. Breathe. Just breathe...

Sammie tucked his face into his knees, squeezing his eyes closed tightly, and sucked in shuddering, shaking breaths. His heart sank back in place, and his chest opened up enough for him to finally take a real, whole breath. He grimaced as a bone-deep ache spread through every limb, and his jaw muscle twitched from tension.

His hands shook as he slowly released his death grip on his legs. Pins and needles tingled in his fingertips, along with an odd feeling like he'd just gripped an electric fence. He gasped, wiping the sweat from his forehead, before he moved up onto the couch. He stared down at his phone for a moment before he shoved it to the side. He had to just stay calm, let Naomi do the work, she'd find Miles, bring him back.

Sammie hadn't felt so useless in his life. Not since...

*

"Help!" His throat was raw from screaming, his hands trembling where he was trying to apply pressure to the massive wound on Miles's stomach. Slick red made his hands slip and slide over too-pale skin. "Someone! Anyone! Please help!" He only heard his own voice answering back.

"Sammie..." Miles's voice, thick and raspy, smaller than Sammie had ever heard. Red spilled over his lips, and Sammie choked back a sob, trying to stay calm, to breathe, to just stay calm, stay calm, Miles needed him to stay calm.

His fingers slipped and he cursed, his hands shaking as he tried desperately to slow the bleeding. "D-don't...don't move. God, Miles, don't move, please, please don't...don't... Please don't...don't leave." Sammie choked out the words around a sob. "Miles, please... Don't leave. I just got you back. Please, please..."

"Move."

He could barely hear the voice through his own racked breaths. He hiccupped, glancing up to find the girl he'd bumped into earlier, looking like she'd just gotten out of a fight, her—her eyes red. "N-no... Stay, stay back."

She stared at him for a moment. "Let me help him. I know how to keep him safe." She knelt on Miles's other side, grimacing slightly, before she shifted the knapsack she was carrying to her lap and pulled out medical supplies and what looked like a bundle of sage, but smelled different, almost damp, somehow. "Trust me."

His hands trembled as her light touch settled calmly over his wrist. He didn't have much choice, did he? "J-just...please, save him."

She scooted closer and immediately got to work. She seemed like she knew what she was doing, cleaning the wound efficiently before moving on to something Sammie had never seen before, something that didn't quite make sense. She covered her mouth and nose and sparked up the bundle for a couple of seconds before stamping it out. She scooped up a pinch of the ashes left behind, then glanced up at Sammie. "He's going to want to thrash around, since this is going to hurt, but I need to do this to get rid of the claim that alpha is going to have on him. I don't have much time to explain, and I promise I'll completely explain everything to the both of you later, but for now I need you to hold him down, so he doesn't rip that wound open more than it already is."

Sammie gulped harshly, gently putting a hold on Miles's shoulder and hip. She huffed, glanced down to Miles, muttered an apology, and rubbed the ashes into the wound. Immediately, Miles shot up against Sammie's grip, screaming.

"M-Miles, Miles, it's okay, you're okay..." Sammie rambled, trying to soothe Miles, not knowing if he could even hear him. The woman pressed against the wound, holding her breath, until

Miles finally sagged, his breathing harsh and wrecked.

"Okay." She relaxed, looking up to Sammie. "Now, I would normally ask him about this, but—" She glanced at Miles's mostly unconscious form. "I can't, and I don't have much of a chance to before it's too late." She settled her gaze on the wound. "I need to put my own claim on him, or it's possible for the other to take. Miles would lose any free will he'd have, and become a passenger in his own body, unless his will is strong enough to fight it. If I make my claim, I can help him, since it's too late for Miles to remain human. I can help him learn control, and give him the option to keep his life as normal as it'll ever be again..." She lifted her head back up to look over Sammie. "I hate to put you in this position, but...I need to do this. For his sake."

Sammie was lost. Nothing she was saying made sense. Miles wasn't going to be human? What was she talking about? "What... I don't understand. What do you need to help him?"

"I need to bite him, like that other one did. I know it's going to hurt him again, but I need to. The less of a chance that alpha has of having control of Miles, the better it is for him." She leaned forward over Miles's body. "Please. I'll explain everything to you after."

Sammie looked down at Miles, taking in his paling skin, the shockingly stark red splashed over it, his closed eyes, his slowly rising chest. "O-okay. I...whatever you need to do." He blinked, his vision blurring as he started tearing up again. "Just please, save him."

She seemed to shift, her eyes bleeding red, her jaw shifting with a pop and wicked teeth flashing into sight before they were sunk into the center of the massive bite wound on Miles's stomach. Miles let out another scream before he thankfully finally passed out.

Sammie felt lightheaded, adrenaline making his hands shake against Miles's skin. He swallowed hard, looking up as the girl lifted her head with a grimace. She wiped her face and spat.

"Are...are you like that monster?"

She glanced up at him, then lowered her eyes. "Sort of. Miles will be too, since that monster bit him. But I'm going to do what I can to make sure Miles doesn't become anything like that, all right?" She reached into her knapsack again and pulled out some wet wipes and a bottle of water to rinse off her face and her mouth. After she was done, she looked down at Miles. "We're going to have to take him someplace safe—I can explain everything to you there." She stood up and glanced down the alleyway before she looked back at Sammie. "Can you walk?"

Sammie trembled but lifted onto shaky legs. A frown crossed her face, and her hands settled on Sammie's back to steady him. "You sure about that?" She glanced down to Miles. "I can probably carry both of you, if you need it."

She was shorter than Sammie and looked to be about fifty pounds lighter. Seeing what he'd just seen, he didn't doubt it, but he didn't want to draw any unnecessary attention their way. "I-I'm fine. I just...have to get my bearings."

She scooped Miles up into her arms easily, then glanced down the alleyway again, another frown marring her features. Sammie leaned against the cold, hard brick of the wall and panted. "W-what...what's wrong?"

"Oh, it's nothing." She shook her head, adjusting her grip slightly before she tilted her head toward the only opening in the alley. "Mostly making sure the way was clear. Don't need to be jumped by anything right now."

Sammie finally willed his legs to move, at which point she started walking alongside him, keeping pace, gray eyes constantly searching over their surroundings. It made sense, considering what just happened; if Sammie had the mental capacity to do more than just keep moving forward, he'd be doing the same.

The walk back to Miles's apartment was long, feeling like days passing between each step. No one noticed or cared—either that or Sammie was too out of it to notice any reaction himself. They'd made it inside the apartment in one piece, and the girl quickly went about setting Miles up in bed to rest.

Sammie wasn't much help, though he tried to do what he could, until she just pulled a chair up beside the bed and ordered him to sit. "I can take care of everything. Just rest." She offered him a warm look, and her voice was soft. "Sleep, if you can. I can wake you up when Miles is up."

Sleep was the furthest thing from his mind. Sammie already felt like he was living in a nightmare. He just wanted to make sure Miles was okay. "I-I'm fine." He leaned forward, his elbows *digging painfully into his knees as his chest constricted, looking down at Miles. He seemed peaceful, but... "I-I'm sorry." The girl paused, and the sound of her prepping medical supplies and various other items to a container at the foot of the bed slowed. Sammie looked up at her. "I—we wouldn't have been there if it wasn't for me. It's my fault this happened."*

"Oh no." She dropped the gauze she was handling, came around the side of the bed, and knelt beside him. "You can't think like that. It'll drive you mad, trust me." She shook her head. "This isn't your fault. There's no way you could've known this would've happened. You can't blame yourself for something like this."

"B-but—"

Her firm hand settled on his shoulder and squeezed tightly. "No. Listen, you have no blame in this. If anyone has blame other than that monster you saw, it's me for failing at my job."

Sammie blinked through his tears, hiccupping. She took a long moment to settle in next to him before she started explaining everything. How there was a different world, how she was part of a force to keep that world secret and to stop it from hurting the human world, how she was there to try to stop the alpha and miscalculated... Sammie didn't speak, he couldn't, he could hardly process everything she was saying. By the end of it, he was staring down at Miles, a weird feeling sitting in his chest; a mix of fear, dread, and something sharp, explosive that he couldn't place.

"I'm sorry you both got dragged into all of this, I really am.

But I'm going to try to make this as painless as I can." She gave him a semi-reassuring look, a good amount of tenseness behind the relaxed expression. *"I'll try to make sure things are as normal as they can be."*

"Okay," he whispered, barely even realizing he'd done so, staring down at Miles with that explosive feeling surging. The feeling left him all at once, before he looked over to her.

"Who are you?"

She looked him over before answering, the words drowned out with the sound of a buzz. It was familiar…

*

Sammie jolted, coming back to the present.

He looked at his phone, his heart hammering in his chest, a glimmer of hope there, Miles's name flashing on his caller ID.

"Miles!" he shouted, standing up, adrenaline pumping through him. "Miles, are you okay? Where are you? Why didn't you answer earlier?"

Heavy breathing came through the line, then it went dead.

Sammie moved before he could think. His feet carried him out of the door and down the stairs as his lungs struggled to keep up with the sudden burst of movement. He didn't know where to start, didn't know where he was going, he just ran. He didn't care if Naomi was on her way. He needed to find Miles.

That same explosive feeling surged in his chest, pulsing, like something living.

Chapter Six

Cinnamon.

Miles knew cinnamon.

His legs itched, his jaw aching. He wanted to run.

Cinnamon, he had to protect that scent. He needed it to be safe.

He felt something like a tether on his throat, and with a shock Miles woke, all his limbs shifting, the air punching out of his lungs. Everything hurt.

"Good job." A hand gripped into his hair and shoved him down. His aching body flared with pain as he hit the muddied ground. Icy rain pelted his skin, and it took a moment to find his bearings. Miles blinked up through the rain as he heard footsteps, and tensed as he saw that man, the alpha, walking away from him, toward the cinnamon scent, toward Sammie. "Stay there until I'm done."

"N-no..." Miles gasped, trying to rise onto his feet, everything aching, his head throbbing.

The man didn't pay him any attention, and Miles grit his teeth as that cinnamon got stronger. He needed to get up, he needed to move, dammit, why wouldn't his legs just move?

"Miles?" Sammie's voice called, and Miles growled, his legs shaking as he managed to get to his feet.

"*Get out of here*!" he yelled before he felt that tether on his throat and his consciousness was shoved to the back once again.

No!

"I told you to stay, mutt," the man snarled. Miles heard Sammie's soft gasp before he became aware of hurried footsteps, that cinnamon scent getting stronger. Why was it getting closer? Why wasn't Sammie running?

"Miles!" His heart sank as Sammie's familiar form broke through the trees. His face was panicked, and his blue eyes flickered toward Miles for a moment before settling on the man.

Miles's heart pounded as the man advanced toward Sammie, eyes narrowing in rage.

I need to get out of his control, I need to stop this!

"Let him go!"

The man murmured something, then he advanced toward Sammie, his features shifting as the first sign of fear flickered over Sammie's features.

No, no, no, no!

Miles willed his limbs to move, willed himself back. He

needed to save Sammie.

He felt something, like a punch to his chest, before he slumped forward. Just as suddenly as he'd been yanked out of control, he was slamming back. He ground his teeth, willing his aching body to move. *"Get away from him!"*

The man, whose hand was twisting into Sammie's shirt to pull him closer, froze. He turned to stare at Miles with shock before Miles tackled him, swinging wildly. His fist connected with the man's jaw. His jaw ached, and an acute headache throbbed just behind his eyes. A glance at his fingers showed his human nails replaced with sharp talons, which dug into his palm as he pulled his fist back. He growled as he felt hands dragging him back.

"Let's go," Sammie hissed, and Miles didn't need to think any more than that, following Sammie as he tugged him away. Sammie was safe. He was going to be okay. His mate was fine.

The word, unprompted from his subconscious, slammed into the forefront of his brain with the intensity of a baseball bat. Mate? That couldn't possibly mean what he thought it meant, right?

"Why'd you stop?" Sammie grunted, tugging again at Miles's arm. "Murderous werewolf guy right behind us, remember?"

Right...

Miles would have to figure that out later; for now, they needed to go. Despite the general ache through his entire body, Miles scooped Sammie up and sprinted out of the preserve, his breath catching as Sammie gasped and stared up at him. The cinnamon scent that filled Miles's head like a sweet, spiced fog grew somehow stronger.

"Why'd you come out here?" Miles muttered, slowing his running as they got closer back to the city. "It's dangerous."

Sammie's eyebrows jumped into his hairline. "Excuse me for caring. You know you've been gone for three hours?" He grunted as Miles froze, his brow furrowing.

Really? He didn't realize it'd been that long...

Sammie wriggled out of Miles's hold. He slapped Miles's shoulder when he got settled on his feet. "I told you I had a bad feeling about this. You completely ignored me!"

Miles stared down at Sammie, that familiar cinnamon becoming overpowered by a sour citrus aroma. He rubbed his nose and shook his head. "I'm sorry." He practically tasted the spice, the constant feeling of "other" that resided in his chest flaring with excitement at the scent. "I'm inconsiderate. I'm a jerk." Miles scooped Sammie back up, causing him to yelp. "I'll make it up to you when we get back home."

Sammie's heart rate spiked, and Miles had to practically choke down the pleased rumble threatening to crawl out of his throat. "O-okay. I called Naomi already, so...you'll have to hurry up."

Miles felt that energy in his chest settle. He almost purred in contentment, basking in the sweet cinnamon and burnt sugar scent coming off Sammie in waves. He felt calmer than he had in weeks.

"You know, you can put me down at any time," Sammie muttered, his face flushing.

Miles's lips curled in a feral manner, and he adjusted his hold again. Sammie's glasses shifted to the edge of his nose as he yelped again. "I know."

"Then...put me down?" Sammie whined. "My legs do work, you know."

"Yep." Miles shifted him, nudging Sammie's glasses into place again with his jaw, that scent of cinnamon and sugar getting cloyingly thick. Sammie's flush darkened heavily, dipping under the collar of his shirt. "Don't worry, I'll put you down when we get home."

Maybe. At the moment, Miles didn't want Sammie to be any further from him than this. He needed Sammie close. He licked his lips, grinning as Sammie choked, looking away. Miles's crush was so much worse.

Mate. He could almost pinpoint the different thing in his head, his voice but rougher. His brain felt as if it'd been filled with warmed honey, everything syrupy and clogged through with a cinnamon sugar fog. *Mine, safe.*

The voice seemed to rumble through his chest, to the point Miles was afraid he'd just spoken the words out loud without realizing it. A glance at Sammie and the worry eased, as Sammie simply pouted, allowing himself to be carried with a soft blush dusting his cheeks and nose.

A rhythmic rumble started in his throat before Miles could

do anything about it, and Sammie's blue eyes locked onto him, brow furrowing. "What...what's wrong?"

Miles blinked, clearing his throat. *Was I... I was just purring, wasn't I? Embarrassing.* "Ah, nothing, just...happy you're safe."

Sammie's blush deepened and he glanced away. He dug his elbow into Miles's chest, and Miles had to choke down that purring sound again.

He was so screwed.

*

Miles fully expected to be lectured, or beat up, or something by Naomi when she got back. Instead, her gray eyes, ringed with vibrant red, softened upon seeing him tangled together with Sammie, the latter dozing gently against Miles's shoulder. She relaxed with a relieved huff and padded quietly over to him, then ruffled a hand through his hair. "I'm glad you're okay." She glanced down to his leg, and Miles barely resisted jolting when he followed, remembering the break at the sight of the bruising and spots of flaking blood. "Looks like you healed up all right. If you're tired, I can hang around while you both rest. I have to ask you some things when you do."

He started to nod when he froze. He glanced down to Sammie as he shifted, snuffling into his shoulder.

Mate.

"Whoa." Naomi's softly awed voice drew him out of the

moment. Miles looked back to see Naomi staring at him with a bit of shock. "Has that happened a lot lately?"

"Has what happened?" Miles frowned, glancing back at Sammie. "I mean…we used to sleep like this a lot, but—"

"No." Naomi eased down onto the couch near him. "That…your eyes flashed when you looked down to Sammie just now. That usually only happens when you're close to shifting, or your emotions are too high." She bit her lip, seeming to debate with herself for a moment before she continued. "It can also happen when you've sort of…connected with someone else."

A purr rumbled through his chest, and Miles finally looked up as her words snagged in his mind. "What do you…" He caught the expression on Naomi's face; a wide, toothy, bordering on manic grin. "What?"

"You're in love with him, aren't you?"

A louder purr escaped his throat, and Miles nearly choked on it as Sammie grumbled, twisting into his side with a grumpy snort. "No!" Naomi's eyes drooped into a disbelieving glare. "I mean…maybe, look, it's complicated. And also, none of your business. This is not werewolf junk so butt out!" Miles hissed, ignoring how Naomi's lips curled more with every word he spoke.

"Oh ho ho! But that's where you'd be wrong, Miles." A growl ripped itself from his teeth and she swatted nonchalantly in the air toward it. "Having that type of connection, one that is so strong and one that both bits of you agree with? That's *exactly* werewolf business." She prodded him, ignoring his squawk of protest. "It doesn't happen very often, where both the human and the shapeshifter part of you agree, so when it does, it means you will overcome whatever you need to keep that connection safe and happy." She leaned forward, teeth gleaming in the dim light. "Which also means you can power through even the strongest alpha command. So that rogue asshole has no power over you."

Miles froze, blinking slowly. *So that's how I was able to get myself back in control earlier...* He looked back down to Sammie, warmth coiling in his chest at the sight of him looking like a puppy curling close to the fireplace on a cold winter morning.

"So," Miles started, his voice softening after Sammie wrinkled his nose in his sleep, mumbling grumpily. "So...earlier, when the other alpha was... He had me in the woods, and it was like... It's hard to describe but I couldn't move on my own, like he was puppeteering my body. Then...Sammie came by, and I could smell him first, and it was like... I needed to get to him, make sure he wasn't going to be hurt..." He blinked up to Naomi, whose beaming expression had softened but was no less wide. "That's what I did? I just...willed my body to move enough that I broke through his command?"

Naomi suppressed a soft laugh. "Miles, that's...it's amazing! I couldn't even do that after ten years! You were able to do it in less than ten days!"

All because of Sammie. Miles rubbed his hand over Sammie's shoulder. "Yeah, but...I didn't really do it on my own, did I?"

Naomi scoffed, scooting closer. "You kind of did. That

connection just gives you the power to do it, not the strength of will and all that. It's a lot of willpower and state of mind and your body, heart, and brain being all on board to do it. That doesn't just come from finding someone you click with."

"Shhm." Sammie snuffled, one eye cracking open with a pitiful glare. "Try'n to sleep…"

Naomi held up an apologetic hand as Miles stiffened, his brain whirling at one hundred miles an hour. How much of that did Sammie hear? What if Sammie was disgusted by him, what if…what if Sammie left in the middle of the night because of Miles's completely inappropriate crush on him?

"Sorry." Naomi's soft voice broke through the hurricane of thoughts. She squeezed Miles's shoulder, giving him a reassuring pat with it. "I'll let you two get some rest. We'll talk more in the morning."

Miles waited until she padded over to the kitchen before he gently lifted Sammie up. He tried to keep his legs from shaking as they moved back to his bedroom.

Sammie gave a small murmur as he was settled into the bed. He twisted over to clutch the pillow as he wriggled into the sheets. Miles watched for a few seconds before he shuddered and turned to go to his makeshift bed on the floor.

"Stay," a sleep-addled voice rumbled from the bed, and Miles turned to see Sammie reaching a clumsy hand in his direction, fingers skimming his arm. "Please."

He startled for a couple of seconds, feeling like he'd fallen asleep without knowing it and stumbled into a dream unaware. Sammie cracked open his sleepy eyes, humming and finally reaching out far enough to grasp Miles's hand.

This is it. The point of no return.

Miles was going to be finished either way after tonight, but staying with Sammie, sleeping in the same bed, after finding out that apparently his shiny new wolf self was also head over heels for his best friend... There was no going back after this.

He allowed himself to be tugged down. Sammie scooted the one pillow left on the bed closer so they could share, then threw the blanket over them both. Miles's breath caught as Sammie squirmed close, tucking his face into Miles's neck. It rocketed him back in time to sharing the bed in junior year, over the summer. A younger, ganglier Miles being tugged close to a smaller, somber Sammie.

"Promise we'll never forget each other?" Sammie's voice was different than anything he'd ever heard. Hopeful and sad, bittersweet. *"No matter what happens, we'll always be together, right?"*

Miles then didn't really know what to say; he knew that was what he wanted. But he also knew Sammie—never wanting to stay in one place, always saying he was going to go out and make something out of himself. Miles had come to terms with not always being in Sammie's life. It stung, but it was just a way to save himself from heartbreak in the future. He'd known at that point there was no one else for him. He was young—his mom had called him juvenile—but he knew, deep in his gut, he'd never find anyone who fit him just like Sammie did.

With a tight chest and sorrow behind his teeth, Miles finally answered, "Promise."

Chapter Seven

"**...**love...m...don't you?"

The words swirled into the tired fog of Sammie's brain, not quite enough to lift him from his drifting, but enough to have him trying to listen to the conversation. He could feel Miles's voice rumbling through him, like a stone being skipped over a sleepy pond.

"So, I just...break his command?"

"Connection...gives you power...click with..."

"Shhh," Sammie grumbled, his face smashed into Miles's side making the sound muted. "I'm trying to sleep."

"Sorry." A hand gently tapped his shoulder, and the conversation drawled on for a few more moments before he was being lifted, floating along in a warm, firm embrace.

What he'd always wanted... Sammie let out a contented sigh,

wriggling as close as he could, before he was deposited into a soft mountain of cotton and lavender-scented cologne. He tucked further into the soft, calming space before he felt Miles pulling back.

"Stay," he managed, blinking his eyes open blearily to look up at Miles. Miles looked... Sammie felt caught suddenly, taking in his friend in the soft glow of the moonlight pouring in from the window. His brown eyes soft and sweet, hair a mess, skin sun kissed and looking somehow even more bronze in the gentle lighting, the barest hint of a soft, lovestruck expression on his face. "Please," Sammie pleaded, his hand finally finding Miles's, his skin so warm it almost felt like he could burn him.

Moments passed, feeling like hours, before Miles dipped down, allowing himself to be tugged close. Sammie remembered the summertime, what felt like decades ago, asking Miles to remember him.

Reaching out and hoping to be met in the middle. And falling short.

He wanted Miles to fight for him. It was stupid, a teenage fantasy that the boy he liked, and had grown up with, watched go from gap-toothed to beautiful in every way, would fight to make him stay.

Sammie's eyes watered and he blinked hard, letting out a puff of breath against Miles's shoulder. He must have been hearing things, or misunderstood, or something. Sammie was slowly falling apart at the seams, after everything. His brain was just cooking up things he'd wished for years.

"Stay..." Sammie muttered, closing his eyes and tugging Miles just the tiniest bit closer.

*

Sammie woke up, alone in bed, his skin hot and sweat making him stick to the sheets. He sat up, something sharp and electric brewing behind his ribcage. "Miles?"

"Kitchen!" a familiar voice called, and Sammie sagged, flopping back onto the bed, blinking away the water in his eyes.

Jesus, what's wrong with me, lately? Did I used to cry like this all the time?

"There's coffee and muffins out here." Another voice, Naomi, followed up. Sammie shook himself and jack-knifed out of bed. He checked his duffel, which was haphazardly spilled out onto Miles's floor. It was mostly full of dirty clothes. Sammie leaned down to pick through it and frowned when his hand hit something stiff.

"*Help!*"

Sammie yelled, stumbling back, as his hand came back covered in blood, his own screams ringing in his ears. That sharp sensation shifted from his chest to his fingertips. Something stabbed into his leg and he heard what sounded like an explosion—

"Sammie, hey, Sammie, look at me." Warm hands cupped his face, and Sammie blinked, sucking a sharp lungful of air into his seizing lungs. Warm, inviting pools of brown, the edges of his eyes creased with worry. Miles sagged in relief as their eyes met. "There, hey, you're okay, you're good."

"What..." Sammie looked down and balked as he saw a chunk of wood in his hip, one of the posts of the bedframe splintered to pieces, and the shirt he'd worn the day Miles got bit on the floor in a stiff, crimson heap. "What happened?"

"Not sure." Naomi's voice came from the doorway, and she eyed him curiously. "We didn't know anything happened until we heard you yell. Then the post there just...exploded, I guess."

That...that doesn't make sense. How would that even happen? What's...

Sammie's thoughts ground to a halt as he lifted his hand to stare at it. His fingertips were black, like they were covered in soot, or burnt. A single blue spark zinged across his ring finger, quick as a blink.

"What...the...fuck?" Sammie managed to get out, before he was slumping forward into Miles, everything going black around him.

Chapter Eight

"**G**et back here, you freak! I'll fucking kill you!"

Sammie's lungs burned as he skidded around the corner of the gym, nearly slipping and faceplanting into the wall, before he got his bearings and continued sprinting out onto the court floor.

He was an idiot, Sammie knew he was an idiot, but he didn't realize he was a big enough idiot to call Nicky Vaughn a small-dicked moron to his face.

He could hear footsteps behind him, getting closer, when he was yanked into the locker room, a hand clamping over his mouth as he went to yelp.

"What the hell did you do now, Sams?" a familiar voice muttered in his ear, and Sammie immediately relaxed, slumping back into Miles.

He tilted his head back enough to look up at his friend, feeling all syrupy and melty from Miles's fond, exasperated look. The fingers against his cheek twitched, then tightened as a gaggle of footfalls sounded outside the locker room.

"Can't find him anywhere, Nicky."

An annoyed growl, before something banged loudly right outside the door. Sammie jolted with the sound, and Miles gripped him tighter and calmly hushed him. "Fuck it, he's dead the next time I see him."

The sound of the witch hunt outside dissipated, and Sammie eventually relaxed, letting out a caged breath as Miles finally pulled his hand away. He turned and beamed, something in his chest twisting as he found Miles looking fondly at him with his hands on his hips. "Thanks, I owe you."

"You owe me a lot." Miles chuckled, leaning back into the tiled wall. "So, what'd you say to him this time?"

"Called him a moron." Sammie glanced away, trying to keep his lips from curling as he followed his comment up. "Might've also said something about why he can't keep a girl interested because of his small dick energy."

Miles barked out a laugh, then shook his head, pushing off the wall and cuffing Sammie by the back of the neck. "You know, your mouth is really going to get you into trouble one of these days."

"Yeah..." Sammie giggled, curling into Miles, ignoring how his insides fluttered like a swarm of rabid butterflies when Miles shifted them closer, his hand slipping from neck to his waist. "Yeah, one of these days, it'll probably bite me in the ass, but that's why I have you, right?"

Miles paused, and Sammie's heart jumped into his throat. He tried to work up the courage to look up at him, but didn't have the chance before Miles finally answered, his voice soft and wistful. "Yeah, yeah, you'll always have me."

*

Sammie blinked awake, head pounding and disoriented, his mouth dry and his bones aching. He felt unsettled in a way he hadn't been for a long time.

"You all right?"

Miles's voice was a worried blanket wrapping over Sammie's bones. He tilted his head, blinking the fog from his eyes. He was in Miles's room, tucked into his bed, Miles's warm hand settled over his shoulder through the blanket. "Uh...yeah. Weird dream..." Sammie muttered.

Miles stared for a few moments, then pulled his hand back. Sammie immediately wanted it back, like a kid who had their favorite toy taken away. He pouted, and Miles moved on, gesturing down Sammie's body. "We patched you up. Dunno what the hell happened, but don't worry about it, all right? Naomi took a look, said that you should be pretty much good. Obviously, it's gonna take a bit to heal up, but yeah. Things as normal."

Normal. What the hell is even normal anymore?

"Thanks," Sammie mumbled, shifting and wincing as pain flared up his side. Miles made an odd, bitten-off sound, but when Sammie glanced back, his expression was blank, Adam's apple bobbing as he choked the sound down. "Speaking of Naomi, is she still here?"

"Nah, she left a couple hours ago." Miles awkwardly shifted from foot to foot, glancing away.

Sammie's features pinched, his brows coming together and eyes narrowing. Something was definitely off. "Everything all right?"

"Yep, fine." Miles clapped his hands. The sound made Sammie jolt; he grit his teeth against a hiss and spun on his heel. "Sorry, I'll go get you some painkillers, and some food. Don't move."

Then, Miles was gone, and Sammie was left confused and aching, his blood tingling in his veins. He had a taste like copper and citrus on his tongue. Anxiety and shame all wrapped into one, filling his chest until it felt fit to spill out of his mouth.

"Wait, so...you're leaving?" Sammie could almost hear Miles's voice from all those years ago. Younger, without that raspy quality it had now. "I thought...I thought we'd get some extra time to hang out before you left."

Sammie, the idiot he was back then, just laughed, hiding the pain. He wanted Miles to fight him, to keep him here. It was the only reason he left, because Miles had pouted and rolled over, letting him go.

Now, Sammie sat, feeling like he'd missed his opportunity. He should've told Miles back then, told him everything about what Sammie wanted. Maybe all of this werewolf business wouldn't have happened.

"Sam, everything...oh." Miles's dazed voice brought Sammie back, and he blinked. The skin of his hands felt like it was being taken apart bit by bit by fire ants. Sammie glanced down, eyes going wide as he saw blue electricity sparking along his palms, licking up his wrists, pooling in his fingertips almost like water.

"W-what is...? I—" Sammie glanced up toward Miles, terrified of what he'd see on his friend's face.

Instead of fear, or disgust, or whatever he'd expected, Miles just looked awed, eyes glittering in the gentle light of the lightning sparking from Sammie's fingers. Miles looked at him like...like he was...

"Beautiful..." Miles muttered, taking a step closer.

Just like that the lightning shifted, pooling into his palms and slipping through his fingers like water, before it disappeared, sinking into his skin like it never existed to begin with.

"I...I don't..." Sammie stuttered, tasting something like battery acid in the back of his throat. "I don't know what's going on."

"It's okay." Miles's voice was soft, more than Sammie had ever heard it. "We'll figure it out. You're all right now."

A hiccup stuck in his chest, and Sammie blinked, his vision getting blurry with tears. "I... Miles... I don't..."

Miles hushed him, tugging Sammie into his chest, squeezing

him into a tight, warm embrace. His chest rumbled against Sammie's ribs as he spoke. "It's all right. Sammie, you're okay. Just let it out, it's okay."

Something flashed at his cheek, blue glowing against Miles's tan throat, and Sammie shoved his face into the firm shoulder in front of him, letting a painful sob rip out of his throat.

His fingers sparked before the feeling went numb as Sammie gripped onto the back of Miles's shirt. His eyes burned, and his face tingled with the tiny licks of electricity pouring out with his tears. He didn't know what was happening, but it felt like every emotion he'd held on to since that night he left all those years ago was pouring out now, uncontrollably.

Sammie didn't know how much time had passed when his hiccupping sobs finally quieted, his fingers tingling with pins and needles rather than the foreign sparking feeling. He sniffled, gingerly pulling his face away and wincing as Miles's shirt stuck to his cheeks for a moment. Sammie blanched, seeing the darker char marks on the otherwise clean white. "Shit. Miles, I'm so—"

"It's okay." Miles shook his head, reaching a hand up and wiping at his cheek, eyes so goddamned soft it made Sammie's chest hurt. "It's just a shirt. It's okay as long as you're okay..."

Sammie bobbed his head slowly, watching as Miles's expression brightened, lips curling, lopsided and sweet. *Fuck it.* "Miles, I...there's something I should tell you. I—"

Miles's eyes widened a fraction, dipping into that gold color when he started shifting. "You?"

"I... I think I... Think I lo—"

Crac-creeee

The rest of Sammie's words were drowned out by the sound of rebar and concrete shattering. The pair of them toppled to the floor as the room tilted sideways.

Miles sucked in a panicked gasp, grabbing onto Sammie as he started sliding into the wall. "Hang on!" he yelled, scrambling to his feet before he pulled both of them to the window, feet slipping as the room kept tipping.

A rumble rattled Sammie's chest as Miles tugged him out of the window onto the disintegrating fire escape. They were going to die.

"Miles—" Sammie's words were cut off, and he yelped as Miles pulled him onto his back. "What're you...? Wait—!"

"Just hold on!" Miles cried before jumping into the air, reaching for the building opposite them.

Sammie glanced down, a scream trapped in his throat, and promptly passed out as he saw how quickly the ground was coming up to meet them.

*

"There's something I should tell you. I..."

Oh, oh, is it, is this...

Did Sammie actually...?

Miles barely contained himself, opting for a soft look instead of what would undoubtedly be a manic, cheek-splitting expression. "You?" He couldn't keep the hopeful lilt out of his voice. Sammie's cheeks flushed a beautiful pink, his freckles standing out stark against it. Nothing else mattered at this moment; all the years of pining and wishing were coming true, weren't they?

Miles inhaled Sammie's cinnamon and brown butter, mixed with a strong sweet liquor scent, and something like copper.

Wait...copper? Sammie's never smelled of copper...

"I... I think I... Think I lov—"

Miles's ear twitched as he heard it, before the ground moved under them. A snarl that made his chest rumble, followed by a crash that left his ears ringing. He could hear people screaming on the floors below them, Pete cursing the room over. There wasn't time—Miles couldn't do anything.

Sammie started slipping away from him, tipping with the building, and Miles grabbed him, his mind racing faster than his body, trying to find a way out. He didn't know what happened. Copper stung his sinuses, getting stronger and stronger until it became a cloying, gagging stench of blood.

Window, leave, get them to safety.

Miles was moving before he was thinking, his mouth speaking without his brain registering, his limbs dragging both of them to the window, every muscle burning with adrenaline and the feeling that always overcame his body when he was changing, a painful twitching shift of sinew and bone, held back because even though he was panicking he couldn't afford to hurt Sammie, so he had to keep control.

Sammie screamed in his ear, and Miles realized he'd leaped out of the window. He grasped onto the building opposite them with a bone-rattling impact. Sammie's grip on Miles's shoulders loosened slightly, and Miles was letting go of the brick before he even knew it and grabbing onto Sammie.

"Shit, shit, shit, shit!" Miles squeezed his eyes shut and his body melted from one form to another. When he hit the ground, it was on four feet rather than two. The impact rattled up into his chest.

Copper flooded Miles's senses again, and before he could register it, he was off, dashing away on four legs, Sammie's arms gripped tight around Miles's neck. He didn't know where his legs were taking them, just that he had to run. He could not let that thing near Sammie.

After seeing the blue sparks over Sammie's skin just minutes earlier, something in Miles's hindbrain told him it was much, much more important that Sammie stay well out of the other alpha's grasp.

Chapter Nine

"**E**asy, puppy. I'm not here to hurt your friend. I'm just investigating." A snap and a hiss, and the unfamiliar voice rose in intensity. "Hey! No biting! Your friend might be injured, I'm trying to help, you mangy mutt!"

Sammie slowly blinked his eyes open, lids feeling weighed down with cement, when the voice was answered with a more insistent growl. The sound rumbled through his chest.

Oh...that's a lot of brown fur...it's soft...mmm.

Sammie closed his eyes and tucked his face closer to his comfortable, growling pillow.

"Oy, hey, friend! You're awake, I can smell it. Talk some sense into your little wolfy boyfriend, here."

Boyfriend...?

A bark rattling through his brain was enough to bring

Sammie's mind back into focus. He sat up with a jolt, then grimaced, his head swimming. "H-he's...not... We're friends."

The voice belonged to a deathly pale woman, dressed in a ratty emerald green fur-lined coat, black jeans, and with a multitude of rings and necklaces all over her person. She chuckled. "Well, you may want to tell Fido that. He's acting rather protective over you."

"I..." Sammie stammered, glancing down to Miles, who was still shifted and looking up at him with his vivid eyes and almost—well, looking as pleased as he could like this. "Who...even are you? Where are we?"

The woman stood up and gave an eccentric bow. "I am the one who dug you both out of the trash bins outside my warehouse." She popped up to her feet, and Sammie noticed the light catch on her teeth. They were a bit too sharp, too long, and out of place in some areas. "You may call me Eddie, and also your friend should probably do his whole...howly thing for his boss."

Sammie blinked, tilting his head, and caught Miles doing the same beside him, much to Eddie's delight. "Howly thing?"

Eddie waved her hand, babbling for a moment. "Yeah, you know, the thing werewolves do when they need to get their buddies to show up. The whole howl chain or whatever."

Miles licked his chops, then gazed up at Sammie, nudging him gently with his bulky head as if to say, "Can you believe this? How stupid does that sound?"

Sammie couldn't help the giggle that bubbled past his lips.

Eddie stared between the two of them for a moment before she crossed her arms and grumbled. "Well, someone should get a hold of your leader or whatever they're called. There's been some weird things happening around here lately and...oh."

Eddie cut herself off, tilting her head in the air and sniffing, then leaped back from the two of them before Sammie could blink. In one breath to another, Naomi was there, swinging at the other girl, growling with her eyes a bright-red glow.

"Whoa, cool it, puppy!" Eddie held her hands up defensively. "I was just seeing if they were all good, seeing as they dropped into my warehouse uninvited." She smirked, bringing her hands down as Naomi snarled, and setting them on her hips. "You know, I'm aware the whole 'invited in' thing is usually just for vampires, but it *is* a two-way street. Also, just incredibly rude to come in and start this whole posturing thing."

"Shut up," Naomi snapped, then relaxed back toward them slightly, looking between the three of them before settling her attention on Eddie again. "Who are you?"

Eddie gasped, placing a hand on her chest dramatically. "My dear, sweet lupine friend, you wound me! I ask for pleasantries and get met with rough words and teeth."

"Answer the question."

Eddie bowed dramatically, her brown curls dragging the grimy floor for a moment. "Eddie Dusk, at your pleasure."

"Oh." Naomi relaxed, her eyes shifting back to gray with a shot of recognition. "I know you, Winifred Dusknova."

Eddie immediately scrunched her nose up as if she smelled something rotten. "Ugh, disgusting." She leaned back from Naomi's space, crossing her arms over her chest and almost sulking. "If you know me then you know I hate that name. Eddie, please, I beg you." With that, she exhaled, her entire body tensing and sagging with the motion. "Now that you seem to be a bit less likely to relieve me of my vocal cords, maybe I can ask you what on earth is happening out there."

Naomi frowned. "Not anything you need to know."

"Ooh…" Eddie bared her teeth roguishly, her fangs on proud display. "You're one of those council dogs, aren't you?"

A growl rumbled through Miles's chest into Sammie's, and with a glance he saw Naomi's eyes flicker with red, looking almost like flames. "It's none of your business, vampire! You just—"

Naomi was cut off as Eddie vanished. Wind whipped around them, and long-nailed hands shoved the pair of them down behind a stack of boxes. Miles stumbled after them, his ears tucked against his skull and snout shoving into his neck.

"Ah, Young of Nichols, what a pleasure to see you here. What may I, but a lowly parasite, offer you on this lovely night?" Eddie blurted, acting calm and cool. Sammie glanced at Naomi to see her eyes widening and nose twitching.

A rough voice grumbled, and a chill raced along Sammie's spine as he recognized it. "I'm looking for a pair of boys, a mutt and a witch."

Eddie hopped from foot to foot. "Huh, yeah, I haven't seen

anything but rats here for a while. Actually, I was gonna just swoop out for a bite to eat soon, so if there's anyone you need to track down, I'd gladly help for a small, small fee of a free meal?"

The voice, the alpha, growled, animal and menacing, enough for Miles to wriggle closer into his space. Naomi clamped a sure hand on the nape of their necks. "I'll pass, leech. Just don't kill them if they happen to stroll into your den. There are plans for them."

Eddie gave an exaggerated salute, keeping her goofy sneer on her face until the alpha had left. Her expression fell the second the warehouse doors closed behind him, and she ducked close to them to whisper harshly, "What the bloody hell did you do to get Nikolas Young to hunt you down?"

Naomi hissed, smacking the vampire's shoulder before she stood. "Not your business!"

The vampire gasped, genuinely hurt this time. "Look, oh *mighty* alpha, I just covered for your asses! And that guy, not sure if you all know, but he's bad, *bad* news! He's been going on mad hunts through the underground. You don't mess with him unless you want to be six feet under, if not more."

Sammie blinked, standing up from his crouch lightly. Naomi paced as she grumbled. "What do you mean—do you know him?"

"I know *of* him, and that is more than enough," Eddie scoffed, crossing her arms and tucking her shoulders up to her ears, defensive. "Listen, you get kicked to the curb enough times you learn the places to eavesdrop, and you figure out exactly where to go and who to avoid so you don't end up someone's dinner or worse."

"Do you...?" Sammie hesitated, thinking on the conversation they'd just overheard. "Do you happen to know what he was talking about? Those...plans?"

"Not a clue, but I do know things have been weird, lately." Eddie chewed on her lip, just barely missing it with her canine, something that looked to have happened many times given the scarring of the skin. "There's been a lot of movement, not something anyone would be able to tell unless they were looking in places like this. Supernatural things happening, more of the outlier types moving in."

"How do you know this?" Naomi muttered; her expression was pinched, obviously uncomfortable to be discussing any of this with the vampire.

Eddie drawled, her tone detached and disinterested. "Like I said, if things are bad enough for you when you've lived as long as I have, you sort of learn to look for things that are going to make things worse." Her shoulders sagged. "It's just a matter of time before Hunters start showing up. Surprised they haven't already."

"Shit." Naomi ran a hand through her hair, then looked over to the two of them. Miles slipped his heavy head away from Sammie with a whine. "We should move."

"Or..." Eddie held up a hand. "You could hide. At least until Young is off your scent."

Naomi scoffed, turning toward Eddie, that annoyed

expression back on her face. "Oh, and where should we hide from the thing that can track us by smell?"

"My room." Eddie leaned into Naomi's space, making the alpha step back, her nose wrinkling. "Didn't ya wonder why he didn't pick up on you lot when we were talking? The great thing about vampires when it comes to you bunch of bloodhounds is that we cover up the scent of pretty much anything else. All the blood drinking and the unholy essence in our blood. Fantastic camouflage."

The alpha frowned and sniffed the air once, then furrowed her brow as she glanced at Sammie and Miles. "Oh…"

"Yeah." Eddie clapped her hands, pulling back with a smirk. "So, up to my room it is! But…first I'd like to ask for a quick…bite, if I could?" Eddie turned her gaze to Naomi, and Sammie watched dumbfounded as the alpha flushed.

"I— Yeah, sure, whatever. Just let them get settled and I can figure out getting you fed." Naomi seemed to be *actually* blushing. She cleared her throat before turning to face the two of them. "Both of you, up there, quick. Before any rabid alpha comes barreling in."

Miles glanced up with an expression that Sammie would read perfectly, even with Miles's current lack of human features. *"Yeah, sure, that's the only reason you want us out of your hair."*

"Git!" Naomi hissed, and Sammie had to bite his lip to stop from giggling. He'd never seen her so…human. Usually, the alpha always had an air of cool confidence, so seeing her flushed and off balance was refreshing.

The two followed Eddie's directions up to the little loft area she'd made from the rafters of the warehouse ceiling. Given what it was, it was more than a little cozy: a small hoard of soft blankets and half working Christmas lights gave the area a muted, sleepy feeling; and pillows and random T-shirts and jeans folded haphazardly in a horseshoe shape made a nest of sorts. Sammie settled down into the pile, letting out a satisfied purr as he sunk into the warm fleece bed made from blankets and mismatched pillows.

Miles let out an odd sound, something between animal and human. Sammie blinked an eye open to see Miles was half turned back, shaking his head out as he shrunk, dark fur melting away to pale skin dotted with moles and beauty marks like stars. Sammie's breath caught in his chest, and Miles looked up, his eyes glimmering gold for a moment before fading to familiar brown.

"Okay?" Miles's voice was rough, gravelly, and deep, and Sammie's mouth was dry, his heart trying to beat itself out of his chest.

"Yeah…" Sammie's voice sounded so far away in his own ears. He vividly remembered what was happening just before everything went to shit. He glanced down to Miles's mouth, then back up to match his gaze as he got closer. "Uh…"

Warm skin brushed up against his cheek, and Sammie's eyes went wide as Miles's fingers weaved through his hair. "Sammie…?"

"Y-yeah?"

Oh...he's leaning in... Is he leaning in? Did Miles just...yeah, he definitely just looked down at my mouth, oh... Is it happening? Is this—

Bang

Sammie shrieked, and both of them jumped back from each other. He glanced over to see Eddie cackling at them from the ladder with the most impish look he'd ever seen in person. "Aw, am I interrupting my little love birds?"

She looked refreshed, somehow more vibrant and full of life, her once near-white lips now pink like they'd been glossed. Her eyes had some more dimension to them, and there was even a soft little blush on her skin.

Eddie grunted as she was shoved upward, letting out a rather unhinged cackle as Naomi grumbled. "Get a move on already. The sooner we can sleep through this the sooner we can get out of here."

The vampire, much to Naomi's audible dislike, trilled and toppled onto the floor, fluttering her lashes at the alpha as she clambered up. "You say that like my hospitality is a bad thing, love."

Bizarrely, Naomi's face went beet red, and she simply huffed, turning away. No arguing, no nothing.

Sammie and Miles locked eyes again, a playful mirth on his face, and Sammie tuned out Eddie's teasing voice as Miles's cheeks dimpled with joy, a rough giggle bubbling out of him.

Maybe things would be okay. They'd figure everything out, eventually. For now, it was Sammie and Miles together, and they were safe and unharmed. So long as they were together, along with Naomi, things would be all right. He had to believe that.

Something warmed in his chest, almost sparking through his veins, like before in the room. This time, though, it was controlled, hot and coiled around in his ribs like a furnace, or a fireplace. Miles's hand rested next to his, adjusting himself slightly to settle against the wall of pillows, and the feeling sparked when Miles stretched out his pinky to loop around Sammie's.

It was especially easy to put all the fear and pain aside then, with the feeling of contentment so deep it felt like it was blending into his bones, and the gentle chatter from Naomi and Eddie. Even though they were barely touching, the closeness of Miles was that final piece, their fingers interlocked as he basked in the heat Miles now naturally radiated, and Sammie was drifting to sleep, that feeling coiling through his blood and dragging him down to sweet, temporary peace.

Chapter Ten

A siren screeched by, loud and grating. It wasn't the first time a siren had woken Miles from a dead sleep, but it was the first time he'd jolted awake ready to fight the closest threat. His jaw ached, and blood slicked his fingertips when his claws burst through his nail beds suddenly. Every muscle tensed; his eyes weren't even focused properly before he was up on his feet, snarling.

"Hey, no, you're all right." A firm, familiar voice snaked through his consciousness, tugging him back like a lead around his neck. Firm, but gentle, maybe more like a hand on his shoulder, something easy to shake if he needed. Definitely not a lead, not like that...

"Miles?" a second, groggy voice mumbled, a little further away, and Miles focused his vision, blinking several times and letting his body relax as he realized where he was. Naomi was right by him, hands raised carefully, a mirth-filled look on her face as he came back, Sammie still curled up in the little nest of blankets, blinking the sleep from his eyes.

"S-sorry..." Miles stammered, shrinking back. "I...guess I'm jumpy...after yesterday."

"I mean, given the fact you lot are being tracked down by an ex-Council dog, and one that seems to have gone off the deep end, *and* lost your home..." Miles twisted around to see Eddie strolling by them. "Yeah, who could blame you being jumpy." She ended with a shrug, and the barest shift in the air caught his senses, like a burnt corpse on a rainy day.

He wrinkled his nose, fighting back the urge to sneeze. "How do you even know all of this?"

Eddie answered easily. "Like I said before, I like to keep my ear to the ground for anything in the vicinity that can be danger-ous. You kids who just happened to fall right at my doorstep have made that extremely helpful, given that jolly ol' Nic there could and would tear me limb from limb if he knew I had you."

"So..." Sammie spoke up, sounding slightly more awake, hav-ing sat up from the mess of blankets. "Why did you? Hide us from him, I mean. You could've saved your own skin by telling him ex-actly where we were. Why put yourself at risk like that?"

The vampire pouted before slumping forward. "Funny enough, I have a heart. And this entire thing...it seems a little fishy, like something you don't want to just stand by and let happen. I'm excluded, but not enough to think that if something major happens then I'm not going to be affected by it."

Naomi went quiet, her expression thoughtful before she stepped toward Eddie. "So, you keep saying you were hearing something going down... What do you know?"

Eddie hissed through her teeth. "Lots of different things. Of course, that Young just stopped working for the council, which is odd as hell, because all I'd heard of the guy *before* was that he was one of their more loyal and ruthless. Now he's mostly just lurking around in the dark and apparently turning as many as he can for a while."

"Shit." Naomi started pacing. "Let me just take a wild stab at this... He stopped about a month or so ago?"

"Yeah." Eddie glanced between Sammie and Miles, her frown deepening. "I'm gonna take a guess of my own that's when they got dragged into this?"

They both nodded, and something shifted again, but this time it felt like the air around them had been electrified. The fine hair on Miles's arms and the nape of his neck stood on end, and a chill shuddered down his spine. He glanced toward Sammie to see him almost curled up in on himself, and looking at him was all Miles needed to get the wave of acrid, burnt lemons scent of fear.

Miles scuttled over to Sammie, knelt, and wrapped himself around him protectively with a low rumble rising from his chest. Immediately, Sammie relaxed in relief, glancing at Miles gratefully.

"So, with that news," Eddie continued, now joining Naomi in her pacing. "That probably means Young was looking for them specifically. But I'm guessing that neither of them had any clue of any of us existing before then, and so...why them? What would they have?"

A zing ran along Miles's arm, and he caught the lull in conversation as he glanced down to see those little blue wisps of light coiling around his wrist and up his arm. It was warm, gentle, but tingled like the moment before touching an electric fence, a caress of sparks and energy.

"Oh... That's it..." Naomi almost sounded breathless, and Miles looked up again to find Naomi and Eddie looking at them, both absolutely distraught.

"What?" Sammie stiffened, and Miles started rubbing soothing circles into his back, trying to calm him down again. He had sort of put two and two together; given his perfectly fine bedpost had exploded into splinters when Sammie was alone, it had to have something to do with this. Which meant it was probably best to keep Sammie as calm as possible.

"Sammie's not *just* human," Naomi explained, grimacing before she continued. "It means...well..."

"Our bodies aren't really fit to hold too much energy in them." Eddie picked up where Naomi had trailed off. "Up to a point, things start exploding out."

Naomi winced, then took a steady breath before continuing. "As creatures that have human forms but hold more than human abilities and powers, we're already nearly at capacity for the human body to handle. It's why transformations for Miles and I sometimes go a little wrong or we get injured shifting; it's just hard for the human body to get used to. Adding something else to it pushes it past capacity and—"

"And your meat suit splits open into a magical overload big enough to take out New York," Eddie finished bluntly. Miles looked up, but the admonishment on his tongue died at the expression on her face. She looked almost haunted, eyes faraway and mouth pressed into a thin line with the force of her jaw clenching.

"You've seen it before, haven't you?" Sammie's voice was small, that sour sting to his scent shifting again to something like salted lavender.

Wrapping her arms around herself, Eddie groaned, her jacket for once making her look so much smaller than she was. "I've been alive for a while and seen a lot of terrible, terrible things. When I first became...this, the man who did it was horrible, could barely be called such. I've had to watch people be tortured, gutted, maimed, and rearranged. All because of a power hungry and insane asshole who was bored." Eddie grimaced. "I've seen it, only once, because most aren't stupid enough to do it. But when your toys start disobeying you, the crazies decide to test the fates."

There was a very distinct sadness to her voice. Sammie squeezed closer to Miles, a distressed sound dragging from his throat.

Naomi shifted, just barely stepping toward her before Eddie

straightened, dropping her hands to her hips and shaking out her great mane of hair. "That's the past, nothing to change it. This, however, we can stop."

The alpha blinked then, freezing in place. "We?" She let out a soft laugh. "What happened to keeping your head down?"

"I like these kids," she stated simply, then leaned toward Naomi. "And you, my love, could use some backup. I know, you're a big strong alpha who doesn't need help." She gripped Naomi by her biceps, smirking as Naomi groaned and attempted to wriggle away. "I would love to assist you, at least to take some of the pressure off of you."

Naomi scoffed, finally shoving Eddie away with a grimace. "As much as that sounds like an absolute nightmare—" Her entire body sagged. "More help can't really be a bad thing."

Eddie let out an excited squeal. Miles glanced at Sammie, who met his eyes. They both wore the same conspiratorial expression. Without much more prompting, Miles giggled, glad Sammie had picked up on Naomi's mild skittishness around Eddie.

"Stop it," Naomi scolded them, hands on her hips. Hilariously, Eddie copied her pose behind her. "Enough of your laughing at my expense—we should start moving out."

"We're leaving?" Sammie blinked, sitting up a bit straighter.

The vampire murmured, "Probably a good idea, given that Young already started snooping around here. Though, since this place is basically flooded with my scent, we'd probably do well to start planning out stuff first."

Naomi narrowed her eyes as she turned her gaze to Eddie. "Good point. How about everyone start gathering things as we start coming up with ideas."

"Can I suggest something that'll probably make things a bit easier?" Eddie asked before any of them had even started moving. "I have a bunch of spare clothes that I've kept, just in case, you know? They're probably soaked through with perfume d' Eddie. Could be good to kinda dampen the trail?"

Naomi stood up straighter, crossing her arms over her chest. "Why on earth would you keep a bunch of spare clothes, and where did you get them? I don't really want to play dress-up with any of your trophies."

Eddie spun back around and stared the alpha down, offended. "I thrifted them, like a normal person... What, you think just because I drink blood that I'm a weirdo serial killer?"

"I'll take some clothes, thanks." Sammie's voice cut through the awkward atmosphere. Eddie beamed at him and guided him over to a very much falling-apart dresser.

"You have a thing against vampires, Naomi?" Miles teased, standing up from his crouch by the nest. "You've been pretty short with her when she's basically just been trying to help us."

Naomi's expression fell. "No...just...I'm tense about everything and I'm not as ready to trust the first person I meet like you all."

Miles bumped the alpha with his hip. "She's fine. Eccentric and odd, but she really does just seem like she wants to help."

Naomi seemed to let the words sink in before she spoke, soft and sounding a little far away. "I'll try and play nice. No promises, kinda hard to break years-long habits, but I'll try."

Sammie laughed, and Eddie squealed and praised him as he spun around in a ridiculous ensemble of a long, rich red cloak, something that looked like a pirate shirt, and sparkling, black glitter slacks. That little entity in Miles's brain rumbled with glee, seeing him so happy. Naomi made a soft sound, and when Miles glanced back, she was looking almost longingly at them.

"It's all right," Miles whispered, gently knocking their elbows together. "Just...you can relax a little. We can all watch each other's backs." He caught the flush on Naomi's cheeks and the small spice of cayenne and ginger floating up from her, getting a hair stronger as Eddie cackled and spun Sammie in a new, over-sized shirt that seemed more like a dress. "And maybe take a leap, with her..."

"What?" Naomi looked up then, flustered and stammering, much to Miles's amusement. "I... There's nothing... I don't..." She growled, shoving at him. "Stop it!"

Miles chuckled before jogging over to the others, winking at the blushing alpha, and turning back to find Eddie looking past him toward her, expression bright and happy.

If things are as bad as they say they are, then what's a little matchmaking before all hell breaks loose?

Chapter Eleven

They left late. The moon was just starting to crest in the sky, barely visible through the lights of the city, streaking across the inky black. They'd all dressed in Eddie's collection, apparently smelling of her death-like scent. He'd only heard snippets of their plan: move out, keep off main streets, and pick up info about Young's movements and plans through the underground Eddie had mentioned.

"Here." Eddie turned to them, her dark-green jacket swishing behind her as she pointed with a flourish to a heavy, steel storm door. There was no sign to indicate what was past it, only the sound of a steady thrum like music rattling through the door. "Remember, heads down, don't stray, and don't talk to anyone. Let me do the talking." She settled her gaze on Miles, raising her eyebrows. "I mean it, pup. I've heard enough about you. No taking things from anyone in there, or drinking anything… Basic club safety, all right?”

“Is that what this is?” Sammie leaned forward, ignoring Miles's pouting. “Our plan to get intel is to hit up a club?”

“Hey, hey, hey! Don't doubt, my lovely little taser.” She winked at them. “Supes love to gossip, and what better place to gossip than where everyone is loose and uninhibited.” She knocked, a musical *tap-ta-ta-ti-tap,* and with a shift through the air that Sammie couldn't see but could definitely feel, the doors swung open, letting them through. It almost felt like they were being embraced as they stepped down the stairs, the sound muffled until they were underground. His ears popped as the music thrummed through him, the beat rattling his ribs and pounding against his skull.

Eddie led them down the steps. The door shut behind them with a heavy latching *thud.* Lights and mist swirled through the air, and Sammie felt that odd tingle through his fingers as they stepped down to the main floor. It was packed, something vaguely familiar to his life in New York partying in college, but the clientele was obviously different.

Scales, horns, fur, fangs, wings—all shapes and sizes to the most literal degree. Something human and the size of his finger zipped by his face, and a high-pitched giggle echoed in his ears. They made their way past another, much taller creature, skin red and a tail whipping behind him. His eyes narrowed at them as they squeezed by, horizontal pupils dilating as he turned. Sammie stumbled after Naomi and Eddie. Miles's hand reached through the light pulsing along his fingers.

Various people, each looking like they stepped from their very own fantasy novel, or movie, or anything other than the real world. Some were immediately recognizable as fairies, pixies, satyrs, harpies; others not as much, like the one they were heading toward now.

"Eddie, welcome! I see you've brought friends!" The person—a humanoid with several features like a rabbit, light gray fur over their skin, eyes glittering and wide in the lights, long ears peeking through their slightly darker hair, nearly black markings on their cheeks and a little animal nose greeted them, showing off small, sharp teeth. "Tell me, business or pleasure? I must know what I should present with my new friends." They had an accent, thick and rough, not at all fitting for their appearance on the outside, which presented someone sweet and loving and doting, complete with an outfit reminiscent of a maid's dress.

"Ah, just here for business, Ryise. Just checking to see if there's been any interesting word going around."

Ryise's long ears twitched as they leaned close. "Of course, my friend. You know these ears of mine hear all. Come, come. Your friends will find it more comfortable in the private room, I believe." They glanced up to Naomi, lips splitting wide. "Especially one representing our *beloved* council."

A brief look of concern flitted across Naomi's face before she schooled her expression. She followed as Eddie led them along with Ryise. Something twisted in Sammie's gut, the club around them suddenly suffocating. He could feel eyes on them, though when he looked, the groups of creatures around them were absorbed in the pulsing music and their conversation. Not a single eye on them.

"Something feels weird," Miles whispered. His hand circled around Sammie's, and the electric tingle through his fingers sank into his skin as Miles's firm thumb traced circles into the back of his hand.

Sammie chewed on his lip, too nervous to speak, and followed them, pushing through the crowds that parted around the taller, rabbit-esque Ryise. They opened thick, heavy velvet curtains and led them into a small room filled with plush cushions and a set of chaise longue chairs, made with the same sort of velvet as the curtains. The room was filled with a soft, pinkish smoke, making the air sticky and sweet on his tongue. His head felt clouded.

The curtains swung shut behind them, and the noise of the rest of the club became muted. Sammie tasted something like sugared lavender and thick, rich honey. His head was starting to spin, and Sammie could barely see Eddie and Ryise settling onto one of the chaises, huddled together. His vision was so cloudy—and so suddenly...

"Ah." A voice, unfamiliar and low, hissed into his head. "So observant," it drawled, and a shudder ran up Sammie's spine. He blinked, and he wasn't in the room anymore; everything around him was dark, only colored by the light smoke in the air. Sammie gasped, reaching for where Miles's hand had just been, only to grasp the damp mist that stained his hand with a sticky pink liquid.

"W-what…" Sammie spun around, trying to find something to get his bearings, only meeting mist and blackness. "Who are you? What did you do with them?"

"Not a thing, my dear little morsel…" The voice rattled through his brain again, and Sammie gasped as he spun around to come face to face with a constantly shifting form. The only notable feature that stayed was its gray, iris-less eyes, bottomless pools of coal that felt like they were boring through Sammie's skin. In one breath to the next, it shifted from something indescribable to something similar to Ryise, side-blinking lids flickering over its eyes before it melted from gray to the dark buttons of coal like the one he was just in the room with. "In fact, I barely moved a muscle… Simply…allowed you all into my domain and let my scent do the work to separate you all…"

Electric sparks ran through Sammie's fingers, his heart beating against his ribs as the creature leaned into his space. A forked tongue flicked out to run over his cheek. "W-what do you want?"

The being giggled, and the sound sent chills along Sammie's spine. "Oh, I have the feeling you know…" It shifted, faster than it should've been able to, running a hand along his throat. Sammie jolted; sparks jumped along his arm and arced into its hand. A sharp hiss made him wince as it retreated. Its skin shifted, turning an odd reflective purplish shade as it shook its hand out. "Ah, so they weren't lying when they mentioned your little spark. I should be getting a good sum from you."

Something shifted in Sammie's chest; his heart hammered so hard he could feel it in his throat. A sharp sting rose from his skin, and static made his hair stand on end. An agonized hiss caused his ears to ring. All at once, the room came back. Sammie felt drained, and the furniture was singed. The velvet curtains burned with little blue streaks of lightning arcing through them.

"Sam?" Miles's voice was rough, and Sammie turned to find him blinking, an odd pink cloud fading from his eyes. "What—what just happened?"

"Son of a bitch," Eddie hissed, crouched to the ground near Sammie, drawing his attention to the creature twitching at his feet. Blue lightning danced along the creature's skin, which violently shifted with each writhing motion it made. "A shifter... Great."

"I take it your friend isn't usually like that?" Naomi growled, rubbing her nose harshly as that same pink faded from her eyes.

"No, dear, I don't make the habit of making friends with fucking shifters." Eddie spat, standing and grabbing Sammie and Miles's arms. She lowered her voice. "This isn't good—we should go."

"No shit," Naomi snarked, and Sammie glanced to Miles, who thankfully seemed just as lost as he was.

"Can we get any sort of explanation of what the hell just

happened?" Miles whispered, digging his heels in as Eddie tried to shove them out of the room. "Who was that? What was she talking about?"

The vampire and the alpha both growled, nearly in unison, and shoved them. "Later!" Naomi muttered, then stopped as they stepped out of the room into the club. It was dead quiet. Several mannequin-like things stared them down, their gray eyes like burning coals in the darkly lit club. Every single patron they passed from before was now replaced with the constantly shifting beings they just encountered.

"Shit." Eddie started sprinting, her hands still gripped on their arms, dragging Miles and Sammie through the crowd. It was like blood in the water of a shark tank; every one of the beings descended on them, slamming into Sammie's chest and knocking the air from his lungs. His skin stung, like several small brands biting into his flesh. Eddie's cold hand slipped from his arm, and Sammie yelled as the beings converged, dissolving into something like a shifting dark goo crashing into him, sinking into his open mouth as he screamed.

Sammie gagged, trying to force the things back out, his vision blurred, lungs burning, stinging touches against his eyes as they crushed in on him. He was going to die; he was going to drown if he couldn't get free. Sammie struggled, but it felt like trying to dig himself out of thick tar.

A roar reached his ears, and suddenly he could breathe, his throat burning as the things were yanked out of his mouth.

Sammie coughed violently as his vision returned. He saw Naomi throwing some of the black masses into the wall, and Eddie was trying to pull him free.

"Miles, clear a way!" Naomi shouted, rushing back to help the vampire. Sammie gasped, feeling like his skin was being peeled back as he was slowly pulled out of the mass.

Eddie and Naomi surrounded him, and Sammie blinked the sting from his eyes to look up as they pulled him backwards. He stared in horror as the thing bubbled up from the floor, shifting and groaning, sucking in any nearby objects. Anything it touched shriveled after a few moments.

Miles yelped, and Sammie spun about, grimacing as his skin felt as if it was being pulled over his bones to the point of breaking, everything sensitive and sore. That magic in his chest pulsed, blue sparking over his skin. Eddie and Naomi both hissed in pain as it nipped at them. As soon as Sammie's eyes locked onto Miles the other two faded into the background. Miles swatted away at the monsters, trying to peel back the goo that crawled up his arm, his skin turning a sickly white wherever it touched.

"*Miles!*" Sammie screamed, magic bursting out of him in a wave like before but turned up to eleven. His vision faded to white for a second as light erupted from him. The creatures screeched as they got knocked back and melted into the ground.

Sammie slumped forward, gasping and shuddering. Firm hands grabbed his shoulders before he hit the ground. Miles's brown eyes, worried and wide but thankfully aware and bright, swam into his view for a second before Sammie fell into sweet unconsciousness, the aches and pains all over his body fading along with everything around him.

Chapter Twelve

"Sammie!" Miles's yell was cut short as the black forms dragged over his skin, trying to get away from the wave of blue energy bursting out of Sammie. His skin stung for a second before it faded to an odd tingle, a lot like the sensation when wounds healed since he'd been turned. The light crashed over him, and the oxygen was pushed out of his lungs. Like a cozy campfire or a heated blanket being draped over his shoulders.

Eddie and Naomi both stumbled as Sammie slumped forward, his entire body going limp. Miles didn't think, sprinting across the room where he was trying to break through the wall of sludge blocking their way. "Sam?" Miles's voice was shaky to his own ears, and he caught Sammie by his shoulders, his hand skirting along his throat as he felt his pulse.

"Holy hell," Eddie muttered, staring around the room. "Your

little taser there ain't so little after all."

A moment passed, just long enough for Miles to fully tuck Sammie into his arms, before Naomi hissed, "It's not safe here. We need to move."

"Right." Eddie tapped Miles's shoulder, kneeling in front of him. "You good to go, big guy?"

Miles spared just a moment to glance at the remains of the monsters. Several of the doll-like forms from before were scattered across the floor of the club, twitching and writhing as the blue currents from Sammie rolled through them. Just how many were there? How had none of them noticed something off? Especially Eddie, if she frequented the place so much.

The air was sickening now, like burnt sugar, pushing past the point of sweet to scorched.

Naomi peeked out of the storm doors, scowling and waving them through. Miles gladly sucked in the non-sticky air, crisp and cold, a much welcome change from down below.

"What the hell was that?" he muttered, once they were all safely above ground.

The alpha glared at him for a moment before turning her attention to Eddie. The vampire looked frustrated, crossing her arms as Naomi's red eyes settled on her. "I know you're going to scold me, but it is not the time," Eddie hissed before Naomi could even open her mouth. "We need to get somewhere more secure. Just believe me when I say I had no idea what we were walking into, I swear."

Naomi narrowed her eyes, staring Eddie down for a few moments, before she let out a frustrated rumble, turning on her heel to stomp down the alleyway. Eddie sagged, looking to Miles for a guilty second before following.

Miles adjusted his hold on Sammie's unconscious form. Sammie would probably die of embarrassment if he saw how Miles was carrying him, almost bridal style, with Sammie's head protectively tucked into Miles's shoulder.

"At least buy me dinner first, Miles..." He could almost hear Sammie teasing, almost see the flush coloring his skin. Miles shook his head, trudging along after the other two. He had to focus on getting them to somewhere safe, just like Eddie said. There was a time and a place.

*

It was roughly an hour later that Sammie stirred, mumbling softly into Miles's skin as they walked. They still hadn't found anywhere safe, apparently. At least, not anywhere near Naomi's standards.

"Mmm...Miles?" Sammie murmured, and Miles tried not to trip as Sammie blinked his eyes open tiredly.

Time, place, not here and not now.

"Yeah, it's me," Miles answered, then immediately felt like an idiot. Duh, of course Sammie knew it was him. Like Miles had to clarify.

"Oh...good." Sammie sagged into him. "I was a little afraid you were just a friendly goo monster."

Eddie choked, and Miles glanced up to see the vampire giggling before looking away quickly.

Miles cleared his throat, adjusting his grip on Sammie. "Nope, no, just your friendly, neighborhood Miles..."

Sammie gave a tired little chuckle that made Miles's chest swell. Something like pride or just plain old affection swirled like a hurricane inside him. He had to swallow a pleased rumble at the sound. "You're adorable..."

This time, Miles did trip up, though thankfully Eddie was there in a blink, cackling like a menace as she shoved him back to his feet, Sammie and all. "Relax, loverboy," Eddie mouthed before giving them some distance again.

Time. Place.

"So...uh, how are you, um...how are you feeling?" Miles asked after he managed to get his bearings back. He just had to focus on one foot in front of the other—pay no attention to the sleepy, soft, utterly heart-wrenching boy in his arms. Easier said than done, considering Miles's entire crush problem.

Time. Place.

"Drained," Sammie muttered, tucking his face into Miles's throat and wrapping his arms loosely around Miles's neck to pull himself closer. "Where are we going?"

Miles swallowed, shuddering as he felt his Adam's apple brush Sammie's lips with the movement. "I-I'm not sure. Let me ask."

Time place, time place, timeplace—

"Naomi?" Miles prodded, thankful that his voice didn't come out as shaky as he felt. "Uh, do you...have a destination...in mind? Or are we just..."

The alpha growled. Miles winced as if she'd given an actual command. He glanced at Eddie to find her much less amused, seeming to try to shrink in on herself.

Sammie twisted in Miles's hold slightly to look at Naomi with a puzzled expression. They were winding further away from the city, trees and greenery becoming thicker as they trekked, cement being replaced with worn stone before shifting to dirt paths.

It was another few moments of quiet before they crossed some sort of invisible wall. Miles froze, and Sammie similarly stiffened in his hold.

Eddie had also stopped with them, though she seemed to know exactly what they'd just stepped into, if the further paling of her face was anything to go by. "No."

"You're the one who wanted somewhere safe," Naomi gruffed, turning toward them and planting her hands on her hips as she glowered. "This is the place I know."

The vampire stared ahead, and Miles followed her gaze only to nearly drop Sammie again at what he saw.

Ahead of them, seemingly appearing out of nowhere, was a massive tower, reaching into the clouds through broken shafts and swirling staircases that shifted with every second. It seemed new, futuristic, and ancient, all at once. Smooth iron at one moment, and worn cobblestone the next, then all rainbow glass before shifting to more and more appearances. Constantly.

Miles felt a dreadful sense of déjà vu at the sight, though Naomi seemed to be at home. Then something clicked.

"You took us to the council?"

Naomi rolled her eyes. "There aren't many other options. It's the closest place."

Sammie gaped, then tilted his head. "It's just…in the middle of the wilderness of Washington?"

"No," Eddie grumbled. "It's in the middle of nowhere, anywhere you find it." She brushed past Naomi, suddenly angry. "That's what all of you council gofers say, isn't it?"

Eddie stormed along, and Naomi gave an agitated grumble before following.

Miles and Sammie glanced at each other before Sammie slumped back into Miles's shoulder. *This is going to be long and dreadful.* Miles had a feeling Sammie got the same impression.

He just hoped they weren't walking from one trap to another.

The sensation that passed over them as they entered was odd, to say the least.

It felt almost like they'd walked into an electrical room, hot and open wires all over, the energy enough to make Miles's hair stand on end. Sammie drew in a sharp gasp, squirming for a moment before he wriggled out of Miles's hold. He certainly looked like he had a bit more color to him, more energized and more himself. It would make sense for Sammie to experience a sudden burst of energy, given how Miles felt like he was getting overloaded with it.

"First time?"

The voice made him jump, and Miles glanced over to see a gentle-looking figure; another rabbit-like one, this one much younger, and considerably different than the fake they'd just met. Pale-lavender fur, a smattering of freckles across the animal bridge of their nose, dark-purple hair in a complicated series of braids with various natural adornments like feathers and vines and flowers strewn throughout. Their eyes were pupilless. Miles realized a moment later that it seemed their vision was impaired as they stared blankly past his face, eyes never meeting, but pouring all their attention on the newcomers.

"Uh...yeah, how could you tell...?"

They chuckled, bangles and beads clinking as they raised a hand carefully to Miles's shoulder and patted along until coming to his nape. "Scent. You have a fading scent of human to you, a little bit of cedar and spices, which tells me you're one of Naomi's pack, right?"

"You can tell all that by scent?" Sammie shouted, bumping into Miles's side in his excitement and dislodging the gentle hold.

They laughed, sweet and kind, nodding somewhat timidly. "Yes, when you come to rely on it as I have, you have to have it well trained like that." They tilted their head, their friendly features soft as their nose twitched. "Where is your alpha, young one? Figured she would be keeping a close eye on you."

Miles blinked, then turned to where he'd last seen Naomi.

Nowhere to be seen. Same with Eddie, now he came to look. Miles had a feeling that didn't bode well.

"I'm not—I don't know. She was just here a moment ago. We should probably—"

"Ah, yes. She must be on one of her missions." They gestured further into the tower. Miles finally took in their surroundings to see it looked oddly like a lobby. Sort of. Discounting the shifting stairways, the magic swirling throughout the place everywhere he turned, and the colorful cast of occupants themselves. "She probably went to see her contact. You can ask one of the Guides to take you there from the pedestal in the center. Let her know Cas would at least like a 'hello' if nothing else."

"Thanks. We will," Sammie answered before Miles could. He tugged Miles along in the direction they'd pointed—a pedestal, just as they'd said. It was circular and filled with softball-sized glass orbs, a dim light shimmering in the center of each. Sammie frowned, glancing about before he leaned forward and prodded one of them.

They both jolted as it sprang to life, lifting from its resting place and chirping, the light shifting from dim gold to a multicolored show that constantly changed. After a beat, the orb floating in the air in front of them, it chirruped before bumping into Sammie's hand again, an odd, almost childlike voice calling from within it. "Destination, please."

"U-uh...wherever...Naomi Chae is...?" Miles stuttered out, and the orb chimed, spinning in place before it started floating off.

When they didn't immediately follow it, it paused, lights shifting within it, almost as if its featureless form was turning to face them. "Please, follow me. We ask you do not stray from my path. If your destination is in an area restricted from non-Council members, I will take you as far as possible and send a message to someone who may assist you further." It chirped again, waiting in place, making another more musical sound as Sammie finally moved. Miles followed.

"What is this thing even made of?" Sammie mused aloud once they'd left the main lobby area, going down one of the many hallways stemming from the main entrance.

"I am a Guide. I am created by Astaria Séverin, Arch Mage of the Council as of the year 1932," the orb—or the Guide—answered, leading them up one of the many stairways. "Watch your steps, please. Astaria built me with the purpose of making the Council building more accessible for any newcomers seeking our aid. Each of the Guides she created with their own personalities and with care and many hours dedicated to every single one of us."

Sammie blinked, glancing over to Miles. "A mage. Is that...?"

"Mage is the term used in the Council for those capable of using magic, and who are able to form it into a physical matter, like myself." The Guide paused, floating in place, before the lights shifted toward them again. "According to records, there are no mages fitting of your description in the Council records. As per the Preservation Act of 326, please go to the Records Department at your earliest convenience, so this issue may be rectified."

"They're really serious about their secrecy, huh?" Miles muttered after the orb continued bobbing along on its way. Sammie had stopped, however, his brow furrowed as he stared ahead, his scent turning sour and sharp like strong citrus. "Sammie?"

Sammie blinked, then shook his head. He glanced about before giving Miles a half-hearted reassurance. "It's nothing. Let's just catch up with Naomi, yeah?"

It was a lie, an obvious one, and one that Miles was about to press him on when Sammie stopped. Sammie wrapped his hand around Miles's wrist firmly, tilting his head in the direction of the Guide. *Right...* If it was something they didn't want to share with the Council, it would probably be best to keep it quiet for now.

The orb led them down another winding hallway after the shifting staircase and finally stopped at a door with the name Damien Blackwood in fancy, shimmery script on the glass. It shifted toward them, chirping musically. "We have arrived at your location; Naomi Chae is inside with Damien Blackwood and Winifred Dusknova. As you need to be registered after, I shall stay outside."

No sooner had the voice finished talking than the door opened. Naomi peeked her head out and glared at the Guide. "I will take them to Records, go back to the pedestal."

"Per Preservation Act of 326, I must ensure that they—"

"Deactivate." Another voice, firm and deep, boomed from inside the room. The orb dipped down, almost as if it was disappointed, before it faded from its colorful array of light inside and floated away back the way they came. Naomi waved them in, opening the door to them to show a tall, well-built man who looked like he'd stepped out of a modern detective noir movie. He was dressed in a crisp leather jacket worn at the elbows, a button-up shirt and tie, and newer-looking jeans. His hair was dark and clean cut, though his hairline where it faced toward them was disrupted by a jagged scar stretching from his eyebrow to behind his ear. He had dark stubble along his jaw.

"Nice of you both to join us for our parlay." Eddie spoke up from the back of the room, almost seeming to sulk.

The man chuffed, nodding to Naomi in thanks as she shut the door and locked it. "I apologize for stealing away Naomi as soon as you all got here, but I wanted to check in with everything since it's been a couple of days since I've had contact." He glanced over at Eddie. "And of course, apologies for getting you dragged into this, Eddie. I know you've been trying to avoid any of our messes."

The vampire cleared her throat. "You know me, just your friendly neighborhood bloodsucker. I see strays and take them in like a withering old cat lady..."

Naomi growled, pinching her brow as Damien let out a sharp cackle. She put her hands on her hips as she turned to the room. "Anyway, to get back on track, I just got to the part I don't know as well, right before the building went down."

Miles winced, glancing at the floor. He didn't really want to rehash all of that. The whole place only went down because they were there. All those people had died because Young was after them.

Sammie laced his hand with Miles, his thumb tracing a calming back and forth across his knuckles. Miles gasped shakily and choked down the minor nausea crawling up his throat. "Um...well, Sammie and I were in my apartment... We were talking, and it was something sudden. I smelled the...blood, I guess, before I heard the building going down."

Damien shifted, a frown creasing his features, highlighting even more small scars along his face and jawline. "So, it was like he'd just appeared out of nowhere? No lead-up to the scent or anything?"

Miles paused, lifting his head up and blinking. "N-no... Not that I remember."

The frown deepened. He gestured for Miles to continue.

"Well... I mean, there wasn't much after that... The second we started going down I was kind of...moving without thinking. I just knew I had to get Sammie to safety. Even if everyone..." Miles stopped, swallowing harshly, his throat clicking.

"Miles," Naomi whispered, and her sad tone just made him feel worse.

Damien huffed, crossing his arms. "That's the worst part about our kind, how we must live... Danger follows us, like a plague, whether it be someone like Young or otherwise. Just as humans have the bad few who kill the innocent, we do as well." He leaned back against his desk. "It's harsh to say, but you gotta save yourself. Put your own mask on before helping others, you know?"

Except Miles didn't even try. Maybe he could've...

"Well, I feel like this is where I'd step in," Eddie announced, speaking up from the back, sounding full of energy compared to how she looked when they first came in. Her dark eyes glanced toward him, soft and unbearably kind, before she started in on her story. Miles realized he should've been paying attention but...

Stop it.

A voice eerily like Sammie's spoke up, cutting the swirling thoughts of blame and contempt before they could start up again. The cool hold against his fingers squeezed. Sammie's livewire eyes locked with his as he looked over at Miles. Miles nodded softly and received a semi-satisfied expression in return. Sammie leaned into his space and took over from his side of the storytelling.

Lavender, grapefruit, sugary-citrus candy, and the barest hint of cinnamon and burnt sugar rushed through Miles's senses, almost like a physical thing as it calmed him from his climbing spiral. The wolf, that familiar little space of warmth in his chest, curled up content and nearly purring as his mate expertly calmed him.

Miles wanted to tell him he knew exactly what Sammie was leading up to before, all that time before the calm little bubble around them popped. He nearly had to bite his tongue against it.

Time. And place.

I just... I really want to make sure we have the time...

Chapter Thirteen

"So, Nikolas Young is working with Shifters now, huh...?" Damien drawled, drumming his fingers against his desk, his expression dark and troubled. "And you said you'd heard of him up to things before that, right, Eddie?"

Sammie glanced across the room, trying to follow the flow of conversation as well as he could. He couldn't explain how he knew, but Miles was not going to be able to retain it, and at least one of them had to be up to date. Even with the fatigue and the dull panic thumping through Sammie's skull, he had to stay alert and keep up.

Eddie gave a half-hearted shrug, dropping her gaze from the group with a pursed frown. "That's what I'd heard. Though that was from Ryise. Who knows how long those Shifters had been hiding out there... It could've been something planted by them."

"I don't think they would've have known you'd be passing info to us, though," Naomi countered, leaning against the wall with her hands tucked around herself. "You were a good couple miles from where they were. There's not really any way for them to know we'd have ended up on your doorstep."

"Well," Damien started after a moment, "if Young has a Seer on his side, they could've..."

Eddie's breath hitched, and Sammie felt like a pile of ice had hit his stomach. "What...what's a Seer?"

"They can see the future," Eddie muttered, running a hand through her messy curls, looking nervous now. "They can see every possible course of a person's future; tug open every possible thread attached to them. They're vultures, opportunistic and cut-throat monsters..."

Damian pushed off the desk to start pacing. "They haven't been around for a while, hunted out by many of our kind for that reason, or used by Hunters to track us down... It's possible that there's one of them hanging around to help Young out."

"But why would they?"

"Because we're fucked," Eddie mumbled. "A Seer wouldn't join the side with the one that's going to lose out. They gamble, but they make damn sure they're on the winning side every time." She let out a harsh, choked-off chuckle, and Sammie could almost see the anxiety coming from her in waves. "Whatever they're planning—this war or whatever end goal they have—it's going to happen, and there's nothing we can do to stop it."

"You have experience with them?" Sammie asked, edging around Miles, who seemed to be coming back into the conversation. His brow furrowed as he glanced between them. "Maybe... maybe if we can get rid of the Seer then we can—"

"It's no use, Sammie!" Eddie cut him off, her eyes wide, a hysterical edge of red glowing through her irises. She tugged on her hair, looking away and hissing. "Seers were pretty much eradicated for a reason; whatever they saw would come true. They would know all our moves—hell, they probably know we're having this conversation right now. Trying to fight fate is useless. That's it. The second they have that kind of power on their side is the second being on this side is a death sentence."

"Do they...see everything?" Miles spoke up, voice quiet, his gaze shifting away from Sammie as everyone turned to look at him.

"They do, why?" Damien had perked up slightly, like Miles's hesitance was a minor bit of hope for them.

"Well..." Miles rubbed at the back of his neck, settling his eyes on the floor. "When I was under Nikolas's control, he seemed pretty surprised when I was able to break free. If he had someone who could see everything, I feel like he would've seen that coming, right?"

Both Eddie and Damien looked surprised for a moment, and Naomi sucked in a sharp breath. "That's right, I remember you telling me that now." She looked over to Damien. "I don't know a lot about Seers, but he has a point."

"You broke out of your alpha's control?" Damien asked, brows raised, his lips curling as he leaned back against the desk.

"Wait…she's not your original sire?" Eddie followed up with, shifting up to her feet to look over them. "If you're able to do that, that'd be something pretty significant. I definitely feel like they'd see that coming." She paused then, looking over at Sammie with a sort of distant, surprised expression. "Oh, holy shit…"

"What?" Miles shifted from where he'd been slumping in his seat, his much too hot body pressing into Sammie's side. "You look like you just figured something out."

Eddie huffed out a disbelieving laugh. "Yeah. Something with chances even lower than Young having a Seer on his side. They haven't been around for ages, since I got out on my own, but…" Eddie hesitated, then cursed again. "I really fucking hate talking about this shit, but my sire, the asshole that he is, had a Seer—his own personal one, a real garbage piece of work. She's the reason it took me so long to get out from under his influence. And the only reason I did was because of this mage who just happened to be wandering through, who blocked the Seer's powers." She gestured to Sammie. "One who looked a lot like she could've been related to you."

Sammie froze, his brain grinding to a halt. A mage who was related to him? Or might be? As far as Sammie knew, his parents were not in the picture. He'd spent as long as he could remember with his uncle, and when Uncle Matt passed it was just Sammie. There were no other relatives, and no way for him to know anything, considering that his uncle barely even knew Sammie existed until he was dropped on his doorstep.

Miles glanced his way, then spoke up, thankfully taking over for Sammie. "How long ago was this? If they were just passing through, how do you know for sure they could be related?"

Eddie gave an offended little scoff, crossing her arms. "First of all, I might be several years older than everyone in the room, but that doesn't mean my memory is fading like some geriatric. Second, it was a suggestion, because I personally have never in my life met any other mage who could do that, so sue me if I make assumptions that the only two I have spent time with are related." When she was met with an unamused look from Miles she grimaced, continuing in a tense tone. "It was about twenty or so years ago, maybe twenty-three if you want me to put an exact number on it. She looked to be about your age when I met her. And I guess to be fair she didn't really stick around and chat. She distracted the bastard and allowed any who could to run free, as long as they managed to avoid all of his silly little safeguards..." Eddie ruffled her own hair, glancing away from all of them to face the wall. "I do recall her name, if that helps. Ashling Kearney, sort of fiery-red hair, freckles, blue eyes, and the same crooked smile you've got going on."

Sammie dug into his memories, his chest pulsing with energy as he tried to remember anything from his childhood that would point to Eddie being right. He wasn't sure why it mattered now; they should move on. Whether he was related to this person or not was irrelevant, but Sammie spiraled deeper into his mind. His uncle's pinched face at the sight of him, something sad and knowing. The few times Sammie would sneak around their dinky little home and happen to hear his uncle whispering to something. A picture?

Suddenly, it was as if Sammie was there, in his childhood home, maybe a handful of weeks before he'd gotten into school. His uncle stepped out to get them dinner, ruffling his hair as he went. The touch sent a zing through Sammie's spine, familiar in a way seeing an old friend was like. He almost followed his uncle when he stopped, looked into the room he'd just left, then stepped toward the photo he'd just put down.

It was his uncle, several years younger, looking like a fresh-faced teen, huddled up with a woman a handful of years older, violently red hair catching in the wind, blue eyes almost looking to glow from the photograph, and a crooked smile, her nose wrinkling with it, distorting the couple of freckles along the bridge. "Ashling..." young Sammie muttered, his voice from now leaving his underdeveloped vocal cords.

"Sam..." A voice, unfamiliar but almost not, whispered in his ear. "Watch out..."

Sammie rocketed back to the present, gasping hard and nearly buckling from the shock of his mind slamming back into his body. A second later, he crumpled to the ground. A warm and heavy muscled weight settled over him as something whipped into the room, and the door splintered at the frame.

There was yelling, the din in the room making his head throb and his ears drone. He pried his eyes open from when he'd squeezed them shut with the impact and found Miles draped over him protectively, eyes a yellow glow. He grit his teeth, canines sharpening before Sammie's eyes, and a second later Sammie felt a rough tug on his ankle. Something stung his skin as it wound around his leg and pulled.

"Miles?" Sammie yelped as Miles grabbed onto him to keep him in place. "What's going on?"

Miles just shook his head, half shifted, eyes wild. Sammie could hear yelling, then a high-pitched howl that cut like a knife into his brain. The grip on his leg loosened as something splashed over his skin.

"Move!" Eddie yelled, panicked and sharp, and Sammie was being tugged to his feet. He couldn't comprehend anything happening around them, everything moving too fast for his mind to take in.

Sammie blinked, letting himself be pulled where they took him, trying to take in anything. A slick, oil-like liquid was splattered where he'd been lying, a thin streak where his leg had dragged through trailing away from it. A leech-looking creature wriggled on the ground, deep gouges nearly splitting it in two. Sammie took in the sight, following the sounds of more chaos to the door, where it'd been splintered apart, broken down from the outside, and on the other side trying to claw its way in was the alpha...or...no.

"That's not…" Miles muttered, seeming to catch up as Sammie was. It wasn't Nikolas Young, not big enough, missing the scar that Miles had given him. It was just as monstrous though. Dark-crimson spittle flew from its maw as it gnawed through the remains of the door, trying desperately to get to them.

"What the fuck?" Eddie whispered, backing up into the wall along with them.

Sammie stared it down. Red froth spilled along its furry throat as it snapped its jaws, scrambling through the doorway. Its back leg caught for a moment, and rather than take the moment to untangle its limb from the wooden remains, it lunged forward. A pop sounded through the room, making Sammie feel like he was going to be sick as it scrambled toward them, not caring it was practically ripping its own leg apart in the process.

"Corner!" Damien yelled, and Naomi, looking as freaked out as them for once, herded them into the furthest corner of the room. A moment later, something cocked, and Sammie jolted as a gunshot sounded. The creature barely acknowledged the shot scattering into its shoulder, even as whatever had been fired into it began sizzling and smoking. "Christ…"

Sammie dragged his gaze away from the beast. Damien loaded a shotgun and shot at it again, then again. Each time it barely reacted, its claws gouging the flooring as it struggled against its hooked leg toward them.

It was the sixth round of shells Damien unloaded into the thing before it finally slowed, sluggishly clawing at the floor one last time before it stopped, its dislocated leg making a sickening sound as the tension finally let up on it. The only sounds in the room were their combined, harsh breaths and the sizzling of the creature's wounds where it'd been shot.

After a few breaths, Damien dropped the shotgun, his arms shaking. He took hurried steps up to the still wriggling leech on the ground and stomped on it, until it also stopped. Sammie wheezed harshly, feeling like a handful of razors scraped down his anxiety-filled throat.

Eddie was the first one to speak, after what felt like hours. "What in the ever-loving *fuck* was that?"

Sammie wasn't sure if he was relieved that for once it seemed like everyone was on the same page, as far as knowing what the hell was happening around them, or if he should follow his gut and find somewhere to be sick. He stared at the creature, half its face bloody and blistered, eyes clouded but...staring straight at him. He shuddered, nausea clogging his throat, and looked away, tucking his face into Miles for an excuse to hide from the gaze.

"I dunno," Naomi muttered, slumping back into the wall. "But I need to not be in the same room as it."

Miles wrapped an arm around Sammie and tugged him along. Damien exhaled, gingerly moving the thing's leg from the broken door with the shotgun, shoving it out of the path and directing them down the hall. "Go back out to the main room. I'll...figure out what to do about this mess..."

They stepped out, and Sammie half expected to see at least a dozen others storming up the hall toward them. Instead, they found a foamy trail of red leading down the hall. A couple of sturdy-looking, thankfully sane people turned the corner.

"Oh hell, you lot all right?" The taller one, a broad-shouldered woman, asked as they approached. She had crimson skin, horns curling from her scalp, and a ginger braid draped over her shoulder. "We tried to keep them from running off, but they were way quicker than any feral I'd ever seen."

The other was a shorter male packed with muscle, his skin slightly paler than the woman's, his eyes black on gold. He looked over the blood trail, a frown on his face. "Went a lot crazier faster than I'd seen any feral go, too."

Naomi grumbled, rubbing her nose, and Sammie realized that the room must've smelled awful, with all the blood and whatever that oil-like liquid was. "Did they get out of containment or something?"

The two glanced at each other, then the male shook his head. "No, it was one of the folks from your division, Ansel. They stepped in, passed by the Guide stand, then started writhing and screaming before they just...exploded into that thing."

The alpha raised her brows before she hissed, glancing away. "Dammit... All right, well, is there anywhere secure I can have them go? I want to stick around to help investigate."

Miles looked up, swallowing hard before he spoke. "Hey, if you're going to figure out what that was, I want to help."

Eddie whipped about, staring at him blankly. "You mean you

want to continue to hang around the thing that literally just gnawed through a door to get to us? Are you bonkers?"

The woman guard shook her head. "I hate to say it, Naomi, but no can do. Leave it to us. You just keep an eye on your little pack here." She gestured down the hallway, pointedly ignoring Naomi's huff of disapproval. "We'll come by for statements later; for now, you all can hunker down in one of the anti-mag rooms further down. Should be safe enough, though as the name suggests, there'd be no shifting or magic or anything happening in there. One of us can stand watch just in case."

Miles and Naomi both slumped, almost like scruffed kittens, before they all set off following the guard. Sammie felt relieved; a moment to breathe before the next terrible thing inevitably happened around them.

"We can snoop about later," Eddie offered, falling into the uncomfortable-looking armchair, shrugging halfheartedly. "We need to recuperate, get our wits back. Dunno 'bout y'all but that shit is gonna be painted in my nightmares for a while." She glanced up at Naomi, who had crouched and sat on the floor by the door the moment they got in. She tapped her fingers against her jaw as she glared at the ground. "I do get wanting to know what the hell is going on, though, as much as I started today just being along for the ride." She heaved a dramatic sigh, dropping her head back. "There's no way I can just...go on my merry way after this. Between Seers and whatever those leech things are, I have a bad feeling about all of this."

"Yeah." Miles finally moved, pulling Sammie along to the slightly more comfortable lounge seat. "That was... It was almost like Young but...different. But close enough they have to be connected, right?"

"Definitely," Eddie answered. "That and how convenient when we're talking about Seers working along with him, someone in the freakin' council goes super feral?"

"We'll need to move as soon as we can," Naomi muttered, sitting up slightly straighter, running a hand through her unruly hair. "I—I don't know where we can go, but sticking around somewhere with a lot of our kind who could suddenly become feral and bloodthirsty like that? Not going to be a good idea at all."

Sammie sagged into Miles's side, closing his eyes. His head hurt, the throbbing from earlier getting worse. This day felt like it'd lasted for a year, back-to-back near-death experiences draining every last drop of energy from him.

He could hear the others talking, probably discussing what was coming up next, plans, predictions... He should stay awake, listen, but he was exhausted, especially since they'd come to a rest. Miles's warm hand settled at the nape of his neck, its gentle touch dragging up his scalp, massaging, taking a tiny bit of the general ache of the coming migraine away.

"Rest for a bit, Sam," Miles whispered, digging his fingers into the tender bits of Sammie's skull, relieving the pressure from his thumping head with relaxing circular motions into his scalp.

"Thanks," Sammie tried to mutter back, leaning into Miles's

touch like a needy cat.

Between the massage, the bone-deep tiredness, and the calming back and forth discussion around him, Sammie was out almost within the very next minute, blessedly free of dreams or nightmares.

Chapter Fourteen

"We gotta get going, guys."

Miles blinked awake, his arm coiling slightly tighter around Sammie's shoulders. Sammie made a small grunt as he wriggled closer. Naomi's worried expression swam into focus, and Miles grimaced, vividly remembering everything from earlier.

"Nothing else went wrong, did it?" he muttered, sitting up straighter. Sammie let out a grumble as he roused.

Eddie scoffed, leaning up against the wall next to the door, looking just a tiny bit more flushed than he remembered, lips and cheeks dusted with a soft pink rather than ivory. "Not yet. Nae-Nae's contact basically gave us enough time to rest up before he kicked us out."

Naomi rolled her eyes, glaring and snarling at the vampire. "Call me that again and I'll kick you."

Sammie sighed. Miles couldn't help but agree.

"Let's just get going, yeah?" Miles suggested. "Do we know where we're going?"

"Nope," Eddie answered, popping the "p" with a toothy smirk in Naomi's direction. "Just that ol' lap dog Damien is going to be babysitting us."

"Oh, shut the fu—"

Sammie let out a frustrated grunt before he snapped his fingers at them, both of them going stock still as an arc of blue light sparked from his fingers. The hair on the back of Miles's neck raised with the sudden static in the air. "Stop it! Jesus, you both are like children."

Both muttered quiet apologies, and Miles shook his head and hopped up to his feet, pulling a still adorably sleepy Sammie along with him.

Miles popped the door open, pointedly ignoring the quiet jabs Naomi and Eddie threw to each other behind them, only stopping when he nearly bumped into someone on the other side of the door. Damien seemed surprised, glancing over Miles's head to the two further in. "Everything all right?"

"Peachy," Eddie answered, practically shooting out of her little corner of the room and wriggling past him. Miles tugged Sammie along to follow her.

"Naomi, what the hell happened?"

Sammie whistled to get Eddie to slow her pace a bit.

"Eddie, what's wrong?"

The vampire just groaned, waiting for them to catch up, wrapping her arms around herself with a sort of pinched expression. "I just... I don't like the idea of moving with even more council people." She glanced up at them and lowered her voice. "I know you both don't have any reason to be cautious, and Naomi seems to be one of the few good ones, but most of the people here are passive at best. They're not here to help—they're here to keep us secret by any means necessary. And they'd rather let people like us suffer than risk the human world know anything about us."

Sammie frowned, glancing around before he leaned close. "Then why stick around with us?"

"Because it's you." She gestured lazily. "I wasn't lying before when I said I liked you kids, and I don't know if you've noticed but I don't really have a lot of friends. This is...it's huge, and I can't... I wouldn't be able to live with myself if I just walked away, knowing that you two could get hurt. And as much as I tease her, Naomi, too."

Miles blew out a breath, feeling a tiny sense of ease that Eddie wasn't fighting with Naomi out of actual hate or anger or anything. He strained his ears to listen for Naomi's footsteps behind them. After a beat with nothing, Miles glanced back. He stopped in his tracks when he found the hallway behind them barren, even doors he knew they'd just walked past gone. "Uh...guys?" He turned back toward Eddie and Sammie, only to find them gone as well. The much too long hallway stretched out forever in either direction, which sent a thrill of ice through his chest. Frosty panic gripped his heart, making it pump harder.

"Miles...is it?"

He spun around, choking back a yelp when he came face to face with a middle-aged woman. She wore her fiery-red hair in a messy ponytail, and her blue eyes had eerie golden pupils glinting in the dim light, almost looking like a play of the light off her glasses. She felt familiar somehow, but Miles had never in his life ever seen her. "Who are you?"

She simply smiled, ducking close to him, gaze unblinking as she dragged her eyes over him. "It's rather rude to answer a question with a question, love. Now, just to make sure I'm talking to the right one; you are Miles, correct?"

"Y-yes." The word felt like it was physically dragged from his throat. The woman seemed pleased at his obvious discomfort. "I...I apologize, for...for ah, being rude."

He choked out the words, trying to fight them on the way out. The woman seemed more and more pleased with each one. After he'd finished, she giggled, eyes still wide and dry as she stared him down. "That is much better, puppy. Such a good little boy you are."

A growl rose from his throat, but the woman snarled, and the sound got blocked in Miles's throat, along with his air. He panicked, just for a moment, before she stopped, giggling. Her lips stretched further than they should've as she leaned close. "See how easy you are to manipulate, my dear? I barely have to try. It's laughable, really, how easy you lot can be used. Mutts made to be given orders."

"W-what do you…? Are you…?" Miles struggled to get the words out, willing his arms and legs to move, to do something other than hold him in place. "Why…?"

"Because of your tiny, little puppy brains." She tilted her head, her eerie sneer twitching into a frown before she exhaled dramatically. "Of course, I'm not allowed to do anything yet. Just give you a warning. So boring."

Miles opened his mouth, trying to speak, to ask what the hell she was trying to warn him about, only for his voice to die in his throat. A pathetic croak squeaked out instead. The woman tilted her head the opposite way, goldish pupils dilating as she smirked again. "Aw, silly, stupid dog. You don't speak unless I let you speak." She bared her teeth, snarling manically. "Listen, *mutt*, there's a war coming, soon, so figure who you want to side with. One side will ensure you and your little *plaything* make it through unscathed. The other…" She poked her tongue through her teeth, staring holes into his eyes, before she finally blinked and—

It almost felt real, but it came over him so suddenly he knew it couldn't possibly be. Visions of Miles holding a bleeding-out Sammie, blood and guts and viscera all over his hands, Sammie's lifeless eyes, and Miles trying to hold his own insides in, Eddie and Naomi's headless corpses…

Miles collapsed, bile rising up his throat and out before he could stop it.

"Miles?" Sammie's voice was panicked, and Miles realized he

was back from whatever the hell that was. He gagged, shaking his head like it would banish the images burned into the back of his eyelids. "Miles, what's wrong?"

He shook his head, spitting the acrid taste from his mouth before gulping down his fear and anxiety. A war, it was exactly what they expected, from the sound of it. He couldn't be sure, of course he couldn't, but he had a sinking feeling that the woman he saw was the one puppeteering everyone.

"We should go," Eddie mumbled, and Miles glanced up to see a sort of faraway stare on her face, gaze locked on the hallway ahead of them. "I...I'm getting a bad feeling."

A much too cool hand settled on the back of his neck. Naomi's familiar scent cut through the copper of blood from the vision and the stinging sourness of stomach acid. "She's right. Come on. Damien says he has an idea of somewhere to go."

Miles let himself be lifted to his feet, focusing on the familiar scents around him to center him to the present. He...they could prevent this. He just had to believe that.

*

"Better?" Sammie offered, quiet, his hand tangling in the hair at the nape of Miles's neck. He'd never seen Miles look so off-kilter, even after the first step into the supernatural world. It was weird, Miles freezing in place out of nowhere, his eyes clouding over, and the moment they'd noticed he crumpled, mumbling about blood and death and a war.

"Mmm." Miles blinked slowly, his hand coiling around Sammie's side.

Sammie chewed on his lip, wanting to ask what the hell had happened. Obviously *something*; he just had no idea what would garner that sort of a visceral reaction from him.

They'd all piled into an SUV (Damien's council vehicle apparently), and they'd been driving for at least three hours at that point. Everyone barely spoke; Naomi and Damien provided the only conversation over the classic rock playing through the speakers. It was severely uncomfortable, making Sammie feel like everyone was waiting for the next terrible thing to happen to them, everyone knowing but not saying while Sammie waited in the dark.

"Miles?" Sammie whispered, waiting to continue until Miles looked at him. He glanced over to him softly, trying to offer some reassurance. "I just... I care about you, you know. I know we never really got to talk too much about it but...I..." He glanced away, feeling Miles's gaze softening. "After...after all of this, I just... Maybe we can go back to that coffee shop, you know? Have a date, go see a movie?"

A spark of anxiety tingled in Sammie's fingertips before Miles let out a soft exhale, leaning close, and pressed a gentle kiss to Sammie's jaw.

He whispered into Sammie's ear, sending a chill along his spine. "You mean like we have no worries? Normal lives?" Miles chuckled, pulling back slightly. "I would like that. I just... I want to have time with you, catch up like we were supposed to." He paused, licking his lips and grinning, eyes flickering down to Sammie's gaping mouth. "Actually make up for something I should've done years ago…"

Sammie let out a nervous little giggle. He reached his hand up to the nape of Miles's neck again to focus on something, anything but the little electric flurry of raging butterflies in his stomach. The last thing they needed was for Sammie to tase everyone accidentally because he was flustered by some flirting.

"So where is the supposed safe place you have in mind, Dame?" Eddie spoke up from the middle row of seats, leaning forward between Damien and Naomi.

"Just somewhere isolated. I have a cabin out away from everyone that I usually go to when everything at the council is getting a bit overwhelming." He let out a halfhearted chuckle, glancing in the rearview at the three of them. "Feels a bit fitting to head there now. Though admittedly there's really not enough room for everyone. We just need to get some sort of a gameplan in place."

"Oh," Naomi drawled. "I think I remember it. I didn't realize you still had it."

Damien answered quickly, settling his gaze back on the road. "No reason to get rid of it. Obviously still useful, and unfortunately overwhelming kind of comes with the job."

"Why stay there, then?" Miles spoke up, leaning forward slightly. "Doesn't really seem worth it."

"I want to help," Damien answered simply. "I've been there

for so long, I've seen so many terrible things, I just... I want to do whatever I can to help."

Miles leaned into Sammie. Damien glanced back again then. When he spoke, his tone was curious. "Are you asking for a reason? You wanted to help with the feral one from earlier. I'm guessing you're interested in that?"

Sammie let out a tiny breath, glancing at Miles only to meet his warm, chocolate eyes, a gentle look in them that made Sammie's heart skip. A spark of blue light zinged along Miles's scalp where his fingers were digging in. Miles didn't flinch, or wince, looked entirely smitten. "Maybe...there's a couple things I want to do first."

Eddie turned around, fake gagging. "Criminy, I can practically smell you two eye-boning. At least wait until we're not all crammed in a car for who knows how long."

Heat flushed his skin, and Sammie cleared his throat, leaning slightly out of Miles's space. He resolutely looked away as the rest of the car blew up with a mix of cackling and yelps as Miles kicked at Eddie with an embarrassed growl.

"You're the worst, you know that," Miles said.

"No, the worst is how sickeningly sweet you two are. I'm practically barfing rainbows right now."

"You're one to talk, I saw you making goo-goo eyes earlier."

"No one has said goo-goo eyes in ages, maybe update your insults before you try that again."

"Eddie!"

As much as Sammie tried to tune out the bickering, he was admittedly relieved. Things seemed a little bit normal; everything didn't feel as...final.

He really wanted everyone to come through this—whatever this was. Whatever was going to happen next, he didn't want to lose anyone.

Chapter Fifteen

This is a freakin' shit show…

Eddie grimaced, tapping her nails against her aching teeth. She hadn't eaten in a couple of days; there were some wacky goings-on with Seers which she always so enjoyed…

"You hungry?" Sammie was a saint, all things considered. Sweet boy, utterly cavity inducing. "You're looking a little pale, and you never know when we'll get a chance to just relax like this again.

Oh, sweet, innocent boy.

"I'll just bother Nae-Nae." Eddie shifted where she was perched on a desk in the homey little cabin Damien had brought them to. He was right when he mentioned it was cramped; two rooms and a den/kitchen area where the alpha in question and her other wolfy little friends were scrounging for food. "No need to offer your neck up. I'm pretty sure Miles would skin me alive if I were to try anyway."

Sammie blushed, and Eddie softened at the sight of him. Young love. So adorable. Like fruit gushers, a burst of sickeningly sweet sugar on her tongue. "I-I mean... I think he'd understand."

"Oh love." Eddie ruffled his hair. "That boy is ass over kettle for you and I'm pretty sure I'd go into diabetic shock if I were still human just being in the same room as the two of you."

The boy's face grew a delightfully vibrant shade of red, and he cleared his throat, shaking his head. "Still—"

"Still nothing." She leaned close. "Besides, I'm fine. I'll find something. Don't you worry your pretty little head. Save your energy for if anything tracks us down."

Sammie mumbled, settling back against the wall. He glanced into the kitchen with a small frown before he looked back at her. "Do you... Have you seen anything like what happened before we left?"

The vacant look on Miles's face before he collapsed was burned into her brain, sickeningly familiar. "I have, unfortunately..." She slumped back again. "That's some Seer trick, something cruel. Our little friend probably probed into Miles's head and fed him some doomsday imagery. They absolutely love their dramatics..." She hissed in a breath through her teeth, grimacing. "To be fair, they usually only show things that are entirely possible. Just...maybe not in line with where we're heading. But you know they can see all."

Sammie was quiet for a couple of moments before he tilted his head back. "I'm scared. I've never... Miles didn't even look like that after he was bitten. He's never looked so..."

"Haunted?" Eddie finished, sucking on her teeth. "Seers are good for that. I can only imagine what they showed him. We just...you know, gotta thread the needle."

"Right." Eddie dreaded the next words she knew were coming. "What do you think the odds are that we actually succeed?"

Pretty much nothing. "Not high," she answered instead, watching the three in the kitchen. Naomi was bullying Miles out of the way of the little cast-iron cauldron they'd scrounged up. Damien cackled as Miles squawked in outrage. She wanted them to succeed, more than anything she'd wanted in a while. Hell, it might even be more than when she was stuck in the utter hellhole that was Constantine's lair. "I think...they might need some help," Eddie muttered, gesturing into the kitchen, trying to keep the small tremble from her voice. "Why don't you go. It's been ages since I've eaten food, so I know I'd be utterly useless."

Sammie shot her a look—the little mage was way smarter than he looked—and stood up, giving her shoulder a squeeze as he went by. She sighed, closing her eyes, taking a moment to drag through her thoughts.

Constantine... She hadn't thought about that asshole for years. Of course, Seers cropped up completely unrelated with the monster currently at her throat. Then again, she hadn't heard of Seers being involved with anyone other than Duskheart—either the ancient jerk had all the others killed to keep his precious little special one to himself or they were just really good at hiding. But it didn't make sense for a werewolf to be involved with them, too...

She remembered her time at the old Duskheart estate; the one time a werewolf had gotten too close, Constantine had made an example of them, butchering them to use as décor. There was no way he'd willingly work with wolves.

"But why the hell would there be Seers again?" she mumbled to herself, chewing on her nail to distract from the circling thoughts. It made no damn sense. He definitely wouldn't let the one he had loose, and even if it wasn't the same one, he'd keep the line as tight as he could.

"Food's on," Miles crowed, and Eddie blinked up. She huffed out a gentle chuckle as she watched Miles duck away from Naomi's reaching hand. Naomi snatched a piece of bread from his bowl. Sammie grinned, splitting his piece in half to share, because of course he did. Eddie shook her head, glancing back at Naomi and freezing when she noticed the alpha giving her an odd look, something much too soft.

Yeah. No way.

Eddie shifted, moving to push from the desk when she froze, the hair on the back of her neck rising, a stone of anxiety dropping into the base of her stomach.

"They're here."

The voice was quiet, soft and familiar in the barest sense, and Eddie felt like everything was moving in slow motion.

She looked past Naomi's shoulder, catching the barest glimpse of a flicker of silver before she was up and moving, sprinting and tackling Naomi before she heard glass shattering. A sudden cacophony of roars and wails came from outside.

"I thought you said we were isolated!" Eddie hissed, looking up, trying to find Damien and seeing only Miles, Sammie and Naomi with her. "What... Where'd?"

Her words were drowned out as wood split from something huge slamming into the wall. She cursed. Naomi shoved her away with a growl as the alpha sprung to her feet. "Keep an eye on them," she snarled out, before, stupidly, dashing out of the door.

"Naomi!" Eddie yelled, scrambling to her feet. "You're being a moron!"

Ridiculously, Miles was chasing after her. Both Sammie and Eddie caught him before he could get very far, thankfully. "She needs help!"

"It sounds like there's a ton of those feral things out there—it's suicide."

"Miles, don't."

The wolf glanced at them both for a moment before he shook them off and sprinted out of the door despite their cries.

"Shit..." Eddie ran a hand through her hair, panic swelling in her chest. This was that fucking disaster of her escape all over again... She needed to not get close to anyone.

It's like I'm fucking cursed.

"Eddie?" Sammie's voice knocked her out of her head, the

small, panicked thing it was. The boy looked small, like some terrified little prey animal. "What do we do?"

Hide, run, be anywhere but here cornered in a crummy little shack. Eddie gasped shakily, running a hand through her hair before she shook her head and bit out words she never would've said before. "Let's go help."

Sammie's eyes went wide, then he walked out with her into the absolute chaos outside.

Screw it, I've had a good run so far.

Eddie grit her teeth, grabbed a bit of the broken wood of the door, and motioned to Sammie. "You do your thing; I'll play defense if anything gets a bit too close."

The boy looked terrified, but he nodded, his scared blue eyes glowing before that light started sparking through his hair and racing along his shoulders. He turned toward the closest snarling, rabid beast. "Got it."

The vampire panted, pressing her back to the little taser, her hair standing on end as magic coursed through him, a flash of blue lighting up behind her. She grunted as she stabbed at one of the creatures lunging toward them. Maybe...maybe if she could find the others, they could just hoof it out of here.

Yeah, sure. Like they'd run. Idiots, they are.

And here she was with them. All for some passive charm she felt toward two complete strangers and their...Naomi...

Eddie was never known to make good decisions for people she trusted: the vampiric asshole in the back alley talking sweet words into her naïve human ears; her ex long, long after that, who cheated and ran off with her new fling and all of Eddie's cash and anything she could pawn off. Now a grumpy as hell werewolf who seemed to have a penchant for running headfirst into danger.

The strength and power beyond my wildest dreams Constantine promised when he turned me sure would be useful right about now...

"Eddie!" Naomi's voice was harsh, high, and panicked, so completely unnatural for the usually calm alpha. Eddie glanced her way, only to be jerked in the opposite direction. Something sprinted through her vision before the world spun out of focus. There was a beat before Naomi was there, snarling and snapping at one of the beasts, one with...

Huh... That nail polish looks familiar...and that ring...

Eddie dropped her gaze to her hand, only to feel the cold drip of nausea run through her when she saw a bloody stump left behind. It was as if her brain wouldn't comprehend what had happened until she saw it, and a scream wrenched out of her lungs unbidden with the wave of pain boiling through her blood.

She wished she could pass out. What fucking use was all this cursed vampire bullshit if she had to deal with this?

"Fuck, Eddie..." Naomi's voice was rough. The alpha's eyes were rimmed with red, crimson bleeding into the gray storm of her usual eye color. She was pretty...

Naomi's rough hands cinched around the wound, and Eddie glanced down again, whimpering as she saw how gnarly the thing was. Her skin was twisted and coated in her thicker, darker blood, looking almost like an ink blot. Naomi seemed to be trying to stave off the bleeding. She took her hands away to rip her shirt off over her head and tore a bit of the fabric away with her teeth. She cinched the cloth tightly above the wound, and a sickening squish accompanied the flare of red-hot agony through Eddie's left side.

"We need to go." Sammie's voice sounded far away, though Eddie could feel the boy's too-hot fingers clamping on the back of her neck and seeping his miracle juice magic into her bones.

"But Damien's probably out there somewhere..." Miles's voice seemed even further away, strained, like he was pushing against something heavy. "We can't just leave him."

Damien... Shit, that's right. He just upped and left us, right before the attack... Almost convenient how that timing worked out...

"I... I don't—"

Go!

The word was shoved into her mind, making her spine straighten and the words clog in her throat. Oddly enough, Sammie's hand tensed, and she saw Naomi jolt at the same time.

"Miles, come on!" Naomi shouted, scooping Eddie up from the ground. Sammie's healing touch was ripped away, the floaty feeling his magic created replaced with butterflies in her stomach and pulsing fire in her arm.

"But—" Eddie didn't hear the rest of Miles's words—the deafening sound of crackling lighting cut him off. She blearily looked over Naomi's shoulder and caught Miles staggering to the side away from one of the feral beasts. The thing twitched with residual energy from Sammie's magic. She watched just long enough to make sure they were both following before she tucked her face into Naomi's shoulder, squeezing her eyes shut to try to block out the pain beating through her with every step.

*

Everything you touch is destroyed.

Everything you care about will be hurt.

Just knowing you, people will die.

The words were running circles in Naomi's brain, much to her annoyance. She glanced down to the small heap of people in or around her lap, trying to break the gloomy track of her thoughts.

Eddie, curled up close, head in Naomi's lap, her eyes closed but very much awake.

Sammie, right next to her, carding his fingers through the matted, tangled mess of Eddie's hair, little electric wisps of magic sparking through the strands every so often.

Miles, basically trying his best to crawl inside Sammie, nose pressed into the mage's shoulder, scenting him, probably to calm his nerves.

You're a burden, a curse, you always will be.

That mean little voice, always there in the back of her thoughts, waiting to pounce and drag her back down to her lowest.

Naomi shook her head lightly. She lifted Sammie's fingers from Eddie's hair, gently tugging at the vampire's nape. "I think a meal will help her now, more than anything else."

Eddie made a small, wounded sound before she opened her eyes and sat up slightly. She looked pale, more than usual, almost the same white as the walls of the abandoned hospital they'd found cover in. "Careful now, Naomi," Eddie practically wheezed, flashing a tired, lopsided smile her way. "You keep offering yourself up like that I might start thinking you care..."

Naomi set her jaw, glancing away before settling her gaze on the two boys. "How do you guys feel about scrounging around for supplies, and maybe finding us a secure place to rest up?"

Miles gave her a tired look but didn't make any argument. He stood up with Sammie and left the thin hallway they sheltered in through a set of creaky double doors. Naomi looked back to Eddie. She tugged down her collar on one side and tilted her head back. "Take what you need."

Eddie offered a genuinely grateful look before she shifted herself up, being careful of her injured side, and ducked down to settle her mouth on Naomi's exposed neck. There was no immediate bite. Instead, Eddie dragged her lips along the vein there, the barest press of her fangs making Naomi freeze in place. "Eddie."

"Gimme a minute," Eddie murmured, gripping Naomi's bicep with her remaining hand. "I want to pretend everything isn't terrible, and you smell like a relaxing as hell summer, so...just, let me have this..."

Naomi grimaced as the vampire chose that moment to bite down. It was gentle, like a kiss, and it made her shudder involuntarily. She hadn't ever felt like this—handled like something fragile. Eddie's hand loosened, skimming up to cup the opposite side of her neck, nails running over her skin soft like feathers. "Ed." Her voice came out way huskier than she'd expected, and thankfully Eddie had chosen that moment to pull back, licking her lips, a tiny bit more color to her cheeks. The wound looked marginally better. At least the bleeding had stopped, thanks to Sammie, and with some energy back from feeding it looked like she was able to start healing over the damaged skin.

"Yeah..." Eddie murmured, following Naomi's gaze to the remains of her arm situated in her lap. "This is going to wreck my street cred."

"You don't have to do that," Naomi blurted, meeting wide brown eyes as Eddie looked up at her with a surprised expression. "You don't have to turn this into a joke to save face or...whatever."

Eddie simply huffed out a laugh, giving Naomi's shoulder a short squeeze. "I mean... I feel like this is one of those 'if you don't laugh, you're gonna cry' type situations. And unfortunately, one of the gross things that happen with vampires is literally crying blood so...jokes it is." She licked her lips again, slower, eyes hooded and staring into Naomi's soul, it felt like. "I'd never want to waste the taste of you, anyway..."

Naomi looked away, swallowing around a sudden lump in her throat. "Eddie..." She tried to come off as scolding, but between the tightness of her throat and the ache in her jaw it was more of a whine than anything else.

Eddie threw her arms up, fingers of her right hand splayed in a placating gesture. "Sorry. Always get a little flirty after feeding. Though…" She paused, shaking herself. "Hell, seems like we're going by each day fast and loose here, so…if you wanted, you know… I wouldn't say no."

Naomi glanced back, gulping hard at the sight of the scarlet blush along Eddie's cheekbones, her deep eyes not looking away. Confident, but…no…

She took a breath in, closing her eyes. Beneath the constant off-copper scent that hung around the vampire, there was something like cinnamon, a spicy mix of cloves, cardamom, wine; something that Naomi had a hard time pinpointing. Obviously from Eddie, and so strong it almost stung her sinuses. What was it?

"Or…or you know, you could just pretend I didn't say anything, and we can go back to…friends? I hope we were friends before, or—"

"Eddie." Naomi opened her eyes again to settle her with a firm glare.

The vampire paused for a moment before she shook her head, rambling on again. "Or you can just pretend I don't exist! I can help you guys and then get out of your hair, and—*mph!*"

Naomi, for the first time since she first ran into Miles and Sammie in that alley, acted impulsively, wrapping her fingers around Eddie's jaw and tugging her forward. She leaned in and jammed their lips together. It was awkward, Eddie's teeth digging into her lips just enough to sting, the copper of her own blood still there to taste but...

It was nice.

Eddie was still for a moment before she relaxed, bringing her hand up to rest against Naomi's cheek, gently shifting until the kiss felt better, more natural. She let out a rumble. Eddie broke them apart just long enough to giggle against her mouth before she dove back in.

It was bliss to pretend the rest of the chaos outside of them didn't exist, even for the few seconds they had. An almost purr-like growl involuntarily bubbled out of Naomi, before she wound a hand in Eddie's hair and tugged back, earning a gasp. She let that spicy scent from before flood her senses. "I think...I'm okay with being maybe a bit more than friends. If that's what you want."

Eddie's eyes were wide, nearly sparkling in the dim light. She huffed, leaning into Naomi's hand with a lazy smirk that made Naomi's mouth water. "Oh, I am one thousand percent on board with that. Now come here..."

Adorably, Eddie made a little trilling sound, her thumb drawing a slow line along Naomi's jaw before she dipped back down and nipped at Naomi's bottom lip before diving in.

Which, of course, was the exact moment Sammie and Miles came around the corner. Miles squawked out a surprised sound as Sammie just smirked in Eddie's direction.

Damn her luck.

Chapter Sixteen

Miles was staring. He knew he was staring. He couldn't help it, really. What else was he supposed to do when the grumpy, practically stoic girl he'd been around for the past couple of months was cuddling with the girl she'd been spending the last couple of weeks snarling at? He was all for either of them being happy and all, but it was just...weird.

Like...watching your older siblings making out on the couch in front of the entire family. Not, together, or anything, just...

"Miles, if you don't stop staring in the next second, I'm going to bite you," Eddie purred, not moving from her place tucked up against Naomi.

He jumped, looking away and finding Sammie on his other side giving him an amused leer. "Oh, shuddap," he groused, pushing him with his knee. "I was just zoning out. It's been a long week, don't I have more than enough reason to do that?"

"Uh huh," Sammie mused, the jerk, leaning close, washing his spicy citrus scent over him. "Why don't you just...turn in for the night?" He glanced up at Naomi and Eddie, then lowered his voice slightly. "Besides, I sort of...wanted some time alone with you, if that's okay...?"

Miles could almost hear his thoughts screech to a halt, his eyes bugging out as he stared at Sammie for a moment before he nodded, trying not to gape like a fish as he spoke. "Oh, uh...yeah, yeah, that'd be...yep, we can do that."

Eddie blew a raspberry their way, but Miles could not pay attention to her now, not with his heart and that feral energy in his chest both running circles through his brain. That raspy, not quite his, voice chanting "Mate! Mate! Mate!" as it went. His eyes ached, the telltale sign they were shifting to that sort of gold color his other form had. Sammie led him out of the small room Naomi and Eddie had claimed and dragged him across the way to a hospital room they'd sort of picked up. An uncomfortable cot with a slightly damp mattress was the only thing there. Not that it mattered at all, since Sammie was looking at him like Miles had hung the moon and stars just for him.

"So...we haven't had much time to ourselves for a while, huh?" Sammie commented, settling onto the mattress as he reached for Miles's hand and interlocked pinkies. "I know we talked about doing something after this all but..." He glanced away for a moment as he traced his thumb along Miles's knuckles. "To be honest, I don't know if we'll have an after."

Miles opened his mouth to counter that, to disregard the idea that they might not make it, then stopped. It was a real fear. Miles could heal quickly, but if anything hit him fatally, he didn't think he could recover in time, and Sammie might have magic, but he was still vulnerable. The scabbing on his hip from his bedpost all those weeks ago proved that. They *could* die, the Seer had made sure to remind him of that, even though Miles didn't want to believe it.

He sucked in a shaky breath, turning his hand to interlock their fingers before he settled next to Sammie, nervous despite himself. "All I can say is I will do everything in my power to try to make sure we make it to that after. And... And I... I can also tell you exactly how I feel, so we don't leave that hanging in the unknown or anything." Why was he so nervous? He knew how Sammie felt, he knew Sammie knew, so why did his heart still feel like it was pounding out of his chest?

"I love you, too," Sammie said, beaming when Miles's head whipped up to stare at him. "I have since middle school, I think..."

"Really?" Miles's voice was soft, so tender it made his chest ache. "I...don't think I realized until recently, but you've always felt like my other half. Like when you left, I felt empty, even though..." He tugged Sammie's hand up to hold his chin. "I don't really feel like I should've. I was a chicken back then."

Sammie laughed, soft and sweet, making Miles ache even more. "If you were a chicken then I was worse." He touched his forehead to Miles's shoulder as he spoke. "That night I told you I was leaving, I wanted you to stop me. I could've told you how much I cared about you, how I felt, and instead I hoped you'd just know and tell me not to go." He giggled; the sound caused that purring rumble to start in his chest. "We're both idiots."

"Yeah…" Miles leaned back, tipping Sammie's head back to look up at him. "We sure were."

Sammie beamed, bright and happy, his blue eyes glittering in the dark room illuminated only by moonlight. Miles responded by doing what he'd been wanting to do for weeks.

It wasn't like the movies, not like some burst of fireworks behind his eyes or some massive shift in the universe. But it was *right*; Sammie's slightly dry, bitten lips just felt…right. Miles brought his hand up to cup Sammie's cheek, not wanting to move for anything.

Every good thing comes to an end, though, but somehow Sammie's thousand-watt expression was even better. "Wow…" Sammie whispered, then cackled. "I really was an idiot, if I could've been kissing you this whole time."

Miles giggled, his nose brushing against Sammie's for the moment he shifted forward. "Yeah. Both of us were…really dumb." He pulled back and brushed his thumb along Sammie's jaw. The starry-eyed glimmer in Sammie's bright-blue gaze warmed him better than any fire, or magic, or anything. "Sam, I think I have to ask Naomi about it, since I don't know exactly what it means, but… My wolf calls you mate. It feels important." Sammie's soft look had bloomed into something impossibly bright, almost blinding to look at. "It feels... If you're not close by, I feel empty. If I'm losing control or lost, I can pull back because of you. Like...you settle me to the ground and keep me here."

Sammie grinned, then paused, his eyes going wide for a moment before he chuckled, almost breathlessly. "In the woods... when Nikolas was there. You were able to break out of whatever control he had when I got there."

"Yeah." Miles tugged Sammie closer and pressed a gentle kiss to his cheek before he rested his forehead against his mate's. He felt at home in a way he never had, even when he was younger. Everything was in place, right where it belonged, and Miles's eyes burned just from how right he felt. "You saved me." He pulled back, needing to look into those sapphire eyes right at that moment. "You brought me back, Sammie."

A wet giggle bubbled up from Sammie, his eyes shimmering so bright Miles was almost blinded.

Everything was right, despite all the chaos outside. Despite the knowledge that they'd have to figure out where to go from here, they had no place that was safe. He was safe *now*, with his love in his arms.

Miles would give anything just to live right here, for the rest of his days.

Sammie pulled him in, mashing his lips clumsily against Miles's, cheeks damp and aching from his joy, just like Miles's.

Chapter Seventeen

Naomi woke up to the sound of screams.

Dread settled heavily and like an illness in her gut. The ragged sheets of the hospital bed stuck to her back in the darkness. Eddie sprinted out of the room as she looked up.

"Eddie?"

The alpha stood up, feeling the ice-cold sweat on the nape of her neck, her hands shaking no matter how much she told herself to calm down. Something was wrong.

It's your fault, you did this, you always do this.

She winced, shaking her head violently. She had to be calm; she had to be.

Deep breaths, deep breaths, it's not—

A high-pitched whimper, dizzyingly familiar, brought her thoughts to a halt. Her heart pounded in her chest. *"Miles*?" She sprinted down the hall toward the sound, her eyes aching and her claws popping through her nail beds in a harsh stabbing pain. "Where are you?"

You did this to them. It's your fault.

"Stop it!" Naomi yelled, slapping a hand into her temple, trying to silence that stupid voice. She needed to focus.

"*Help!*" Sammie's hysterical scream had her running again, not even realizing when she had ever stopped. She streaked around a corner of the hospital floor, barely stopping herself from barreling into the wall with a bloody hand. "*Help, please, help!*"

"I'm coming! Just hold on!"

Where the hell was the exit? It felt like she'd been running circles in a maze, just passing the exit every time! Where the hell were they?

She growled, skidding around another corner and freezing. There was a woman down the hall, fiery-red hair almost down to her waist, standing with her arms out and her back to Naomi. She smelled...like nothing.

"Who are you?" Naomi's voice was shaking. She tried to speak again only to have the words back up into her throat. She coughed, then stopped breathing.

The woman laughed, turning slowly as panic gripped Naomi's brains. Her heart beat a staccato rhythm in her ears, and her vision blurred as she struggled to get a breath in. The woman's gold pupils glittered in the dim light, a manic set to her face as she cackled.

"Naomi!"

She gasped, shooting up and coughing, trying to gasp in as much air as she could. She jumped up and attempted to run after the woman, then felt something try to shove her back.

"Naomi, *Naomi*! Calm down!" Eddie's voice swam into her brain like a lazy wave at a pier, slow and quiet, building up in even measures. Naomi gazed around wildly before she settled on Eddie's wide brown eyes. Eddie and Miles were looking at her with worry. They pressed her back to the bed. "You're okay... Nae, you're back with me, you're okay."

She wheezed harshly, trying to calm her racing heart somehow. She felt like she was going to throw up, her heartbeat pounding in her throat. "I... I thought..."

Eddie's brow furrowed, then her gaze darkened and she snarled, showing off her longer canines. *She needs to eat*, Naomi thought randomly.

"Son of a bitch..."

Miles frowned, then narrowed his eyes at her, like he was really looking her over. She wanted to hide, scrunch in on herself. It was an odd feeling, something she hadn't felt in years, and especially not with Miles. "Naomi...did you... What did you see?"

"I..." She jumped when she felt something cool press to the back of her neck. Sammie's calming touch seeped into her skin like a balm. "I woke up. I thought I heard screaming. I tried to run out and find one of you, but it was like you were always just barely out of my sight. I turned a corner and saw this...this woman." She looked up at Miles, pausing when she saw how pale he was. "She—she had red hair, and these odd...golden eyes. Pupil and all. And she was just laughing, cackling almost."

Miles gulped, collapsing down into the other cot in the room. "Shit."

Eddie growled, the sound sending a shock of something she couldn't name zipping along Naomi's spine. "A Seer."

"No, the Seer," Miles mumbled, looking up at Naomi with a tinge of fear that made the beast in her mind seethe. "That's the same one I saw. She...likes to get inside the heads of werewolves, said we're easier. It has to be the same one."

"We should make a plan," Sammie said; the calm voice of reason Naomi should be but couldn't bring herself to be at the moment. "We need to stop this. Miles said she'd mentioned a war last time. We need to stop that."

Eddie frowned, her eyes rimmed red, hand hovering over the nub of her other arm. "We're only four people. She has at least several feral beasts on her side, and gods knows what else." She hissed, sitting up straighter. "But she's a raging psycho bitch who is messing with my friends, so fuck it."

"Yeah." Miles leaned forward, still pale but expression steely. "We can figure out what their aim is, figure out a way to make them weak so we can stop them."

Naomi chewed on her lip as she glanced Eddie's way again. She looked terrified, smelled it, too, but there was something else under there. She was determined, and pissed, and...something that made Naomi feel just a bit more herself, a bit braver and tougher. "You're right." She let out a breath, looking around her small, jumbled pack—the thing she'd never wanted, never sought out, and stumbled into anyway.

That little voice of self-hatred and blame and fear had quieted, not completely gone but somewhere Naomi had to strain to hear it. Maybe...maybe they could do this. Seer or no, they could be the deciders of their own futures. They could die trying to stop this, or whimper and hide with their tail between their legs and die as cowards. Naomi was tired of being the scared little girl she was when she was turned.

"Let's get them."

*

Eddie had never felt more at ease with herself, despite knowing that they were all probably preparing their own graves. Naomi squeezed her remaining hand under the table, giving her a hopefully comforting expression as she spoke through what they knew. Eddie had seen red that morning, once the panic of Naomi shooting out of bed like it was on fire, screaming her head off, had faded. Eddie knew so little about Naomi, but enough to be absolutely livid at the witch putting her through more misery.

"Eds?" Naomi whispered, and Eddie focused back, letting out a pleased hum as Naomi nuzzled close. "You're up."

The vampire glanced at the group, all watching her with varying degrees of anxiety and determination. "So, I don't know much about Seers, but I know they can bleed. The one with my sire had been hurt once in my time there, when I was escaping. It was by the one who helped me get out, who seemed like she could somehow block the Seer's powers." She glanced at Sammie, watching him sit up a slight bit straighter. "Like what we assume you can do. So, if we're right on that, Sammie should be able to get enough of a surprise on her to incapacitate and stop her from whispering all our secrets to Nikolas."

"And speaking of Nikolas," Naomi started, looking up at Miles with a touch of trepidation. "Are you sure about your idea for that...?"

Right—the plan Miles had come up with. It made sense, but it was unbelievably risky. Miles would play along, following Nikolas's orders until the Seer was gone, and he would try to take him down by surprise. As far as they knew, Nikolas still expected to have some control over him, even if Miles was able to break it that one time. They would just have to rely on Miles being able to do that again.

"Yes." Miles glanced at Sammie, his gaze softening and something sparking in his eyes that made Eddie ache. "If I have Sammie's scent, I can pull myself back." His voice was bright and happy and so sickeningly sweet. "He's my mate. My wolf would die before it would lose him."

Naomi's brows shot up, and her breath hitched. Eddie glanced over, just catching the alpha looking away from her. "Are you...are you sure? Everything I'd heard about them before they're... There haven't been any mates in ages, not since before we started regulating everything."

A rumble from Miles's chest rattled in Eddie's. "Positive. It's the first thing my wolf thought when I came back to myself."

Naomi puffed out a weak little half-laugh, then shook her head, leaning forward. "Right, okay, so...back to the plan." She cleared her throat, tapping the crude map they'd made on a rickety tool table they'd wheeled over between them. "That's Nikolas and the Seer—what about the rest? We know the ferals, which... Seems like they go down after a good amount of effort." She glanced at Eddie before she looked back to the map. "I'd say I could take over holding them back, but we have no idea what else they have on their side."

Eddie drummed her fingers along her jaw, grimacing for a moment as she remembered. Those awful shifters that had stolen Ryise's face. "We met with the shifters in the club—seems to be a fair assumption they might be in on it, too. Sounded like they were getting paid to find us."

Sammie flinched, and Eddie stopped breathing to avoid the bitter, battery-acid taste of his well-placed fear. "The shifters..." Naomi breathed, glancing up between the three of them. "The thing that attacked us in the council, that had the leech thing attached to it, yeah? And those shifters in the club—they had that black goop. That was a lot like that leech, right?"

Eddie's brow furrowed as she tried to piece together what the alpha was laying out for them now.

Miles frowned, tilting his head adorably as he thought. Sammie sat up, a tiny little gasp catching in the air. "Oh! That's right! I didn't put it together until just now, since everything was happening so fast and we never really got much of a chance to relax, but yeah, they were really similar."

"Oh shit," Eddie whispered, the pieces falling together now. "They're infecting the ferals by feeding them shifter pieces... It's not enough to make them into that bomb they were with Sammie, but it would be enough to make them lose control of their shifting abilities."

The awful writhing thing in the council flashed in her mind, looking like ink come to life, just like the splash of shifting bodies and yawning black maws from the club. One and the same, just different applications.

"There's also the weird way Nikolas left," Naomi started, looming over the table like a detective piecing together their tack board in a mystery. "I remember seeing him, not closely but enough to know he wasn't like this always. It was just a week or so before I ran into you guys. He'd disappeared, and I followed him to Seattle when I got the report that he'd started killing humans." She paused, gesturing as she spoke. Eddie watched raptly and tried to swallow back the desire to kiss her. *Later, not the time, and not the place.* "He'd gone on this case right before he became feral, like something infected him there."

"He's not fully feral, though, is he?" Sammie muttered, glancing Miles's way. "He can shift back and talk like he's normal.

I don't think the shifter goo is tied to him like that."

Naomi's leg bounced with anxiety, and Eddie just knew she was going to say something she was not going to like. She could feel it like a coming thunderstorm, aching in her teeth. "You're thinking of doing something suicidal, aren't you?"

The alpha glanced up. "I want to look at his case file at the council. See where he was last. It might lead us to where they're based, or even what started all of this."

Yep, suicidal and stupid. Eddie pinched the bridge of her nose. The next words out of her mouth were something she hated even more. "Fine. Yeah. Let's go back there." She lifted her head up when a dead silence filled the room. All three pairs of eyes stared her down. She held her one hand up, conceding defeat. "We need to start somewhere. And like hell I'm letting us get separated now. I'm walking proof of what happens when we separate." She pointedly waved her handless arm about. Miles and Sammie grimaced as Naomi's expression softened. "If you think it'll help, then yeah, we'll all head in."

"Thank you," Naomi whispered, her gray eyes unbearably fond, to the point Eddie had to look away or her cold little vampire heart would pop.

"All right," Miles said. "Then we'll head there today, if everyone is up for it."

"We'll prepare, then head out," Naomi finished, tapping Eddie's neck with two dainty claws. Eddie's gums ached with the action. "You guys get ready in your room. I'll make sure Eds is all fed and everything."

The nickname had her blushing like a child. This woman was ridiculous, once she let herself have something. Eddie barely waited for the boys to leave the room before she shifted into Naomi's lap. She didn't go for the neck, shoulder, or anything like that. Instead, she took the alpha's mouth, nipping her lip to a musical little giggle, ducking in to fully commit so that not a drop was wasted. The kiss was coppery and spicy, blood and the alpha's own special chili spice and dark, bitter chocolate taste mixing like the world's best ambrosia.

"Careful, Eddie," Naomi teased in between kisses, red smudged along her lips like her personal shade of lip gloss. "If you keep this up, I'm gonna think you care for me."

Gods, Eddie was dead. Well, deader than she already was. Naomi had that knowing look, the one Eddie used to hate. She tilted Naomi's head slightly, all that blooming confidence from the alpha melting the smell of her to warm sunshine, alcohol mixed with spices and the sharp bite of salt. It was the scent she'd had earlier, the one that Eddie absolutely craved to the pit of her stomach. That smell was all she wanted, ever, when she was trapped in Constantine's hell mansion for ages. "Maybe I do, despite you fighting me every step of the way," she muttered pointedly into Naomi's throat, pressing her lips against the skin.

"Maybe if you didn't fight everything I had to say then." Naomi's voice was breathless, sending a thrill along Eddie's spine. It wasn't breathless in the sense of having a predator against your throat, ready to bite down and feast. More...the type of breathless when you're about to be kissed by a lover, maybe even by the one.

All that talk of mates from those two twisted Eddie's thoughts in a knot. Not that she'd fight them. Not now, not when things were cresting into something that could mean...everything.

Eddie pressed a kiss to Naomi's pulse point and giggled as the alpha sagged and frowned up at her. "Maybe I do care, and maybe I love you." She brushed her thumb along Naomi's cheek, just a peek of red circling her stormy gray eyes, the smells of summer and beaches and eternal sunshine absolutely radiating from her blood. "Maybe, you'll just have to make sure you make it out of this alive to know for sure."

"Eddie..." Naomi breathed as Eddie dove in, sinking her fangs into the juncture of her throat and shoulder. Fresh fruit, semi-sweet spices, honey, rum all swirled together in a perfect blend on Eddie's tongue. Naomi's fingers wound into her hair, keeping her in place. She drank than longer before, and...she felt electric from it. Like she'd taken some of Naomi's boundless energy and strength into herself, rather than just sustenance to keep her dreary existence going.

"Fuck," Eddie cursed, laughing and kissing the dripping blood from her shoulder. "I feel...more alive than I ever have."

Warm hands tugged her up, and Eddie let herself be led up to Naomi's lips, more than willingly.

"Maybe I care, too," Naomi whispered into her mouth, their lips not parting far enough away for the movement to not tickle against hers. "Maybe we should both stick around. You know..."

She smirked, and Eddie pulled away far enough to see the lovingly cocky look on her face. "Just so we both can know, you know?"

"Yeah." Eddie pressed the promise into Naomi's lips.

I know.

Chapter Eighteen

The constant shifting of the council building as they approached filled Sammie with dread. A little unraveling ball of anxiety sat like a fist in his chest. They were going to be in and out, but he knew there were plenty of chances for things to go wrong. Even aside from the feral creatures they'd encountered last time. Damien had disappeared; whether that was purely ill timing or him being in on it, there was a very high chance of him being involved now. At least if their theory on Nikolas was anything to go by.

Naomi stuck to the front of their small pack. Sammie was sandwiched between Miles and Eddie in the middle. All of them were recognizable, but considering Nikolas targeting Sammie before, he seemed to be the most important to keep safe. At least, as far as Naomi and Miles had said.

"Naomi." The rabbit-like person, Cas, calmly greeted them, staring straight ahead as they spoke with an empty expression. "You finally come by to chat? It's been ages."

The alpha tapped the desk in front of them as she spoke. Their milky gaze flickered over to her hand before settling back ahead. "Maybe later. Listen, I'm just gonna go to my office for some things real quick before I head out. If anyone asks for me, just let them know I'm still out, please."

Cas nodded, their gaze sliding over Sammie with an odd intent. Something was off; the hair on the back of Sammie's neck stood up with it. He felt a tap on his hip and glanced down to see Eddie's hand there, motioning out of sight of the desk. *W-R-O-N-G.*

He shivered but tamped down the panic building in his chest. They needed their info, then they'd get out. They were all expecting this. Just, he needed to stay calm until they got up into Naomi's office.

"Of course, my friend. It'll be like you never existed."

The words, spoken in Cas's calm, soothing tone, made Sammie's blood go to ice.

"Thanks, Casandra," Naomi muttered, walking away. She took a beat, as if waiting for something, before she ushered them along.

The walk up to her office felt like hours. The entire building was buzzing with activity, but somehow it felt off, fake, like they'd accidentally walked into an alternate reality that wanted them dead. Sammie closed his eyes, letting Miles guide him along with

Eddie. He just needed to not explode, keep calm, and they could get out. That was all.

"Here," Naomi whispered. She opened a door and pushed them in, then closed the door behind them. She let out a heavy breath as she shook her head. "Shit... All right, Sammie, Eddie, watch the door, Miles, you help me look for what we need."

Eddie steered Sammie by the door and settled her cool hand on the back of his neck. She squeezed for a moment before she let him go. "This shouldn't take long, loverboy. Just make sure your tasers are all charged and ready to go."

The office was quiet, other than Naomi and Miles murmuring between each other as they looked through file after file. Sammie's anxious energy sparked and ebbed along his lungs and throat. He wasn't sure how much time had passed, too focused on the small view of the hallway he had and on Eddie's subtle breathing as she waited along with him for the other shoe to drop.

"I found something," Miles said, his voice loud in the otherwise quiet room. Sammie jumped, glancing back for a moment to see the werewolves huddled over a spread of papers. Miles chewed on his lip as the alpha began to read aloud.

"Nikolas Young, last reported in New York state on a retrieval of council property and illegitimate magic use subjects, found...deceased... Corpse recovered, next of kin to be informed as soon as cause of death is found." Naomi paused, reading ahead. "Recovered body of Young, last seen on council main building, missing, along with other bodies in the anti-mag mortuary.

Investigation to find the corpse will be completed by…by Naomi Chae."

"You're investigating his missing corpse?" Eddie muttered, her brow furrowing as she stared over at them.

"No… I-I was told to just take down the feral alpha and bring him back to council proper…" She flipped through the other pages in the report. "I don't remember this report at all. The original orders I had aren't anywhere in here."

"Who else can get into your office?" Sammie asked, staring out into the hall, his heart sinking into his stomach with the tension pressing in around them.

"Just me, and…and Damien…" Naomi growled, shooting up to her feet. "God dammit! I trusted that asshole!"

Miles hushed her, settling a hand on her shoulder as she tried to sprint across the room. "We have to keep cool, remember? What else do we need to look for?"

"Yeah, we might not have much more of a chance if someone is trying to set you up," Eddie muttered, turning back to focus on her task with Sammie. "Everything still look clear, Sammie?"

He barely bobbed his head in response, listening to the two sorting through more reports and orders and such. Nikolas was dead, but he was alive—at least he was if that was actually the same one… Other bodies went missing, too, right when Naomi was sent to look for him. Something was there, in the back of his mind, almost within his grasp. Something that felt like it might fit some pieces of their puzzle together.

"Is there…any use for someone with magic to have dead bodies?" Sammie muttered, turning to face the two poring over the desk.

Naomi glanced up, then frowned. "I mean, I've heard of some being able to raise the dead but…only in the sense of them not really being around anymore. Like, they got bred out, basically, forcibly extinct." She drummed her fingers against the desk as she spoke, looking more and more perturbed with every word. "From what I know since I started here, the magic users who could manipulate the dead would be trained out of that magic or have anti-mag collars put on. They're the reason we register everyone, especially anyone who can use magic, so those ones could be weeded out."

Eddie was quiet, just for a beat after Naomi finished. "I think my sire knew one, when I was with him…" Everyone's gaze fell on her and she dropped her eyes from the group to focus on her nails where she thumbed along the ragged cuticles. "I don't remember details—any dealings like that he usually kept his spawn out of. But I do remember someone coming to the manor one day, with a marching group of these people that looked like death warmed over." She blinked hard, as if to force the memory away. Sammie settled a hand on her arm, trying to comfort her. "I…I didn't think anything of it, especially since I was already barely making it through each day then, but…looking back now, I think it was more something like that man had brought back corpses to puppet around."

There was a moment of silence, just a breath, before the hair on Sammie's neck rose, tension zipping along his spine, and an almost phantom feeling of a warning shoving him out of the doorway.

He stumbled back, Eddie falling along with him, just before the door burst open in a mess of splinters and black sludge. Shifters.

Sammie's heart stopped for a second, a sensation like choking and his vision dimming before magic surged out of him into the black. His ears rang, the cracking sound of thunder mixed with his pure panic at the sight of the shifters again making the surroundings and voices around him dim.

A strong, firm hand grabbed his bicep and hauled him to his feet. Sammie blinked, once, twice, and it was like the flick of a switch. He wheezed in air, and sound rushed back in.

Somehow, the first thing he could hear was a woman's voice, different from Naomi and Eddie, but hauntingly familiar. "Run, Sam, you have to run."

"Come on, Sammie, we have to go." Miles's voice followed the woman's and Sammie nodded deliriously, trying to take in the sudden chaos around him before they left.

There were a lot of those black leeches all over the floor, in a gory spray from the doorway. Some were singed and some stomped to death, a few wriggling weakly. In the center of the room was a hulking, mutated version of the wolves they'd seen before, its maw ripped wider and its body twitching with blue lightning sparking through it with the aftershocks.

Miles pulled him out, and Sammie cursed sharply. Naomi and Eddie were far ahead of them, sprinting down the winding stairway, avoiding a wave of the shifter goo flowing down the stairs after them. "This way, come on!" Miles urged, pulling him down the opposite stairway. Sammie jumped, hearing something smack into the door of one of the offices nearby, before that door splintered. He didn't look back, just started running along with Miles with the sound of an inhuman clicking screech ringing through his ears.

"*Sam-meee!*" something eerily like Miles's voice screeched, just behind him. "*Stop, let me taste you!*"

"My-uhls..." another voice, familiar in a way that made Sammie feel sick, called. Miles's mom's voice, soft and sweet and nearly identical to Sammie's memory of her. "Why would you... run from your...mother?"

Miles stumbled, and Sammie grabbed him around the waist. "Don't, Miles, you know it's not real."

"I know! I know."

"Miles, Miles, MilesMilesMilesMilesMilesMiles—" Her voice started getting louder, and louder, and Sammie chanced a glance back, only to see how close it was behind them.

It was horrifying; a wretched abomination of Miles's mother, and Sammie's friends, Miles, Naomi, and Eddie, and a woman Sammie couldn't put a name to, but was so achingly familiar he stumbled, rolling his ankle and pitching forward. He slammed into a stair neck and rib first. Pain shot through him, ripping a gasp from his lungs. A numb, pins and needles sensation washed over his legs at a terrifying speed.

A roar cut through the ringing in his ears, and Sammie looked up, wincing in pain as his side flared with red-hot agony. Miles was half shifted, eyes gold and fangs on full display, claws tearing through the black ooze, roaring at the thing before he tore away the black licking at his leg and hiked him up onto his shoulder.

Everything ached; Sammie's leg was numb, and the left side of his body was in searing pain. But they still had to get out of here in one piece, and while Miles was much faster, the thing was still too close for comfort. Sammie could slow it down, at least until they were safe. If they were.

Using all his willpower to stay awake and fight off the black spots dotting his vision, Sammie concentrated his magic in his palm. He lifted it up and blasted all his energy directly into the mashed-up face of Miles and that woman the creature was leering at him with. He heard a wounded screech, just before he lost consciousness. At least he could buy them some time, if nothing else.

The electric-blue eyes of the woman danced in his thoughts as he drifted off, her fiery-red hair and freckled nose so achingly familiar.

*

Sammie surfaced slowly, like coming out of anesthesia. Careful fingers ran through his hair, each pass waking him more and more.

Blinking his eyes open, Sammie expected to see the hospital, or the wilderness, anything other than a quaint bedroom. Pale-lavender lace curtains fluttered in a light summer breeze from the cracked window. The walls were painted pastel blue, with a scattering of charcoal sketches pinned up on the walls. The bed underneath him was covered with a well-loved quilt that smelled like freshly baked cookies and lemonade. He could hear a song playing somewhere in another room, something he remembered his uncle singing to him those first couple of nights to help him get to sleep. "Blackbird," he thought was the name of it...

Sammie felt those fingers tickle along his scalp again before he looked up to find that same woman watching him with a serene expression. She was beautiful, a little older as evidenced by the gray hairs in her red braid and the crow's feet around her eyes. She was dressed simply: a worn green plaid shirt with a plain gold necklace. Round, gold-rimmed glasses framed the freckles on her nose, making the bright-blue eyes behind them all the brighter. She hummed gently with the song until Sammie sat up, then smiled at him, her grin crooked.

"Sam, you're not supposed to be here yet." She sounded like she was scolding him, yet her voice was calm and made Sammie feel at ease.

"Where am I?" Sammie asked, finding himself leaning into

her touch as she skimmed her fingers down along his cheek. "How did I get here?"

"You overdid it." She looked at him peacefully. "You're not really used to your abilities yet, my dear." She had a hint of an accent, something a lot like his uncle's, a bit of a southern drawl on some of her words. "This is only temporary, I believe. Just gotta let you rest up and you'll be back in no time."

Her voice and demeanor were so achingly sweet Sammie's eyes teared up. She tutted quietly, brushing a thumb along his cheek. He had to swallow down the sudden lump in his throat before he could speak. "Who...who are you?"

She cooed softly, dimples popping in her cheeks and eyes wrinkling. "You can call me Ashe. I'm just an old part of your life, before you can remember, probably." She tapped his cheek gently, tilting her head to the side as she spoke. "What's important is getting you back to your friends, your family now. Unfortunately, you're in this now, despite what I've tried to save you from." Ashe tilted him forward, tapping their foreheads together as she whispered, "Now, Sammie, I need you to close your eyes, breathe deep, and brace yourself. I'm going to make sure when you wake up next, you're back in your body with them." There was a beat, the record in the background playing fuzzy feedback, and Ashe's voice sounding faraway and melancholic as she finished. "I'll keep you as safe as I can from here, my little star."

*

The next breath Sammie gasped in tasted distinctly of ink and blood. He coughed, tears in his eyes for more reasons than the stench in the air.

Miles's hands immediately went to his shoulders. "Sammie? Oh, thank God, you weren't breathing."

He swallowed, feeling like his throat was bruised with the action. His chest ached, and his ribs were cracked and sore. "I...I was dreaming... This, I think..." The words clogged in his aching throat, and Miles hushed him gently.

"Just rest, we have to get moving. I only stopped right outside to try to get you back. Come on."

Miles hiked Sammie up onto his back. Normally, Sammie would be losing it at this point, blushing and stuttering. He couldn't bring himself to focus on anything but that woman, Ashe, and her parting words.

The same words he could've sworn he heard before, years and years ago.

A time he could barely remember; he couldn't really pinpoint an age or time of year or anything. All he remembered was a kiss to his head, the sound of a door breaking down, and a woman sobbing into his hair with those same words. "Be careful, my little star."

Chapter Nineteen

Eddie was, admittedly, exhausted.

Between finding out that they were being stalked by a walking and talking corpse someone was probably puppeteering around along with the Seer; the stress of being in the council and knowing that something was very, very wrong; and the knowledge that the council could be overtaken by shifters as easily as it was, she was surprised they were all still standing. Though Sammie was touch and go; the poor thing had completely sapped his battery with the last blast that nearly knocked the building down.

He'd woken up looking completely devastated, though he hadn't explained why. He'd mostly kept around Miles since he woke up, clinging like a lamprey and being even more sickeningly sweet than usual.

Naomi was currently on the mission to get them a vehicle so

they could get to their one lead, the one that happened to be across the country, because of course it was. Eddie had never been to New York; the closest she'd been before was Pennsylvania, where Constantine had settled. She'd never intended to go back anywhere near there but...here she was. Everything was lending more and more to the idea that the bastard was involved in this, somehow.

She didn't know about anyone else who would find as much glee puppeteering around the dead for his bidding. The first decades of her new life were more than enough to show that.

"You all right?" Miles's husky baritone startled her out of her head, and Eddie looked up to find the two of them watching her carefully. Sammie, the adorable imp he was, offered a small, comforting—albeit tired—smile. "You look a little...out of it. The wound bugging you?"

Eddie glanced down; it'd just about healed over completely, only a bit of pinkish scar tissue left, thanks to the generous feeding with Naomi. It was still weird, almost like she could still feel the missing appendages. "It's fine." She wiggled the fingers of her remaining hand. "I'm just thinking. You know, the typical stuff. How we're probably gonna die, just how much everything could go wrong, how much of an asshole my old sire is. You know...basics."

Sammie frowned, leaning out of Miles's space for the first time since they settled. "You keep mentioning your sire—do you think he'd be involved in this?"

"At first, no." Eddie grunted, drumming her nails against her teeth in agitation. "Now I'm not sure. It could be his Seer who's doing all of this—sounds like it might be the same one, and Constantine had no respect for the dead. If he found a way to use them as puppets, he'd be all for it."

"Is he still around?" Miles asked, scratching along his jaw and looking away when Eddie glared toward him sharply. "I mean, you haven't seen him for a few years, right? He might've left the area."

"No." Something rumbling and harsh bullied its way up Eddie's throat. She cleared it, shaking her head almost violently to get rid of the scared, angry little thing that hadn't cropped up in years. "I mean... I can tell he's still close-ish. Some sense that he's still there to come collect me when he pleases." She couldn't stop the bitter words before they left.

"Not if I can help it." Naomi's easy drawl broke through the sour fog clouding Eddie's head. She relaxed, turning to find the alpha looking her over, a fierce little glint in her stormy eyes and an adorable crease in her brow. Eddie and her damned heart were falling every time the woman opened her mouth nowadays.

Miles perked up, almost like a puppy watching their master come home. "Any luck?"

She huffed, plopping down on the ground next to Eddie and leaning her head against Eddie's knobby knee. "Nope, every rental place is closed, and my Jeep at the council has mysteriously vanished." She frowned, and Eddie reached out with very little thought to dig her fingers into Naomi's short, choppy locks. The alpha relaxed under her touch, just a little, but enough to convince

Eddie to keep her hand there, running her fingers through Naomi's hair and scratching at her scalp.

"Can we steal someone's?" Sammie piped up, and Eddie's touch froze, along with Naomi as they both looked up at the mage. He blinked, glancing at Miles who smiled fondly at him. "What?"

"Nothing, just…" Eddie chuckled, continuing her ministrations. "Didn't expect you to suggest crimes."

Sammie's brow furrowed, and he tilted his head. "I know I'm small, but I did spend a lot of my high school life barely dodging the cops."

"Yeah, you slashed the principal's tires for your own personal senior prank."

"Just three," Sammie corrected with obvious pride. "Mr. I-Made-Every-Girl-At-The-School -Uncomfortable-With-My-Comments had to pay all of that out of pocket."

Eddie glanced at Naomi. The werewolf shared the same look she must have on her own face, a bit of disbelief, shock, and a distinct sliver of fear and respect.

"Well, um, unlike some of us, I don't have much experience in grand theft auto, so I wouldn't be much help with trying that."

"Oh." Eddie lightly scratched her fingers through Naomi's hair again. "I do. I needed a way to get the hell away from Constantine as fast as I could, so I hotwired the first car I found." She winced, holding up the stump of her arm. "Only issue is I did it with two hands the last time—I dunno how well that'd go now."

Sammie giggled and stood up, cracking his knuckles. "I have

a slightly crazy idea…"

*

"So, how sure are you that doing this won't just fry us?" Eddie whispered as she and Sammie snuck along the road near the preserve, where they'd camped out to get out of range of the council. According to Naomi, any of the council people kept their private vehicles in unmarked lots near the thin spaces where the council building would appear. It made sense, but it seemed a little silly, and maybe unwise on the owners' part, considering what she and Sammie were going to be doing now.

"Like…ninety-five percent?" Sammie scanned the lot before his eyes settled on his mark, blue sparking from his mouth with his exhale. "There, that should work, yeah?"

Eddie glanced; it was a decent sized SUV with a wild array of bumper stickers and a custom license plate that read "SRYNSRY". She gave Sammie a dull look, raising her eyebrows.

"What?" Sammie hoofed it to the driver's side and waved Eddie over. He waited until she was right there before he tried the door, laughing lightly when it popped open with no problem. "See? Perfect."

She rolled her eyes, then hopped in the driver's seat. She reached under the wheel and got to work, removing the part that covered the wiring she needed and gesturing for Sammie. "Hold this so I can strip the wiring." She used the edge of her sharpened nail to split the material covering the wiring, then hopped over the console and watched Sammie as he slid into her place. "Should be enough, you sure this won't channel through and hurt us?"

Sammie shrugged, then grabbed the wire, a small spark of electrical energy running through his fingers, just enough to connect the two exposed wires to spark the ignition. The engine roared to life, and Sammie pulled back his hand to reveal a thin braid of magic left behind tethering the wires together. "Holy shit," Sammie cackled, then shut the door. He barely waited long enough for Eddie to let out the breath she'd been holding before he slammed the car into reverse and peeled out of the lot. "I can't believe that worked!"

"Same." Eddie sagged into the seat, looking over at Sammie in relief and buckling herself in. They just had to swing by the little alcove they were hiding in before to get the other two and they were off. Hopefully, they'd luck out and the owner wouldn't be out for a while.

They spent the rest of the drive bursting into random fits of giggles, giddy over something finally working for them. After a while Eddie started fiddling with the radio. She settled on something loud and energetic before she relaxed back, feeling pretty damn on top of the world.

Once they stopped for Naomi and Miles, Naomi followed Eddie's instructions to get a more stable wiring situation for the SUV, and Eddie settled back in shotgun with the alpha beside her once Sammie got it started again. The Energizer Bunny and his boy both cuddled up in the back, and they were off with their limited provisions. If Eddie could get herself out of her own mind enough, she could even pretend they were just on a road trip.

"Nervous?" Naomi asked, voice quiet under the music, her gray eyes flickering over to Eddie. "Your leg's been going faster than we are."

Eddie glanced down, then clasped her hand over her jiggling leg and shook her head. "It's the closest I've been to Constantine since I left."

Immediately, Naomi's face hardened, and she let out a tense exhale. "I can get the nerves, then. The one who turned me, he was terrible, everything I never wanted to have someone experience again. It's why I took Miles in right away, because if I didn't..." She sighed, drumming her nails into the steering wheel with a grimace. "I never really wanted a pack or anything, I only got to be an alpha by facing off my original alpha and killing him. That alone was such a bloody, horrible ordeal, a lot of people from the council got hurt or killed in the process. I always thought if I had to take care of a pack, I'd mess it up somehow."

Eddie watched as she spoke, tension building up as she did, shoulders hunching by her ears. She reached out and settled her hand on Naomi's thigh. When the alpha turned, she squeezed gently. "If it's anything, I think you're doing pretty well so far."

Naomi scoffed, glancing into the rearview, her expression softening right after. "Yeah...maybe you're right."

She turned to look at the two in the back, laughing to herself as she saw them cuddling close, Miles even sort of purring as

Sammie's head rested against his chest. "Glad they're at least able to relax a bit."

"They've been through so much in so little time," Naomi commented, drawing Eddie's gaze back. "I think they deserve a little bit of it."

So do you.

The words stopped on the tip of her tongue. Naomi looked her way for a moment before focusing back on the road.

They still had a long road ahead of them. She could save any of those sappy thoughts for later...

"So..." Sammie's voice broke through the sudden silence in the car. Eddie turned to find him worrying his lip and looking unsure of himself. "This might be...weird to bring up but... When I passed out, I had this strange dream."

A clear sense of dread fell over the car; Naomi and Miles had already had dreams or visions from the Seer. Eddie was hoping futilely that Sammie would somehow be protected from them but apparently, she was wrong.

"What was it?" Naomi spoke up first, her brows pinched and jaw tight.

"I was in this bedroom I've never seen before. There was a woman that I think..." He paused, visibly composing himself for a moment before he continued. "I think she might've been the woman who helped you, Eddie?"

The vampire blinked, spinning around as much as the seat would let her to stare at him. "You serious? That was so long ago, though... I doubt she'd still be alive."

"She called herself Ashe, had red hair and a crooked smile." He lowered his voice, his gaze sliding to his hands in his lap. "She knew me... I think she might've been..."

Miles squeezed Sammie's shoulder reassuringly. Eddie waited a bit before she turned forward again, catching Naomi glancing away from her as she went. She picked at her jeans, a frown tugging her lips down as she stared ahead. It was a bit of a bittersweet feeling; she'd been throwing out an idea she didn't really believe when she'd suggested Sammie was related to the same woman who helped her. The idea that she'd somehow run into a relative all these years later astounded her.

Eddie never believed in fate—she didn't want to think of herself being destined to live the life she got, but...things like this made it harder not to.

As for how Sammie met her... Eddie didn't know anything of an afterlife, but she had last seen her fifty years ago. For her to still look as young as Sammie described...

She didn't know where else Ashe could've been, as much as she wished otherwise. Eddie knew well enough wishes didn't work.

Chapter Twenty

Miles felt like they'd been on the road forever, the dull routine of stopping to stretch, grab food, start again with nothing in between. He was glad about it, given how insane the last couple of weeks had been. They seemed to be close if the road signs were anything to go by, the last one finally showing New York City. Granted, Naomi had mentioned it was worth avoiding the city itself; the report seemed to be leading to the place Nikolas was killed being in the surrounding wilderness. It didn't narrow it down a lot, but they knew the state, at least.

"We're gonna take a break," Naomi grumbled, blinking her bleary eyes with a wince. "The lines are starting to blur."

"Want me to take over?" Miles asked, starting to lean forward then stopping when Sammie's head slipped from his shoulder. Sammie grumbled and grabbed Miles's arm to keep him in place.

"No, we should stop for the night." Naomi merged over to take the exit and pulled out into what Miles assumed to be a little pin drop of a place on a map, a handful of local restaurants and a single motel with a spattering of houses around them. She pulled into the motel lot and parked, rubbing her eyes wearily.

"I'll get the rooms," Eddie offered. She started to get out of the car, but Naomi stopped her. "What?"

The alpha huffed, turning to the two of them in the back. "We shouldn't be separating more than we have to. Let's just all go in."

Sammie opened his eyes sleepily and leaned away from Miles with a mumbled acknowledgement. Miles hopped out right after him, bringing up the rear as the others started off to the somewhat sketchy motel.

The exterior of the place looked like it was built in the thirties, with it not having been updated or maintained properly since the eighties. The once bright pop of sky-blue paint was now peeling and faded, a whisper of color buried under years of weather damage. The roof at least looked decent, in the sense that he didn't think it would collapse on them as they slept. The interior wasn't much better: ripped, peeling wallpaper in a poppy floral that made his eyes cross. The furniture inside seemed to creak and groan just by looking at it, and the gaudy faux chandelier had the majority of the bulbs on it either broken or burnt out, if not completely missing.

The clerk behind the counter looked as exhausted as they did, a younger man practically drooling onto a magazine as he zoned out. Naomi cleared her throat, and Miles would've thought the guy had been shocked by how high he jumped from his seat.

"O-oh, hello, what can I do for you?"

Naomi arched a brow at him, then stepped up closer to the counter, pulling out her wallet from her pocket. "We need a room, two beds."

The teen tiredly checked them in, and Miles glanced more around the place. He desperately wished he didn't have heightened senses at that moment. The scent of decades of lingering smoke stuck in the carpeting and curtains, and the overwhelming stench of sketchy humans soaked in alcohol and drugs and sex was starting to make his eyes water.

They finished up, and Miles sucked in a greedy lungful of fresh air when they stepped out to go around to their room. Second floor, Room 213 around the back, in the non-smoking area to their combined relief, if the way everyone else sucked in deep breaths of cool, night air meant anything.

The room itself wasn't much better aesthetically: powder-blue shag carpet; gaudy gold bed frames; gold and neon-blue pinstripe wallpaper; and a bathroom with complete powder-blue tiling as far as the eye could see, and worst of all, more of that well-worn shag.

"Who the hell designs a bathroom with a carpet in it?" Eddie grumbled in disgust. "Nobody whip out a black light or anything. I'd rather be blissfully ignorant to how much grody shit is in here..."

"Let's just get some rest," Naomi mumbled, tugging Eddie down into the bed. The vampire let out a small "oof" as she flopped back. "We're just stopping so we can finish the rest of this without crashing."

Miles grumbled, glancing to the other bed to see Sammie gingerly plucking at the bedsheets before he looked up at him. "I think I'm good, sleeping over the covers. You run hot, anyway."

He flushed, ridiculously, got in bed with Sammie and pulled the mage close. Sammie fell asleep almost at once, tucking his face into Miles's throat, his soft breaths washing over Miles's skin and leaving behind goosebumps. He murmured softly, carding his fingers through Sammie's hair for a moment before he pressed his lips to Sammie's forehead. He closed his eyes to the sound of his mate's steady breaths, and the sweet, citrusy cinnamon scent of him blocked the vileness of the room as he drifted off to sleep.

*

When Miles woke up, the sun was barely peeking through the thinning blue velvet curtains. The clock on the nightstand read just before six a.m. He groaned, rubbing his eyes and glancing at Sammie who was starting to stir along with him. His blue eyes blinked open before he stretched with a soft sound that had Miles's brain flatlining for a moment.

"Mnhg," Eddie mumbled, and Miles glanced over to see the vampire sweetly drinking from Naomi's wrist. The alpha looked hardly more awake than she had the night before.

"Morning..." Miles sat up, leveling Naomi with a sympathetic look. "Want me to drive for now?"

She didn't really respond, simply gave a small grunt of approval and continued to let Eddie feed happily.

It took them a bit of time to get going. Naomi especially seemed zombie-like as she shuffled to the car. Eddie checked them out after some minor cleanup. They grabbed food and were back on the highway in about half an hour.

"So, you said the wilderness seemed more likely, right?" Miles asked as they started their second hour since they left. Naomi was much more awake in the back after a quick nap, not surrounded by overwhelming scents, and a full stomach. "Do you have any guesses for where? We're not seriously just going to comb the entirety of New York state looking for this place, right?"

"We'll be able to tell," Naomi answered, tapping her nose. "People who work with the dead carry a specific stench, same with the bodies they raise—at least according to any old reports I've seen of them. They smell like blood and rot. That will be easy to track down within a good couple of miles."

Eddie looked a little small in the rearview. She sat up. "I have an idea. No real reasoning why it'd be right but... With Constantine working with them, I'd assume they'd have to be within close distance. Traveling with a lot of corpses you're puppeteering around can't be easy without being seen. No idea if they're the same, but it's a start."

"All right, so in that case, where should we go first?"

"Head toward Afton, there's a forest preserve near there. Constantine was just about on the state line about half an hour from there so..." She shrugged, glancing away from Miles's eyes in the mirror. "It's a guess, but hopefully it's right."

Sammie punched the directions into his phone to guide him. Miles took the exit Sammie told him to. He glanced back to see a black SUV following them.

Miles's heart slammed into his ribs, something about the vehicle behind them setting off alarm bells in his head.

"What's wrong?" Sammie asked, looking back where Miles was staring into the mirror, a little bit of nerves shooting into his tone.

"Shit," Naomi muttered, following his gaze. "Fucking hunters. Miles, drive!"

Though the command wasn't in that huskier tone of Naomi's that suggested he listened, Miles slammed his foot into the gas pedal. The car jerked as it went from sixty to ninety in the blink of an eye.

They shot ahead of the SUV for a few moments before they started speeding along with them. Other cars on the highway parted out of the way of the two, much to Miles's relief. He felt like his brain was five miles back; no way could he think far enough ahead to avoid anyone on the road.

His racing heart was already threatening to choke him with nerves. A gunshot ringing through the air, and the back window shattering had him nearly sick with panic. What the hell could he do to get them out of this?

A sharp exit off the highway caught his eye, and before Miles could think it through properly, he was slamming on the brakes and swerving over into the exit lane. The SUV behind them squealed by, nearly going up on two wheels as it turned to try to follow them just a hair too late.

"What the fuck?" Eddie whined while her one hand gripped Sammie's seat so hard her knuckles were going white. "Where the hell did you learn how to drive like that?"

Miles swallowed the lump in his throat as he followed the exit to a backwoods road, not much around them aside from trees. "No clue—where the hell are we?"

Sammie looked around, his eyes catching on the side mirror as he cursed. "They're coming. What do we do?"

"Try to find somewhere we can lose them!" Naomi barked, and Miles grit his teeth as he pushed the gas pedal to the floor. The tires spun for a moment before the car peeled out of the way. They didn't get far down the road before another gunshot rang out. The car juddered, and the wheel jerked out of Miles's hands. A screech of the remains of the tire against asphalt was their only warning before the SUV around them started tipping to the side.

A moment of electric panic ran through Miles. Sammie's hand slammed into his shoulder and, miraculously, the vehicle stopped, slowly settling back on four tires again.

Miles stared at Sammie, who stared down at his own hands before a ringed hand slammed against his window. The man on the other side of the glass leered at him, his eyes glinting behind his gold-rimmed sunglasses. The expression distorted the large scar running across the bridge of his nose.

"Oh no..." Eddie muttered, and the man motioned for him to roll the window down. He rolled his eyes and took his gun from his holster when Miles didn't immediately move.

"Relax, I'm not going to shoot." The "yet" of his words hung in the air, turning Miles's stomach. Not that they had much of a chance to get away now. "Just wanna talk, specifically..." He leaned back, waving delicately at Naomi. The alpha looked incensed and incredulous at once. "With Little Miss Fugitive back there."

Naomi audibly swallowed before she ground out through clenched teeth, "Listen to him, Miles."

The dimmed window juddered down, and the man nodded in thanks, ever present smirk there as he leaned forward. "Right. So. I'm sure you recognize me, Chae. It hasn't been that long since we last saw each other. Imagine my surprise when I'm minding my business, and an order from the council to take you out comes across my desk." He mimed holding a paper up and lifting his glasses to squint at it. "Insurrection? Surely not! Faithful, loyal Naomi Chae? Couldn't be the same one!"

"Boss?" Miles's heart jumped into his throat at the voice of another hunter who stood at Sammie's side. His gun was raised but not pointed in Sammie's direction. Miles's gaze worriedly locked on his mate. "This is the mage the report mentioned."

The man scoffed. "I can see that, Peters. Just..." He leaned back, whistling. "The lot of you, back to the car. I can take care of this."

The man stared at Sammie a bit longer, his fingers twitching around the gun. Miles's jaw ached and a migraine popped with the force of a baseball bat into his eyes. A growl ripped from his throat unbidden.

The hunter jumped and stumbled back. He shot into the ground with a yelp as he slipped. Naomi hissed as the main hunter cursed, then came around the car to cuff him on the neck and shove him back toward the car. "Jesus, get him out of here, Jaime." He waited until the rest of the hunters dispersed before leaning against Sammie's side, the smug expression falling from his face. "Listen, I'm not here to hurt you guys. I'll do what I can about the others, but I swear on my life, no harm will come to you from me." He tapped the window with his knuckles, waiting for the window to be lowered before he continued. "Something about this whole thing is off... I knew it since I saw your name on the report."

"So, you're not here to kill us?" Sammie muttered, and Miles reached out for his hand, swallowing the lump of anxiety in his throat. He wasn't anywhere near as talented as Naomi was with scents or pinpointing details with his hearing, but this guy's heart was steady. There were no signs of him being anything other than human like with the shifters. Miles was unfortunately gullible, something he knew all too well, but he felt like at least this man could be trusted.

"I'm here to figure out why this whole thing is throwing me off." He leaned close. "If something is going on with the council that's off, that can only be bad news for all of us."

"How do we know we can trust you?" Naomi hissed, leaning forward between Sammie and Miles. "We've been through hell and back, Booker. We can't just—" She froze mid-sentence, and Miles sucked in air only to fight back a gag at the scent that suddenly pooled around them. Blood, lots and lots of blood.

"What?" Booker leaned back, concern coloring his features. "You two have the look like something's wrong…"

"Miles?" Sammie's voice was quiet, worried.

A gunshot from behind them made Booker and Sammie flinch. Miles looked back in the rearview to see some of the hunters leaping from the SUV, yelling and shooting at something before a flash cut across them. The men fell to a heap with a fresh wave of blood washing through the air.

Miles and Naomi were out on the next breath. Eddie and Sammie quickly followed suit. Booker took one glance back at his group before he started running after them. "What the hell is that?"

Eddie glanced back before becoming somehow even paler, looking nauseous. "No…" She was the quietest Miles had ever heard her. He looked back to see a man dressed head to toe in black, mouth and throat painted in blood, flashing them an unhinged, gory smile as he strolled after them.

"Constantine…" Naomi whispered, scooping up Booker and

Eddie onto her back before she shifted in one fluid moment and ran full speed ahead of them.

Miles cursed and tried to follow her example as best he could, grimacing at the creak of his bones under the rushed shift. Sammie gasped, gripping the fur that sprouted from the nape of Miles's neck as he fell to all fours in a gangly gallop.

Need to run. Get away. Keep mate safe.

Miles growled. One of Sammie's hands slipped from his fur before the shock of his magic electrified the air, and Sammie cursed. By the sound of Sammie's continued attacks, though Miles couldn't look back, he could tell they were still being chased. The sound of a gun told him Booker had become stable enough to try to push Constantine back.

He couldn't help feeling like this was all a trap, that they were being herded somewhere. He couldn't voice his concern, and they couldn't stop.

Eventually their luck would run out. Miles prayed this wouldn't be the end of it. They were so close to ending this. He hated feeling this helplessness, but all he could do was run, follow his alpha, and hope.

Chapter Twenty-One

Naomi grit her teeth and shook out her limbs once they'd found somewhere seemingly safe. She had a sinking feeling in her gut, like just before peering over the edge of a cliff, the tell-tale sign that something was wrong. Not that she needed her gut to tell her that.

Constantine had led them here, to this little shed in the middle of nowhere, before he disappeared. Once it was clear he hadn't been sticking around, Naomi and Miles shifted back, Sammie using a bit of his magic to heal Miles after he'd shifted in such a rush.

"You okay?" Naomi glanced up at Booker's voice. He was hanging around Eddie carefully as she crouched in the corner of the cabin, hugging her knees and looking a thousand miles away. Both of them had been dragged into this mess. Naomi couldn't help the overwhelming guilt that clogged in her throat at the thought.

"Eds?" Naomi whispered around the lump, kneeling by the vampire and gently reaching out to her hand. "You with me?"

Eddie's brown eyes glanced up at her and she let out an unneeded breath before she acknowledged Naomi. "Yeah. I'm fine."

She could smell the sourness of a lie from her, something most definitely not needed for her to know that. Her sire was here, from the sounds of it. Eddie carried a mountain of traumatic memories from her time with him; of course she wasn't fine. Naomi would have been concerned if she had been otherwise.

Booker exhaled heavily through his nose and flopped onto the floor next to them. "Well, this is a fine mess we found ourselves in, huh?"

Naomi frowned before she dropped down to sit next to Eddie. She snaked her hand between her chest and legs to rub her thumb over Eddie's knee for whatever modicum of comfort she could provide. "I guess you're due an explanation by now." She glanced up at Miles and Sammie, the two hovering by and looking nervously in Booker's direction, to which she waved them off. "He's fine. He helped me out when I was first getting out from under the alpha who turned me."

"Every person we trust seems to either backstab us or die," Sammie muttered, full on staring Booker down.

The hunter, to his credit, just raised his hands. "I get it, trust me—you all have obviously been through a lot. You have the council and an infamous vampire lord after you; your allies are going to be few and far between." He settled back, dropping his hands to his sides and slumping against the wall. "If I turn on you, you have my full permission to shock me until I pop."

Sammie narrowed his eyes, grumbling and turning back to Miles. He busied his hands by fussing over him. Miles relaxed, settling into Sammie's touch and gesturing Naomi's way.

Booker was facing Naomi now. "All right, so, we should probably go back as far as possible."

Naomi recounted everything: from her assignment to recover a feral Nikolas; to Miles's accidental turning; the two boys being tracked down until they were forced to flee with their building toppling down; Eddie taking them in; every turn of the way trying to find solace or a way to stop everything being met with danger. The set-up at the council, and Damien…

The hunter heaved a tired sigh once they'd summed everything up, pushing his glasses up to pinch the bridge of his nose. "And of course the council put out a call for you since you found out their little scheme. So, someone with a decent amount of power is working with this necromancer and seer," Booker grumbled, slumping back against the wall. "Which is just great for our futures. The whole reason the council exists is to prevent your kind from causing a panic among us, and with this it just sounds like they're purposefully going to be drawing attention to you lot." He frowned, glasses falling back into place as he crossed his arms. "Sounds like they're trying to take us back to medieval times.

There's going to be a lot more death ahead if they follow through with this."

Naomi grimaced, squeezing Eddie's hand as Eddie—now a bit more relaxed—brushed along her knuckles in comfort. "Yeah… definitely sounds like someone is getting us to hunt one another again."

The small cabin flooded with a sour stench, anxiety and fear combining into something that had Miles and Naomi wincing. Sammie shuddered, leaning forward from Miles's side slightly. "Is there a chance there's someone you guys know who would want that? There's always some…alternative ideals at the fringe of societies. Anyone you guys know of who would be looking to take us back to that?"

"Just Constantine…" Eddie mumbled. Naomi had to choke down a pained sound at Eddie's small voice. "He always hated humans and couldn't stand that we had to hide or be hunted by all of the council."

"Mikhail Ilya." The name tasted sharp and bitter as it left her mouth, and Naomi swallowed the lump in her throat before she continued, ignoring the pitiable look from Booker. "The alpha who turned me, he was the same. Because I was born human he treated me like trash, took me just to have a mutt to abuse. He would've lived for all of this…"

"Yeah, but he's…he's dead…" Booker furrowed his brow. "Which wouldn't matter much, if there's someone raising the dead."

The realization spoken out loud made a cold sweat spring along Naomi's body from head to toe. She could scent the spike of anxiety from herself, could taste copper and acid from the intense shift. She'd been trying not to think about it, trying to avoid contemplating the possibility of having to see Mikhail's face again.

It was sudden and painful, how quickly she felt like the terrified, traumatized teen she was when she last saw him.

Damien and Booker were both there, along with a couple of other council people who had helped to put down the near feral alpha. Naomi, as a panicked, cornered seventeen-year-old who had put up with years of abuse and terrors, had dealt the final blow. She'd lashed out without thinking, biting out his throat while he was distracted and his grip on her arm had loosened. She was bloodied and nauseous and her body was changing in a way that was painful and exhilarating all at once.

The hunters were working with the council to clear out his den. Damien and Booker had been kind and caring with the fresh alpha who was finally freed from her tormentor. She hadn't been able to pay attention to much, scared and lost as she was.

"Naomi?" The voice jolted her out of her thoughts. Booker looked at her with a worried expression. "You with us?"

Miles and Sammie were closer now. Miles especially looked concerned, tentatively reaching out for her. Eddie hadn't let her go. Her features were somber as she squeezed Naomi's hand back.

Naomi responded to Eddie's touch. "Yeah. I just haven't thought about him for a while, is all."

Booker grimaced then, and she raised her free hand before he could apologize. "Save it, it's nothing. Better to prepare myself for it here than if I come face to face with him again." She cleared her throat, taking a modicum of comfort from Eddie before she moved on, breathing in the vampire's scent of overripe fruit and rich, coppery wine to center herself. "So, with Mikhail being dead, we can assume he's a puppet, and not a mastermind of this, if he's involved. Constantine is more likely to be someone who's pulling the strings of this." She glanced at Eddie, frowning. "But...you mentioned before that he'd met up with someone who was puppeteering the dead before you left, right?"

Eddie inhaled sharply. "Yeah, he might be involved with some of the inspiration in everything but...I don't think he's leading it." She unraveled her hand from Naomi's and bit lightly at her nails for a moment. "I think...whoever is raising the dead is more than likely the main one plotting everything. He probably met up with Constantine for the Seer." She glanced over to Naomi then, her brown eyes wide and worried. "With the Seer, he can make sure whatever plan he makes is flawless. Constantine gets what he wants in the form of chaos and the freedom to gorge himself without consequences, and the Seer gets to win." She huffed, glancing down to her knees and chewing on her nails again. "She's probably still pissed after Ashe had wrecked her visions with me."

It was subtle, but there was a spike of something sharp and bitter like shock from Booker at the mention of Ashe. Naomi glanced his way, finding the hunter staring at Sammie with a deepened furrow to his brow. "What is it?"

Booker glanced up, then shook his head. "O-oh, I just… Shit, damn your nose, Naomi."

"What is it?" Sammie mumbled, sitting up, catching the shift in the atmosphere and glancing his way. "It's about Ashe, right?"

Booker groaned, then held up his hands. "Okay, Jesus, nothing gets past any of you, does it?" He faced Sammie again, lifting up his sunglasses before he spoke. "So, I'd met this mage, a rather damn powerful one, some several years back, not long before the Mikhail incident. I was a young, reckless idiot then, and this woman came up to save my skin. She'd refused to accept any sort of thanks or anything like that, had just told me to make sure her son got to the hands of her brother safely. I'd asked her why she couldn't do it, and she'd just smiled all crooked like and told me she was simply making sure her little star could be safe from all of her problems."

Sammie gasped, his scent going electric and stingy in her sinuses. Booker continued, giving him a vaguely guilty look. "She'd told me where to find the kid, and where to go, and when I tried to find her again when I went back to her place, it was ransacked and bloodied." The hunter's expression fell as Sammie teared up. The small cabin filled with the cloying scent of sadness. "When I went to follow up on her at the council, they'd put up an announcement of her death."

"Shit," Eddie whispered, dropping her hand with a grimace. "So…did you look into anything else with her?"

"Yeah, I looked into her registration. I wasn't able to get onto the group investigating her death, but the council was tied up with Mikhail around then. They couldn't afford to pay attention to their archives while everything was out hunting him down." He took a moment before continuing. "I was right with my first assumption, that she was a strong force to be reckoned with. She dabbled in a bit of everything as far as magic and could do a bit of precognition." He pointed to Sammie. "That's how she knew to get her kid out; she knew someone was going to go and hurt her. She knew that if she kept running from them, her time would run out at some point. She got her son out while she could."

Naomi glanced over at Sammie, who was slumped against Miles with a sort of far off look on his face. It would explain a lot; how Sammie was ridiculously skilled already with his magic, after not being able to use it for most of his life, and if she could, Naomi would guess his mother would find a way to make him stick out a bit less by subduing his power somehow.

"So...wait," Miles muttered, wrapping his arm around Sammie as he looked up at the rest of them. "Sammie's mom, Ashling, she was part of the council?" Booker nodded, and Miles continued before he could answer verbally. "And she'd messed up this Seer's plans at least once, right?" He gestured Eddie's way, and the vampire slowly bobbed her head, her brow furrowing. "So...is there a chance that Ashling and this Seer knew each other before that? Like, how often did Ashling get in the way, if she had the ability to block their powers? If the Seer was pissed enough about that, is there a chance she'd want to get revenge from that with her closest relative?"

Booker paused, making a vague wandering sound. "If I remember right, she'd been working against Constantine for a while before she died. The infiltration to free his spawn and help them acclimate was a couple of weeks before her death, actually."

"Shit," Eddie muttered, running her hand through her messy curls with a grimace. "Sammie, I—"

"It's fine," Sammie grumbled then sat up, his blue eyes staring Booker down, so intense even the hunter with decades of experience under his belt withered. "So, this Seer, the one who killed my mom, she's the one behind everything?"

"Theoretically, yeah?" Booker cleared his throat. "We can't be one hundred percent sure but...it seems that way?"

The air filled with static, and Naomi sucked in a sharp breath as Sammie inhaled deep, his eyes flickering with blue energy that washed down him in a wave as he exhaled, jaw clenched and hands curled into fists against his lap as he settled. "So...if we take care of her, this whole issue is solved, then."

"We can't kill her." Miles spoke up, soft and careful, and Naomi watched, near slack jawed, as Sammie shifted from a white-hot rage to something calm and disappointed. "We'd be just as bad."

"You all shouldn't be involved in this in the first place," Booker continued, pointedly not looking Sammie's way as the mage puffed up in anger like a dangerous, nuclear house cat. "I can take care of the Seer. If she's trying to destroy the council, she's going to be killed on site anyway. That should be my job, not yours."

"I—" Sammie started, eyes filling with that electric blue again, and Naomi could sense it as his gaze flickered up to the window behind Booker.

Blood. Decay. Rot.

Naomi got up to move. She pushed Eddie to one side as she tried to grab Booker and pull him back from the window, just a second before something broke through the wall, and Booker was yanked away, a sickening pop filling the air.

The hunter was gone before Naomi could blink, and the next thing she could see through the hole left behind was feral wolves surrounding the little cabin. Circling them, like sharks in a tank filled with blood.

They weren't going to make it to that Seer. She was going to make sure of it right here.

Chapter Twenty-Two

"**M**iles!"

Sammie's shout rang through Miles's ears. A sickening feeling of déjà vu hit him as he slammed into the wall of the rickety cabin. The wood gave way along with his arm as he tumbled across the floor. Pain flared fiercely through his right side. A glance down showed his arm bent the wrong way, the flesh bloody and bruised with the break.

His dream, all that time ago, that felt like fantasy… Was this because of the Seer? Did she plan all of this before Miles even knew Sammie was back?

"Are you dead?" Naomi's voice floated into the cabin before she crouched in, grimacing at the sight of him.

"Don't say it," Miles gritted through his teeth, sitting up and hissing as his arm throbbed with the action.

The alpha just knelt beside him and gently tapped his swelling shoulder. "This is gonna hurt a lot."

"No shit," Miles grouched, before squeezing his eyes shut, half feeling her hands poking around the break. "Just get it over with."

It was just as painful as in his dream, the twist and pull of her resetting his arm. He barely bit back a scream, tasting blood as he clenched his teeth against it. "Sorry," Naomi mumbled before she paused, waiting for him to look at her before she continued. "You should take Sammie and go—let us deal with this."

He remembered in the dream feeling offended, too small and weak to handle things in her eyes. He didn't know anything, didn't know Sammie was here, didn't know how much they'd gone through for the last several months. He shook his head, grimacing as the movement pulled at his sore, healing muscles. "No, I'm not going to just run and leave you guys behind."

She grumbled, like she knew where the conversation was going to go. To be fair, it wasn't hard. Miles was always going to stand his ground, and Naomi would always try to keep everyone else safe before herself. They were predictable. He didn't need some Seer shoving a premonition into his dreams to know that.

"It's not your fault, or your mess, Naomi," Miles assured her. The alpha sagged as he spoke. "We've come this far together. Either we run together and get out of here, or we all go down fighting." He paused, then chuckled. "Besides, Sammie would probably fry my other arm if I tried to get him to leave."

Naomi stared him down for a moment before she shook her head. "God, we really do fit together as a pack way too well…" Miles started trying to get to his feet, knowing he'd won. Naomi just rolled her eyes and stood up. "Don't shift until you heal up. We'll try to do what we can. If we find an opening through the feral, we go. We don't need to die where they want us to."

"Yes, Alpha," Miles teased, just to watch Naomi roll her eyes before she left. Miles sagged back, looking down to watch his broken skin stitch together. He wished his dream had lasted a bit longer, let him know what to expect when he stepped back outside. He'd felt pretty damn useless for most of this; at least then he could've done something to help everyone.

Miles wasn't like Naomi, who was knowledgeable, experienced, could figure things out, and could last more than five minutes in a fight. Eddie was at least smarter; she may not be the best when they had to survive against the feral werewolves or the shifters, but she at least could figure out a way to get them out. And Sammie was so much more useful and helpful and…and powerful than Miles could ever hope to be. Miles felt like he should be a background character in his own life, for how useful he was.

The growling and shouting outside ramped up, and Miles focused back in on his healing limb; the skin was a faint pink where it'd been split open from the inside out. He inhaled deep, trying to get his head right, focus. He stepped out back through the hole his body had made, bracing himself for what he might find, only to step forward and suddenly have a swooping sensation come over him, feeling like someone had tugged a rug out from underneath him.

He stayed on his feet, somehow, though he felt like he should've been sitting or lying down or doing anything but standing when he looked up. He was somewhere completely different from the dark woods and the dilapidated cabin. Soft lilac curtains framed a window with bright skies outside, and the sound of laughter and joy flowed in along with the breeze that smelled like summer rain and fresh laundry. The walls around him were painted a soft sky blue, beneath many, many charcoal sketches. Some of the faces on the sketches looked familiar, Miles realized, as he stepped closer to one. It almost looked like Sammie, a little bit.

"Miles, right?"

He jumped. The soft, southern-accented voice came out of nowhere. He turned around, nearly tripping, before careful hands kept him from falling. A woman with a shock of red hair and gold-framed glasses smiled at him apologetically.

"Sorry, hon, I forget sometimes how jarring this can be. It's been a while since I've brought someone here still awake."

None of what she was saying made any sense. "Who are you? Where am I? What are you even talking about?" A lump of anxiety formed in Miles's chest, sticking in his throat. "Where's Naomi, and Sammie?"

"They're safe, don't worry. I'm watching over them now, along with your vampire friend." She stepped back, gesturing to an armchair Miles didn't remember seeing before: plush cushions with a retro pattern partially covered with a lovingly handcrafted quilt. "Please, have a seat. We have all the time in the world, I promise."

Miles warily watched her as he obeyed, barely stopping from groaning as he sank into the seat. He hadn't realized how long it'd been since he'd sat somewhere that was comfortable; still, he had to know what was going on. "I still don't know if I can trust you."

"That's smart," the woman answered simply before she waved her hand. To Miles's surprise, a tray of snacks and coffee appeared out of thin air. Somehow, Miles could tell they were all his favorites; double chocolate chunk cookies, salted brown butter caramel shortbread, and unsweetened coffee with a splash of cinnamon milk. "Here, have as much as you like. Give me a moment, and I'll explain everything."

Miles, despite himself, could feel his anxiety and fear melting away, the comforting setting paired with the woman's gentle demeanor pushing the idea of this being another trick to the back of his mind. He watched as she padded away, going over to the door that Miles had missed again. She popped it open, then nodded to herself, shoulders sagging in relief. Miles could hear Naomi and Sammie through the door. Eddie's voice washed through occasionally as well as she yelled and cheered, disbelief and relief coloring her tone.

"Now, before you go worrying about everything going on outside of here, you're still up and moving, sort of. Your other half is doing most of the work. I just borrowed your consciousness to chat, if you don't mind." The woman waved her hand again as she strode across the room, and Miles watched, wide-eyed, as a wooden rocking chair appeared out of thin air across from him, its pastel plaid cushions tied with neat little bows to the seat and back. She made a soft sound as she sat in it, whistling before she reached over and grabbed one of the cookies from the tray. "It's a lot less disruptive to the waking world to borrow you, rather than Sammie. And you all need all the manpower you can find."

He stared blankly at her, jaw dropped and bobbing as he tried to find words. The woman waved a hand, chuckling softly to herself. "Oh jeez, sorry. You asked all that and I never answered you. My mother would cuff me by the head if she could see me now." She leveled him with a warm, apologetic expression, crow's feet crinkling and dimples popping into view with her crooked smile.

Oh.

"Ashling...?"

She beamed at him proudly. "Yep, though you can call me Ashe." She settled back in the seat, rocking gently as she nibbled on the cookie she took. "You're...well, I suppose many would just consider this the afterlife. Though, of course, you're not here be-cause you've passed on. I just need to speak with you, all of your group, really, but... I might have a good amount of magical power but I'm not that good."

Miles sagged back, blinking owlishly at her. She gestured to the tray, silent hospitality radiating from her. He shook out his nerves before taking the coffee and the shortbread. Both were perfect, somehow tasting like comfort and love and warmth. His eyes stung as the salty-sweet taste of the shortbread washed over his tongue.

"Good choice, by the way," Ashe commented, holding up the cookie. "The more chocolate the better. That's one thing I wish I could've given Sam as he was growing up. My brother was never much of a baker." She chuckled softly, then settled back. "Unfortunately, neither of us have the time to chat much about things like that. Would've loved to have been able to meet you some other way." She sat up slightly, still rocking as she spoke. "This...Seer problem you have. It's my fault. Not just because of what y'all figured of me foiling her plans." She murmured guiltily, looking away. "The Seer is my twin, Áine. Our parents were from a long line of mages, so when we'd both developed powers they were ecstatic, especially given our brother had little to no magic. Áine had never been able to use traditional magic quite like I could, and when she started having visions, she started...well, losing it.

"She saw our parents discarding her, looking at her in disgust and looking at me with pride. She got jealous. Mattias tried to comfort her as best he could, but...there wasn't much he could do when she saw the worst one." Ashe adjusted, grimacing. "She'd seen the two of us fighting and saw me losing control of my powers and injuring her. She'd antagonized me afterward. Told me to just get it over with if I wanted to hurt her so bad.

"We were young, halfway through being teenagers, so I had all this power but very little control and...I'd lost it. I got angry, and I lashed out, and she lost her sight because of me." She settled back, electric blue eyes shimmering. "I didn't mean to do it, and she'd pushed me away when I tried to help. Our parents threw her out because they thought she'd hurt me."

Miles sagged, staring down at his hands. "Wow...that's..."

"They're awful," Ashe finished, heaving out a breath. "I left not long after, and according to Mattias they both died soon after that. I tried to keep track of Áine, but she didn't want to be found. I couldn't find her until I was well into my council days, had met Sam's father, and I was near three months along. She'd been with Constantine, of all people. I'd begged to be on the team to track them, but they wouldn't let me while I was pregnant with Sammie. They lost track of her and Constantine not long after he'd been born.

"I raised Sammie with his dad for a while, before Alexei left us, much too young for Sam to remember... Then it was just the two of us, but...I couldn't leave Áine alone. It killed me, knowing what I'd done to her. I needed to make things right." Ashe settled her gaze back on Miles as he listened to her, enraptured. "Sam was three when we found where Constantine was based. He'd established himself well, had a massive coven that took us weeks to fix. I'd freed your friend, Eddie, with that one. Áine's sense of predicting me had apparently faded. The mage scholars at the council assumed it was because of just how much she hated and feared me in one. Her emotions were too complicated to predict my actions, which made the natural magical aura I have a handy tool in the infiltration."

Ashe's lips twitched for a second before shifted back on topic. "Which...that brings up something useful for you all. Sammie still has some of that magic in his aura, my own having mingled with his when I saw him for the last time. It means Áine can't infiltrate Sammie's thoughts or use her predictions on him. As long as you have Sammie with you, you should be able to get close enough to her to take her down."

Miles frowned, shifting forward in the armchair. "But...you do realize what Naomi and Eddie—hell, what Sammie is going to do to your sister when they get to her, right?"

Ashe paused, her expression turning melancholic. "I do, but I think by now she's beyond saving. She'll do whatever she can to ruin Sammie and shatter the tenuous peace between us and the humans. This is to prevent a war, Miles, and in war, you have to make sacrifices. Even if they're people you care about."

The words turned Miles's stomach, and he set the snacks aside as he shifted even further forward, dropping his head in his hands. "Sammie and I...we shouldn't be here. Why us?" The words felt like acid bubbling out of his throat, his eyes stinging.

"Oh, Miles..." Ashe's voice was soft, sad and comforting at once. "I know, but nothing is going to change the fact that you are. It's not fair. Gods know if I could trade places with the both of you I would, in a heartbeat. But...it's you." Gentle, careful hands brushed against his knuckles, and Miles lowered his hands to his lap as Ashe brushed away the warm tears that bubbled up over his cheeks. "I don't have much more time with you here, my dear. I can hear you all have found a way out of the worst of the feral beasts. Just watch the shadows, and please, remember...if hope ever seems lost, look for proof."

The words didn't make much sense. Miles furrowed his brow. Ashe simply smiled at him as he felt a tug at his chest, pulling him toward the open door behind him. "Wait. I-I don't understand. What do you mean to look for proof?"

Ashe shook her head, her voice quickly fading as the sound of wind rushing around him filled his ears, and Miles had to close his eyes against a sudden bright flash of light as he was yanked backward. He felt like he was tumbling for a while, fumbling through the air trying to right himself, before he slammed into his body. Everything ached, much like after a really bad, really sudden shift, and the full force of his heightened senses came back in a rush. He hadn't realized he'd been missing them until he could scent the vile rot and carnage smell of the mad wolves, the familiar scent of overheating electronics and rainwater, Naomi's spicy, cayenne aroma, and the gag-inducing scent of lots and lots of blood.

"Miles?" Sammie's voice was close, and Miles pried open his eyes to see his mate's worried expression. The beast in his chest made itself known with a fierce sense of ache in his chest at the sight. "Are you okay? You shifted back really suddenly."

"Uh…" Miles's throat tightened around tears, and he cleared it, shaking his head. "Yeah, fine. I'm fine. What's going on?"

Sammie frowned, opening his mouth to undoubtedly ask Miles what his deal was, only to be cut off by Naomi's frantic shouting. "Hurry up, guys! We don't know when we'll have a better chance to get out!"

Right. They had to escape. Ashe had mentioned that. That part, at least, made sense. Sammie leveled him with a look Miles could read even without the senses, or the knowledge of Sammie's…well, everything. Miles shook his head, mouthing that they could talk later, and scooped Sammie up before sprinting after the other two, down the narrow path between the trees that could at least slow down the much too big feral wolves. They could get out first, then Miles could figure out how the hell to summarize everything Ashe had just told him. He really wished she'd picked someone other than Miles for it, but he'd figure it out.

He definitely could figure this out.

Chapter Twenty-Three

They'd been walking for a while. Sammie's legs cramped with every step until Miles picked him up to carry him wherever Naomi deemed somewhere safe. He had absolutely no idea where they were; he could only hope they were heading in the right direction, and that they weren't walking into any other ambushes, or Constantine or anything.

A giant lizard monster could step out in front of them and Sammie wouldn't even be surprised. Just shrug it off and try to generate enough power to stun it.

"You all right, Sam?"

Miles's low baritone rumbled through where Sammie's chest rested against his back, making him shudder just a little. "Fine." He pressed his face into the nape of Miles's neck, trying to get his focus back. "Just tired."

It was true. He was tired. Utterly exhausted, down to his bones. He wanted to curl up in bed away from everyone and sleep for a year. He wanted to not leave the house for a decade; he never, ever wanted to see another supernatural creature for as long as he lived after this. Not that he had much choice, or a house to go back to.

He wanted so badly to turn back time, go back to before he and Miles stepped out that morning, and just spend the day in bed. But, of course, all he got was stupid lightning powers.

Granted, they helped slightly for more than just tasing whatever monster was trying to kill them next. He somehow could use it to accelerate healing, which was something. Still, a little time magic or something would be great right about now.

Sammie's brain couldn't find a point to stop at, hopping around between thoughts like a kid being unleashed in a theme park for the first time. The Seer, Ashe, Booker's apparent death, guilt over Peter, his uncle Matt, Constantine, Miles, high school, Miles, the weather, Miles.

At least that was one consistent thing from before all the supernatural junk. Miles practically waltzing through his thoughts unbidden but wholly welcome.

"What about you?" Sammie muttered, trying to focus his thoughts back to one place again. "You've been pretty off since we got out of there. Are you all right?"

Miles's thumbs rubbed circles into the sides of Sammie's thighs, much to his heart and brain's utter elation. "Yeah, just…

It's a lot. And weird to explain, and I don't know if I can explain it well enough. And probably shouldn't talk about it until we can find somewhere safe."

The little niggling feeling of panic started worming its way through his ribs, and Sammie shifted forward. Miles grunted slightly under the redistribution of weight on his back. "What is it? Something dangerous? Did the Seer get to you again?"

"No," Miles answered, quick and quiet. "Not dangerous. Just...helpful but a little awkward to know."

Not cryptic at all. "Miles." Sammie's voice came out grumpier than expected, but he was so, so tired. He was tired of the circle talk, of people avoiding the subject.

Miles puffed in resignation, slowing down his steps before he spoke, his voice even quieter. Sammie needed to lean forward so his chin was resting on Miles's shoulder. "I talked with Ashe."

Sammie's breath caught, and he scrambled to get off Miles's back. He had to make sure Miles was telling the truth. He stumbled as he swung around Miles to face him, staring into those brown puppy dog eyes to be certain he caught every little micro expression on his face. "You...you talked with my mother?"

"Yeah. While I was shifted, she said she borrowed my consciousness. She told me who the Seer is." Miles glanced away. "So, uh...Ashe and the Seer are twins. And basically, she's trying to get revenge out on you since Ashe hurt her in an accident when they were younger, and their parents basically wrote off Áine, um, Ashe's twin sister."

Sammie stared, wondering if his brain was broken somehow. The Seer was his aunt? That couldn't be right. Uncle Matt never said anything about any siblings other than his mom, never mentioned anything about Sammie's grandparents or anything. Every picture Matt had of his childhood showed just Matt and Ashe. There'd be evidence, wouldn't there? "Miles..." Sammie muttered, unable to help the disbelief coloring his tone.

Miles immediately sagged, shaking his head and pulling Sammie closer. "Shit, no, I knew she made a mistake telling me. Sammie, I know it's a lot to try to come to terms with, but I'm telling the truth." His hands were warm through Sammie's shirt, sinking into his skin from shoulders down with calming, radiating heat. Sammie knew Miles wouldn't lie, but... "Your mom mentioned she was powerful, like, really powerful. Áine had some magic, the visions and everything, but their parents just... Ashe overshadowed her. She got jealous, and her visions showed Ashe injuring her, and when she went to confront your mom, she...lost control. Áine lost her sight, and their parents were afraid of her getting back for it, so they kicked her out.

"She went with Constantine after that, and Ashe looked for her to make amends." He perked up, brown eyes going wide. "She'd mentioned your dad! Alexei said that he'd left when you were still young. And she'd said that the reason Áine can't get to you is because her...magic aura had mixed with yours? Áine was so torn up about your mom that it's made it so she can't predict her thoughts, and it's sort of made it so she can't with you, either."

"So…" Sammie started, his mind becoming a worse jumbled mess with every word Miles spoke. "The only reason that Áine can't get into my head is because she hated my mom so much that the thought of her or her magic clouds her ability to use her powers?"

"I guess? She also told me to look for proof, if we ever lose hope."

"Proof? You're sure she said that?" A slightly annoyed but resigned look crossed his face, and Sammie winced, holding up his hands to Miles's cheek. "I didn't mean it like that. Just…we've been sleep deprived and we're all stressed out. That's gonna make our memories a little messy. That's all."

He sighed, leaning into Sammie's hand as he closed his eyes. "Yeah, I guess you're right. Sorry for getting offended."

Sammie chuckled, briefly distracted enough to lean up onto his toes to press his lips to Miles's, soothing both of them. "Sorry for making you think I doubted you." Sammie pressed his forehead to Miles's, waiting until those soft baby deer-like eyes opened again. "I love you, Miles. I think the world of you. I just want to make sure we both get out of here alive to get to the part where I can prove that to you."

Miles purred, dipping down for a deeper kiss, making Sammie feel that little constant ball of energy zing through his chest. "I know. I love you, too, Sam."

They spent another second together before they started forward again, only to pause when they realized Naomi and Eddie were gone. "Eddie?" Sammie called, that lightness in his chest growing heavy with dread, sinking like a weight into his gut. "Naomi?"

"They're a little preoccupied at the moment," a voice, eerily familiar, answered from behind them. Miles spun around before Sammie could move, a growl rumbling from him that vibrated through Sammie's chest as Miles pushed him behind his own body.

Nikolas smirked at him, looking human aside from the eerie, dead cloudiness to his eyes and his elongated canines. Beside him was a woman with a shock of red hair, eyes similarly cloudy but much more awake. Clearly alive and aware, her eyes with that sort of milky film like the tissue had died, a slight scarring around her sockets looking like an electrical burn. She looked like...like Ashe.

"Áine?"

The woman was dressed in a torn black tunic and worn black jeans. The shimmery fabric draped over her shoulders seemed to live and breathe as it shifted in the wind. Her earrings and necklace were made of fangs instead of precious stones. Her lips curled slowly, creepy and off as she tilted her head. "Maybe." She tilted her head the opposite way, suddenly and violently, neck cracking loudly in the dead silence of the forest, and Sammie watched in horror as her eyes and lips turned inky black. The fabric twitched and writhed. "Maybe...not." Her voice was distorted, layering over and over itself.

"You seem terrified," Nikolas commented. Sammie found

himself frozen completely as he stared down the woman. She started leaking inky black from every orifice. "Maybe it's best the two of you run."

Miles moved, just as the woman burst into a mess of black, leech-like shifter material all over the woods. A giant mass of black started writhing toward them, making the air in Sammie's lungs freeze and his vision gray from the lack of oxygen. Sammie was lifted from his feet as Miles picked him up and sprinted away.

They were always running. Nikolas's last words felt like a request for a duel, a glove slapped across his cheek. But Sammie couldn't think of anything but the feeling of drowning whenever he saw the shifters. His lungs burned and his throat tried to shove out the mass and the blind panic of being completely and utterly powerless.

He squeezed his eyes shut against the panic, the sight of Nikolas and the horde of shifters chasing after them, and against the choking sense of failure and shame for running away, again. He just wanted these stupid games being played with them to end.

"Run, little sheep, run."

Sheep?

Sammie cracked open his eyes and looked up at the two main sources of his fears for the last couple of months, confused. Nikolas was herding them somewhere, just like before.

Yeah, no. Sammie wasn't going to let that happen. He was tired, and he was done.

"Miles. I'm gonna zap them."

Miles stumbled, obviously hearing Sammie's whispered words even with the cacophony of crazed laughter and the squelching writhing of the shifter. "What the hell do you mean you're gonna zap them?"

"Just listen!" he hissed, focusing on their movements. Nikolas stepped out to the right to herd them around the trees, shifting their path to the left. The shifter coiled forward to ensure where they went. They moved in tandem. If he could just get them to get close together to hit at once, but far enough apart so... "I'm gonna zap them. And you need to turn around and sprint back the other way. Go between them."

Miles was quiet for a moment, then his grip around Sammie's waist tightened. "Got it. I trust you."

Sammie nodded, fighting against the choking feeling in his chest and waiting, watching them until they both moved within a step of each other, trying to kite them to the right. He concentrated a quick burst of energy into his palm and shot it at them. He whooped when it hit right where he wanted, exploding into a wave of electricity and bringing the two off their feet. "Go, now!"

Miles obeyed, immediately stopping and turning before sprinting between the two and shifting Sammie around himself as he kept running, wrapping Sammie's arms around his front. "Hold on, I'm gonna shift so I can get out faster. Just, direct me where to go as best you can. Do you know where you're going?"

He had absolutely no clue. Other than it was possible they were close to the actual Áine and this, well, for lack of a better title, necromancer. Nikolas and the shifter might've been there to lead them off the trail. "I'll try to figure it out."

Miles squeezed Sammie's hand before he grunted, stumbling twice as he shifted. It was quicker than usual, not as flawless as Naomi, but still just as breathtaking as the first time it happened. Miles's neck and shoulders widened as he changed in size, broadening and dropping to all fours. Sammie was at least able to find his grip quickly as fur poured over Miles's skin in the next second, thick and long enough to grab nice firm handfuls. The wolf beneath him rumbled, licking Sammie's wrist before breaking into a full sprint.

He followed his gut, directing Miles with a tug on his fur through the winding woods. They started uphill, picking their way through overgrowth and stone as the forest tilted upwards along the mountain. Sammie had no idea where they were exactly, the last point he could pinpoint on a map being the border between Pennsylvania and New York. That was a while back, before the rickety old cabin that was reduced to support beams during the battle with the ferals. He thought they were heading north, for the most part.

It was only a handful of minutes that felt like hours, but Miles seemed to know to stop before Sammie did. The wolf beneath him growled harshly, padding to a halt as his hackles rose under Sammie's hands. It didn't take him long to understand why Miles stopped; a smell like a morgue assaulted his nose, making him gag and cover his mouth, eyes watering. That familiar sense of dread dropped into his gut, souring his stomach along with the stench.

"Little Star…" A slightly raspy voice cut through the relative quiet of the clearing they'd stopped at, a cave mouth gaping into the cliffside, looking perfectly innocent from outside. Thin gold crescents glinted from the dark, before electric blue shimmered around them, features melting into view as the woman, the one the shifters had mimicked, strolled toward them. She looked older, grey in her red shock of hair, eyes with that film and scarring suggesting the damage Ashe had mentioned, and she wore an expression that was manic and enraged. She bared her teeth, too wide and sharp, as her gaze bored through Sammie's skull. "You're just as I expected you to be. Brave and *stupid*, just like your mother."

Miles growled along with Sammie, words bubbling up in his throat before he could stop himself. "She's not stupid, you're just bitter!"

Áine chuckled, shaking her head. "Bitter. Yes, I am bitter." Her smile was still firmly in place, countering her rage-filled tone as she screamed. "Of course I'm *fucking* bitter! I didn't ask for this. I asked for love, and care, and to be noticed, and I got ignored, beaten, and your demon of a mother blinding me!" She drew back, hissing. "She could've helped me earlier, before she tried to shock my eyes from my skull. It's too late, now." She sagged. The taunting look on her face fell for a moment. "You're here, which means everything is already in motion. And if it was a different time, different circumstances, I would've loved to meet you for the first time."

She turned on her heel and stepped back into the cave. Sammie cursed, clambered off Miles's back, and started after her. Miles snapped his teeth into the back of Sammie's shirt, keeping him in place. His constant rumbling growl pitched up into something more worried, stressed.

Sammie stared after her, a weird combination of emotions—sadness, anger, fear—all bundled together in his chest with a lump of anxiety bullying its way into his throat. He wanted to ask her about everything that happened, wanted to tell her it wasn't too late and she could start over, and he wanted to—as bad as the thought was when it first passed through his mind—finish the job that his mom started and kill her, just to end their combined misery. Sammie sagged, turning back to Miles. "We need to end this."

Miles grumbled, then grimaced, shifting back in a couple of seconds, shaking out his limbs. "We should wait for Naomi." He glanced toward the cave, his eyes starting to glow that partially shifted gold. "It's a trap, we don't know what she has waiting inside. And we have no idea on that other mage."

He was right, Sammie knew it was stupid to try to follow her, but he was struggling to get his emotions in order so he could listen to his brain. Sparks danced over his fingers, and Miles glanced down, before clenching his teeth and slumping. "Miles..."

"I know... You're going to go in anyway, right?" Sammie stared him down. Miles steeled himself, determined to follow

Sammie to the end. "Right. Let's go, then."

They could be walking into anything, but they had no idea where the other two were, and Sammie was tired of running away. It felt like they were always taking one step forward then running four steps back. Maybe...maybe he could do what his mom couldn't and get Áine to see it wasn't too late for her, or he could end it.

Sammie reached for Miles's hand, and the two of them crossed the threshold of the cave together. No running away, no turning back.

Chapter Twenty-Four

Eddie hated the woods. She really did. She missed the city, the tells for the dangerous places and the knowledge that if she got lost, she could easily find her way. What marker was there in the woods to help her find out where she was? Trees? A slightly weirder looking tree?

Turning and finding Miles and Sammie gone, and Naomi suddenly not by her side when she turned back the other way, she was reminded of why she hated the woods so much. Her mind flashed back to running from Constantine, bumbling her way through the forest looking for any sign that she wasn't just circling back to the mansion of her personal hell.

"Nae?" Eddie called, hating just how shaky her voice was. She hadn't been alone in weeks. She'd been on her own for years, and the first moment she was by herself she was a terrified little kid again. She hated it, how small and weak she felt. "Miles? Sam—Sammie?"

"Winifred." The voice was like ice, punching the tiny bit of air from her lungs. She turned, shivering, her legs shaking so much she felt like she was going to collapse. Constantine smirked at her, strolling leisurely through the trees toward her. His face and neck were smeared with blood already, part fresh and part flaky and dried. "See you have lowered yourself enough to associate with dogs. Though..." He looked down at her missing hand and chuckled. "Looks like you know where that leads you. Are you ready to come home, spawn? We can fix that up for you and get you back on better blood than the mutt's."

Eddie couldn't move, couldn't speak—she felt like she was being strangled, a chain around her throat tightening with every word. She wished she was brave enough to talk back, that she could stand up and fight. She was weak, always weak. Compared to everyone else, she really wasn't worth the time. It was evident here, as she shuddered and stared, unmoving and unspeaking.

Constantine cackled, his cold fingers digging into her jaw. "Aw, has the mutt blood really gotten to you that much? Can't even speak to your sire?" Eddie winced as his fingers tightened, shaking her head back and forth. "We'll wash that dirty alpha's taint from you, and you'll even get to watch her get a taste of her own medicine from her old alpha."

Those words shoved Eddie out of her own body as she realized what Naomi was going to go through—any trace of Naomi was going to be erased from her. It made her sick and angry, and she reacted, her brain catching up after and cheering as she jerked her head back enough to be able to get Constantine's hand in her mouth and locked her jaw down. She snarled as her old sire hissed, eyes flashing with fiery anger that would have her shrinking back and bending in any other situation. Now, Eddie simply bit down harder before she yanked her head back again, taking part of him with her, then sprinting after the last place she saw Naomi.

She spat out the bit of flesh and shook her head, blinking hard as she realized everything seemed...more. She was moving faster than she ever had, and she could smell exactly where Naomi was, along with a horrid ammonia-like stench, rot and mold mixing into something she was sure the werewolves would be complaining about.

Eddie emerged through the trees, breathing in sharply when she saw Naomi, looking pale and terrified as she backed away from a hulking feral alpha. The flesh around its maw was rotted and decayed, its throat horrifically mauled. Mikhail, she was sure of it, between Naomi's shocked fear and Constantine's words.

"Naomi!" Eddie called, running toward them. She wasn't running away as she normally would; she was too busy being absolutely incensed. Naomi's pretty, charcoal eyes flicked over to her, and she sagged in relief for a second before she stared, looking a little confused and shocked.

"Eddie... What are you...?"

Eddie stopped between Naomi and the walking corpse of

Mikhail. Staring into his blank eyes, she puffed herself up, an un-earthly hiss vibrating in her throat. She could barely see a reflec-tion in the dark glassy eyes—her body slowly towered over him, her fangs lengthened, the nails on her remaining hand grew into razor-like daggers, her limbs creaked and groaned with the growth. Distantly, she realized what was going on—something she'd seen Constantine do when he was really pissed, usually be-fore she or one of the other spawns got punished. She never thought she could do anything like that. Was it because she acci-dentally had some of Constantine's blood?

"Tell your master..." Eddie started before she realized it, her voice gravelly and eerie. "We'll be coming to clean up his mess." She sensed a shudder from behind. Naomi let out a shivery breath as she settled her trembling hand to Eddie's back, skirting across her knobby spine and stretched skin in a way that had Eddie nearly purring. "Now, *leave.*"

The puppet shuddered before turning tail and running, a glint flitting over its eyes that was almost like *compulsion.*

Oh shit, I just compelled something for the first time. I thought I couldn't do that.

She shuddered, feeling everything settle back into place. "That is *so* weird..."

"Eds?" She turned to find Naomi staring at her, amazed and still with a tiny bit of trepidation. "That...is you, right?"

"Yeah." Eddie pulled Naomi into a tight hug and squeezed hard. "I'm so glad I found you..."

Naomi pulled Eddie back enough to look over her face, which was probably still a little bloody from biting Constantine. Which… *holy shit, I did that, didn't I?*

"I can't believe this," Eddie whispered, chuckling to herself. Naomi, adorably, tilted her head and furrowed her brow. "I just… We got separated, which I'm pretty sure was on purpose, and Constantine was there. I froze up at first but then he started bad-mouthing you and Miles and I just got so mad that I…" She giggled, the sheer unbelievability of the situation getting to her. "I bit the asshole, and I went to find you and—"

Saying the words out loud was like a lightbulb flashing over her head as she realized why Constantine's comments about Naomi got to her so bad. God, she was so dumb, and so unbelievably blind. Eddie mused softly, brushing some of Naomi's hair back behind her ear, the alpha blinking up at her. "And?"

Eddie tilted Naomi's face up and pressed their lips together, more tender than they ever had before. Naomi relaxed into it and pulled Eddie closer. She would've stayed there for ages, if she could've, but…

Something, probably one of her new senses she'd earned through Constantine's blood, was telling her they needed to move. Sammie and Miles were still out there somewhere, and if Naomi and Eddie had to deal with their old nightmares, they were probably close to the same situation.

She sighed as they parted, brushing her thumb along Naomi's jaw and grinning as she got a whine in response. "I can tell you later, but right now we should find the others."

Naomi gave her a look that told Eddie she knew exactly what she was thinking. It made sense, especially if Naomi felt the same way as Eddie. That big *L* word that Eddie used to hiss and spit at. "Got it, but also you should probably tell me now. You know, since this is a suicide mission."

Eddie grinned, so stupidly gone for her. "You're right, my love. How about we move along, and I can tell you just how absolutely and completely lost I am on you, and how deeply and intrinsically in love with you I am."

Naomi barked out a laugh, swatting at her, before she started off into the woods. She stepped backward for a bit as she beamed at Eddie. "Good, because I have the feeling Miles isn't the only one who has a mate in our little group."

Of course, everything about them didn't seem like it should fit, yet here they were, Naomi talking about mates, and Eddie waxing on about how head over heels she was.

They were going to end all this nonsense, if nothing else so Eddie could have all the time in the world to maybe, just maybe, have a little bit of normalcy with her love. Even if she had to bite them all herself.

Chapter Twenty-Five

It felt like they'd walked into a different world when they passed into the cave. The hair at the back of Miles's neck rose, and that alternate part of him curled up like it was ready to strike at the slightest shadow or sound. He was sort of glad, considering how clouded his senses were with the heavy stench of viscera and bad energy. It felt almost like Sammie's, electric but wrong, like how the air felt before a tornado rather than a relaxing late summer night storm.

Sammie seemed to be just as affected, his body tense under Miles's guiding hand. His magic pooled at his hands and occasionally raced along his arms, like he was having trouble controlling it.

To be fair, Sammie couldn't see as well as Miles could, and even with his enhanced sight he was having trouble seeing in the pitch black. He could barely make out shapes of stone, and he could only see the path forward by a dim bluish light far ahead of them.

They stepped into a wider chamber when Miles stopped. He grabbed Sammie by the waist and pulled him close, barely choking down the growl clawing its way up his throat. Something wasn't right, but he couldn't see what, just... He knew there was something in the room with them. He could tell by the barest shift in the air, the scent of severe weather and gore mixed with the merest hint of sugar and lavender, sickeningly sweet like candy.

"Shifters..." Miles muttered, clutching Sammie tighter. "I can't see anything, so I don't know where they are."

Sammie shivered. He lifted a hand up and created a palm-sized ball of light, illuminating part of the room. It was enough for Miles to see most of everything. He shuddered when he realized just how many shifters there were. The entire cave was pitch black because of them. That was the reason he couldn't see; they were planted all over the walls and most of the floors, writhing and wriggling around them.

It felt like a horror movie, watching the main characters walk into the monsters' breeding grounds, thousands of the things suddenly waking up and staring them down. He didn't think—he grabbed Sammie by the arm and sprinted away from the ones around them, barely feeling the wind whipping along his back as some swiped at them.

Like every single horror movie he'd seen, the cave exploded with activity, shifters hissing and chittering as they started after them. Miles heard them gathering up behind them, and despite himself he glanced back only for his heart to seize in his chest at the sight there. They were merging, making a wriggling mass of life-draining monster, bigger than even Nikolas when he was shifted. It crawled after them, the beast splitting apart to open its maw and snap at them.

It was getting so big it was going to be hard to avoid it, and the shifters not in the mass were blocking the path they'd come from. Miles looked around, frantic, trying to find some way to get them out of here in one piece.

There's no other opening, where the hell has Áine even gone if there's no other—

"Sammie, you trust me, right?"

Sammie was panting, his legs visibly shaking as he kept up with Miles, but he still looked unsure as he nodded. Miles scooted Sammie up. He darted off to the side to the center of the cavern. It was small, barely wide enough for them to fit through together, so he had to correct his stride and slide at just the right time to slip into the hole without the shifters catching them. "What're you doing? Miles, we're not going to fit in that!"

"Trust me—" He ducked to avoid a massive, gooey hand swiping over their heads. "I'll make us fit."

"Miles, that's not—!" Sammie squawked as a tendril whipping past his face. Miles jerked him out of the way just in time. "It's right behind us. We're not going to have time!"

"I'll get us in, keep as close to me as you can."

"Miles, wait, we—!" Sammie yelped. Miles dropped into a slide and caught the opening just right for them to slip in mostly seamlessly, his legs aching slightly from the minor battering against the walls.

Sammie screamed, clinging to Miles as they slid down the tunnel, the descent growing steadily steeper. They gained speed at a worrying pace, despite Miles trying to slow them down. He couldn't see how far they had to go; it felt like half an hour of falling before that blue glow sparked into view, and they fell out of the tunnel into the lit chamber. Miles landed on his ankle wrong, and Sammie cried out from the impact.

"Shit, Sammie, what's wrong?" Miles grit out, twisting about with his broken ankle to check on his mate. Fear and worry pulsed in his brain, his own pain overridden by Sammie's.

"I-I landed on something…" Sammie stuttered, shifting, and Miles's stomach swooped at the sight. A pool of red stained Sammie's shirt around his ribs. There was a jagged blade underneath him coated with a goldish substance, little specks of black around it. He couldn't smell anything from it other than Sammie's blood.

"It's not too deep, but there's something on it. Can you heal yourself?"

Sammie shakily raised his hand up to his side and seeped his magic into it as they slowly rose to their feet. "Where are we?"

Miles helped Sammie up and looked around; the smell of bodies and decay was strongest here. Given the scenery around them, it made sense. It looked like they were in some sort of morgue and operating room. There were bits of vials of materials and a massive tome and rune right next to it, making it all the more obvious they'd just found the mage who had been raising the dead, or at least their base of operations.

His eyes caught on one of the beaten-up tables left in the center of the room. A white cloth was draped over it, something or someone clearly underneath it. Something was screaming in his head to get out, that there was something wrong, but at the same time... Miles knew they needed to find this necromancer and Áine; they needed to put an end to this. If they could find any clue or sign of them, it'd help, right?

Without much more thought than that, Miles stepped toward the table, Sammie following close behind. Miles grabbed the cloth and pulled it back, and he grew nauseous at the sight of Booker on the table, pale and bloodied, a deep gouge in his chest. "Shit."

"He's not...alive, is he?" Sammie muttered, and Miles shuttered out a harsh hiss as he pressed his fingers to Booker's pulse point, feeling for anything. He was cold, his skin clammy and oddly waxy, and there was absolutely no pulse.

Miles opened his mouth to answer, turning away from Booker's corpse, when a hand wrapped forcefully and tight around his wrist. Booker's hand, attached to the definitely dead body. Those lifeless eyes popped open, and Miles felt like he'd been submerged in ice water when the corpse lifted from the table, maintaining its death grip on Miles's wrist.

"Miles... I'm so glad you finally came," Booker said, his voice slightly off, almost like any emotion had died along with him.

"Miles!" He heard Sammie gasp, and he realized finally that Booker's other hand was holding a wicked-looking blade, coated in the same substance as the one Sammie got cut with. He jerked back when the blade skirted his stomach. Immediate, agonizing pain ripped through his core. It was the worst thing he'd ever felt; his skin bubbled and hissed with whatever poison was on the blade.

Booker's hand released him, and Miles slumped to the ground, everything zeroing in on the wound. It was barely enough to break the skin—what kind of poison was that strong?

"Wolfsbane." Booker's voice cut through, and Miles yelled as he was yanked back by his hair, his scalp screaming with the action. "One of the few things that can truly kill your kind. Aside from completely decapitating you, anyway." The blade settled under his jaw, not pressing hard enough to break the skin, but an immediate painful rash still bubbled up where the blade touched.

"Now, you get to be witness to something great, Miles. One of the few living creatures to be present at the beginning of the end of our hiding." Booker sneered, his skin stretching unnaturally as he leaned into his face, nearly nose to nose with Miles. "You'll bear witness to Samuel's true calling. And, if you're lucky, you'll get to join him in starting the new era."

Miles tried to jerk back, get out of Booker's hold, but he couldn't get his body to work. It felt almost like Nikolas taking over, paired with the searing pain that pulsed from the wound on his stomach and throat. He tried to move his limbs, or shift so he could get free, and the icy feeling that had been filling his gut spread all over. He felt like he was human, again, somehow. He couldn't shift; reaching out toward his wolf who was always there felt impossible.

Booker's lips turned upward, slow and wider than should be possible, watching Miles as he came to the horrific conclusion that he was completely powerless. The former hunter stepped to the side, hand still wound through Miles's hair, and revealed Sammie, who was sagging into...into Peter, looking much like Booker, crazed smile and empty eyes, covered in all matter of injuries, too many for him to have survived. Another puppet.

"Night, night...Miles," Booker taunted, before slamming Miles's head into the table. Everything went suddenly and terrifyingly black.

*

"Miles." The voice was far off, almost like someone trying to talk to him right out of being put under. He felt something warm drip from his hair, trailing over his cheek, but he couldn't open his eyes, like his lids were weighted.

Every little bruise, cut, and ache flared to life, Miles whimpering as his entire body throbbed with the beat of his heart. Everything hurt, in varying degrees. His skull throbbed like it was split in two. He wondered, for a moment, when he'd feel the telltale pins and needles of his body healing, only to remember they'd somehow blocked his powers.

"Miles, *please*. Wake up..."

Sammie, pleading and crying. Miles grimaced, his pain increasing at hearing his mate sound so distraught. He shuddered out a breath, agony flaring through all of him, and willed his eyes to open. It took every ounce of energy to do so, but after what felt like an hour, he managed to peek his eyes open.

Sammie's watery blue gaze was much closer than he expected, and when he caught Miles blearily staring at him, he let out a distraught sob. Miles reached to comfort him, but stopped, realizing that his hands were bound. So were Sammie's...

Everything around them faded in slowly. Sammie was cuffed to the wall next to him, Miles's right hand barely within reach of Sammie's left. Sammie thankfully looked uninjured, while Miles was littered all over with bruises and scrapes. The worst by far was the cut on his stomach—the skin around it was blackened and seeping, black veins spreading from it. Just looking at it made a fresh wave of pain pulse through him.

There were a couple of people in the room with them, though at a second glance he noticed they didn't seem to be moving or breathing at all. He couldn't see their eyes, but he could guess from how they stood still as statues and covered in what should be fatal wounds that they were corpses brought to life. Miles rolled his head to the side, catching someone else walking into the room, Áine trailing behind them along with Nikolas.

The newcomer was a taller man with grungy, sandy hair to his chin, stubble partway to a salt-and-pepper beard along his jaw. His sharp blue eyes were tired and sunken in. All of him looked drained of life, but not quite like the puppets guarding them, as if he'd exhausted almost every bit of his energy except for the last little bit to keep him alive.

The man glanced up at them then turned to one of the tables filled with vials and scraps of papers in an unorganized mess. "Samuel, you're a lot scrawnier than I expected."

The words were jarring, something out of nowhere that had Miles and Sammie simultaneously turning their heads to stare at him. "What...huh?" Sammie stuttered, his brow furrowing.

The man looked them over, looking vaguely disappointed as he worked. "Your time away from your people made you soft and weak. Ashling made a mistake sending you to live with that powerless man."

Miles stared, trying to get the words to piece together to make some semblance of sense. The man knew Sammie, that much was obvious, along with knowing Ashe and who Sammie had grown up with. But why was he here, doing this, if he did?

Sammie spoke up, voice small and scared. "How do you know any of that?"

The silence in the room made Miles's ears ring as the man settled his lifeless stare on them, not a single change in his nearly blank expression. "I'm the reason you're alive. Ashling and I, we gave you life."

Sammie whimpered, and Miles fought through his memories, the fogginess from whatever poison was in the seeping wound making it harder. "Alexei? But...you're supposed to be dead," Miles muttered, remembering that much. Ashe had told him Sammie's father had left them, he'd died...right?

"In a sense." He looked away. "The council is poison for our kind. Suffocating our potential with their rules and human paranoia. Ashling never saw the light of that—I did." He turned back to the vials, plucked some from their stands, and mixed their contents. The inside of the tubes turned a smoky black that smelled like sulfur and blood. "I was dead, for a moment. A necessary discomfort to free myself from their iron rule. All of those council dogs are blind when it comes to death, especially when it comes to my type of power. A dead necromancer is better than a live one."

Sammie shuddered, and Miles could tell he was losing it even without his enhanced senses. "Why... You...you killed..." His words got stuck, tears brimming his eyes, and Miles growled at the sight, jerking against the binds only to whimper at the flare of utter agony along his ribs.

"Ashling was an obstacle to our vision," Alexei answered, completely emotionless.

Sammie lunged forward, a single spark of blue dancing across his arms. The shackles held firm as he struggled against them.

Alexei grunted, acting as if he had an annoying gnat buzzing around him. "Áine, get me a sample from him." The Seer stepped forward, leering manically as she grabbed a dagger from the array of tools on the table. "It'd be much easier if I could just bring your corpses to where we need and raise you there, but the reaction doesn't occur with dead tissue." He considered a moment. "It's a shame, that council dog was such a prime candidate for it, as well... Such a long line of animalistic energy would level a county if it worked..."

"How did you become so dead to everything?" Sammie screamed, thrashing against the binds, his eyes sparking with tiny pulses of energy. Not enough to do anything. "You've taken everything away from me, and for what? Because you didn't like what the council was doing? How does that give you any right to completely ruin thousands of lives?"

Alexei gave a close-mouthed grunt, nodding to Áine to go ahead. Miles jerked against the binds, trying everything he could to loosen them. He called out, again and again, hoping that somehow his powers would flood back, that he could get them to safety, stop Alexei and Áine and this entire insane plot of theirs to start a war.

They needed time, they needed help, but Naomi and Eddie were lost somewhere in the woods last he knew. As far as he knew they were all alone. Miles needed to get them out!

Sammie yelled as Áine dragged the blade along his cheek. Blood immediately welled to the surface and coated the dagger.

Miles screamed, pulling against the shackles, his wrists tearing to pieces, before everything went red.

Chapter Twenty-Six

Sammie squeezed his eyes shut against the sting along his cheek, yelling out with the pain. Something on the blade made the cut burn more than it should, as if acid coated the metal. His head throbbed, and his entire body ached. His chest felt tight, and his throat closed around his airways with an incoming panic attack. They were both going to die—there was no way out of this. Sammie's own family was going to murder them, because they were failed by the council. It wasn't fair, but Sammie was quickly learning that nothing in their lives was ever going to be fair.

He flinched, jerking back from the blade, when it sounded like something exploded. Sammie fell from the shackles and smacked his head against the ground with a crack that had his gut swirling. He eased his eyes open, grimacing as everything swirled around him with a dizzying speed that made him feel like he was going to be sick.

A growl, low and loud enough to rattle his ribs, filled the cavern, and Sammie's gaze fell onto a huge, feral-looking wolf, maw as big as the table by them, gold eyes burning with an animalistic rage, shackles around its limbs. A sore-looking wound ripped along its ribs, raw and seeping.

It looks a lot like the wound Miles had.

"Miles?" Sammie whispered, grimacing. Speaking felt like a mallet to his brain. The wolf didn't react, snarling and snapping as it advanced toward Áine. The Seer stared in shock.

"Mad mutt," Áine spat, jerking back as Miles roared and lunged forward, barely missing her face. She looked at Sammie, her expression shifting as her back hit the wall. "Sammie, you wouldn't let your precious mutt murder anyone, would you? He'd regret it, you know it. He's…" She jumped back into the wall as Miles sneered, caging her in. "He's, he's soft. He'd hate himself. You should stop him."

Sammie wasn't sure he could. Not that he wanted to. "I think he could live with himself when it came to you."

Áine's face fell as Miles lunged again. He sank his teeth into her side before he jerked away, and Sammie had to look away, fighting the urge to be sick.

He choked down the feeling, squeezing his eyes tight as bile rose in his throat before he looked back up. It was soon enough to see Miles sprinting out of the cavern, his much larger form easy to spot even through the darkness and the spinning of his splitting head. "Miles, wait!"

Getting to his feet was an ordeal; his limbs didn't quite listen as he tried to move. Running wasn't much better, but Sammie couldn't be separated from him now. He had no idea where his father was, or Nikolas. Constantine may even be down here with them—he had no clue, and he wasn't about to let Miles risk being hurt by any of them.

Thankfully, the narrow path wasn't that long, leading to the forest outside sooner than it should have. Nikolas and Miles were right there at the opening, circling each other. Sammie couldn't see his father, but as long as Miles wasn't hurt. Sammie could worry about him later.

"You really need to learn to keep your guard up, Samuel." The words were whispered in his ear. The blade that Áine had earlier pressed along his throat was coated in something smelling strongly of rot. "You are just as bad as Ashling with that."

Sammie choked, his eyes stinging. He was tired. So tired, and angry, and sad, and exhausted, emotionally, physically, and mentally. "I don't have anything left in me now." He held his hands up, sagging. "Just get it over with. Kill me, whatever. Finish it already."

"That's just the problem," the man muttered, pressing the blade a fraction closer. "I need you alive. It doesn't work with you dead. So, you'll come with me, and if you want your friend to live, you'll listen to what I tell you until we get to where we need to. Make a spectacle of you to the humans... We can come to light in a grand display of destruction."

Sammie watched Miles and Nikolas trade snapping bites and claws, listening to his would-be father drone on and on, saying Sammie had a grand purpose to bring about a new age. He didn't care anymore.

"I have a better idea." Another voice, chipper and cocky and achingly familiar, sounded from behind him. The knife was jerked away from Sammie, giving him the chance to turn to find Eddie standing there. She yanked his father's head back by his throat with her injured arm and used her remaining hand to twist his arm until the blade fell. She winked Sammie's way before tilting his father's head back enough to stare him down eye to eye. *"Go turn yourself in to the council and rot."*

Sammie stared in confusion as a glaze fell over his father's eyes. His body went limp, then simply turned and walked with a purpose into the clutch of the trees. It made no sense. His father had a single-minded focus to start a war, yet a couple of words from Eddie could make him walk off to turn himself in? "What... was that?"

Eddie winked, then looked up past him. Sammie followed her gaze to find Nikolas pinned beneath Naomi and Miles both, the alpha dealing the final blow to his throat, the quick end punctuated by Nikolas sagging to the ground underneath them.

Naomi melted back to her human form, shaking herself out and wiping her arm across her mouth. She spat red to the ground before she looked at Miles. He snorted, settling on the ground and shuddering.

"Miles?" Naomi's voice was worried, and Sammie freed himself from Eddie's careful hand on his shoulder, his insides twisting with anxiety as Miles whimpered.

"He was hurt..." Sammie muttered, crouching by Miles's side and gently pushing the fur away from the still raw wound. It wasn't healing at all—unnaturally black and poisonous-looking red seeped into his dark fur. "They—they used some sort of poison on him. He couldn't shift or anything and then he just...sort of burst into this."

Naomi went quiet, ducking down to check over the wound herself before she hissed. "They used wolfsbane. He shouldn't have been able to shift at all with this unless—unless he went feral."

Sammie frowned, tilting Miles's face toward him slightly. His eyes were not quite human like they normally were. The rage was gone, at least, but it felt like his Miles was far, far away. "Miles...?"

The wolf whined, tongue lapping at his hand, almost apologetic. Sammie's eyes and chest burned. "I can try to clean the wound, and maybe we can heal it but..."

Sammie shuddered. The rest of Naomi's words were clear and painful without her speaking them. Miles might not come back, not soon, maybe not ever. Sammie knew enough about what being feral meant when she spoke about it before, all those weeks ago. There was the chance that his Miles might be long gone.

"Okay..." Sammie choked back the fresh wash of tears

stinging through him. "I'll, I'll help, just...let's help him."

Eddie's hand settled against his back as they worked. The vampire hovered over him, trying to soothe Miles as he whined and fought not to flinch back as Naomi wiped away the wolfsbane. Sammie's hands shook as he settled around the wound, his magic sputtering as he willed the damage to heal.

It was a slow process. Sinew and flesh had shrunk away from the poison and pieced together jagged and wrong, and Naomi had to correct it as Sammie healed. It felt like tearing his heart out and trying to patch it back into his chest every time Miles whined and jerked. Tears poured down his face freely. His eyes never seemed to run dry despite the process taking what could have been hours.

Finally, the sun barely cresting over the horizon, the wound closed, and Miles shakily rose to his feet. Sammie held his breath, hope sitting broken and weak in his throat as the wolf shook himself and looked directly at him. He whined, nuzzling against Sammie's throat, before he pawed back from him, looking at him sadly and shaking his head.

A sob burst out of Sammie, and he lunged forward, wrapping his arms around the wolf's neck, feeling hope and relief and all the love he had for Miles, *his* Miles, who was now gone. He screamed, clutching tight, despite hands trying to pull him back.

It's not fair. It's not fucking fair!

"W-we went through all of this! He sacrificed himself f-for us, and he's g-gone!" Sammie bawled, the wolf whining pathetically as he cried. "It's not fair! It's n-not f-fair!"

The wolf rumbled the same way Miles used to in an attempt to calm him, hooking his head over his shoulder. It hurt; the way it was still so much like him. Sammie could hope, and hope, and hope, and he'd have this facsimile, this "almost" of his best friend, his love that he kept missing being able to have, time and time again.

He really was cursed.

Sammie cried, all his limited energy going into mourning. He bawled until his throat hurt, until the sting of his eyes forced him to keep them sealed, until his sobbing breaths quieted to painful wheezes, and until he finally sagged into the wolf, the whine rattling his exhausted bones.

He was broken, after all of this, after all that running and their last push to get through this ongoing nightmare. As he lost consciousness, careful hands and cautious paws keeping him from the ground, Sammie hoped that he could stay in that sea of black. Away from the utter injustice of coming through all of this, just to lose Miles at the end.

Chapter Twenty-Seven

"You okay?" A familiar southern drawl washed over him, warming Miles's chest as he stirred in the bed. Opening his eyes, Miles found himself back in that room, laughter and music and the sounds of life happening floating through the open window. Ashe was seated beside him, her face worried and sad all at once.

He thought over the question. He was; at least he thought he was. He was in one piece, Sammie was safe, Nikolas and Áine were gone... But, examining it now, Miles felt distraught. But why?

A gentle hand skirted along his jaw, and Miles flinched, focusing back on Ashe as she frowned. "You shouldn't be back here, Miles. You're not here fully, and I didn't bring you here, yet here you are." She tilted her head, worry lines and crow's feet deepening as her anxiety about his presence worsened. "What happened?"

Miles had to comb through his memories, the little missing pieces of the last couple of hours. He remembered hanging in that cavern with Áine and Alexei, eyeing Sammie chained up next to him. He remembered Áine stepping forward with the blade, and reaching out for his wolf, trying desperately to shift. He did, but looking back, how did he do that? The poison that Booker's body had cut into his skin should've made it impossible for him to shift, right? Then...

"I...I don't know," Miles finally answered, sitting up slightly, eyes searching the blanket lying over his lap like it could provide any sort of light on the muddled thoughts in his head. "I was poisoned, with wolfsbane, and I saw Sammie get hurt and... I shouldn't have been able to shift but I did. I don't know how I did, but I remember doing it, and I remember breaking free and snapping at Áine. I remember Naomi there to help with Nikolas, too, but...after that it's all foggy."

Ashe went quiet, and Miles looked up to find unbelievable sadness on her face. She shook her head, reaching out to him with careful hands, settling on his arm much too gently. The care made him anxious, like she was trying to soften her words.

"You know what happened, don't you?" Miles asked, his throat clicking as she nodded solemnly. "Just tell me. We can find a way to fix whatever it is."

Ashe grimaced but obeyed. "I think you went feral." She didn't meet his eyes, focusing instead on her hands skimming careful circles onto his arm. "If I'm honest, I don't know a lot about how you werewolves work, but I've heard enough things about them going feral to know that."

Miles sat up fully. "How—how do I stop it? Like, I'm still here, and like you said, I shouldn't be here, so there has to be a way to go back, right?"

"Like I said, Miles, I don't know." Ashe settled back into her chair. "It seems like your wolf had to take over to help the both of you, and in theory you could try to shift back if you can get your consciousness back to your body."

"Then let's do that." Miles scrambled out of the bed, dusting himself off and standing on shaking legs before Ashe, hoping, praying to gods he didn't believe in that there was a way back. "Just do what you did last time and push me back into my body!"

The mage gave him a sympathetic look before she closed her eyes, taking both of his hands in hers. He watched her eyes move behind her lids, the minutes feeling like hours as she worked. There had to be a way. He couldn't leave all of them behind like this, he just couldn't.

After several moments, the laughter and voices outside setting him on edge with every passing second, Ashe sagged, opening her eyes and releasing his hands. "I...I'm sorry, Miles. I think this is beyond me."

A soft sob bubbled out of his throat as warm tears spilled over his cheeks. "N-no. I... Ashe, I *have* to get back. We're so *close*, I... This can't be it."

Ashe shook her head again, standing up from the chair and

heading to the door. He didn't remember it there from the last time he was in this room, and seeing it filled him with a sense of calm and dread all wrapped into one. Finality.

"I can't do anything for you, Miles. I can let you rest, and keep you company, but...I can't help you go back." She tapped the door. "You might be able to find your way through here, but I can't guarantee anything for you. I can't open the door; everything past that doorway is only something you can do." She hesitated for a moment before drawing Miles into a hug. His breath caught in his chest before it bubbled up as sobs.

He didn't want to go. This wasn't fair. They survived for so long, and Miles couldn't even see them to the end. After everything they'd been through, he broke before the end.

Ashe soothed him for hours as Miles cried until his chest hurt, the sunny sky from outside never changing, but feeling hopelessly depressing all the same.

When he calmed slightly, Ashe pulled back, gently holding his face up to look at her. "It's time, Miles. I wish things were different..."

He hiccupped, brushing away the tears on his cheeks before he faced the door. It was plain and looked perfectly in place in the quaint room, but it still felt ominous. Like an ending he wasn't ready for. The knowledge of what that meant sat like an iron weight in his gut, and before he could back out, Miles stepped forward and opened the door.

*

"You okay?"

Miles blinked, his eyes getting used to the sudden shift from the bright, blinding light that flooded his vision as he opened the door, to...a playground?

Miles sniffled, rubbing his cheek and wincing when he skirted over a wound. Red smeared on his knuckles. His hand was a lot smaller, and it took him longer than it should've for Miles to realize he was somehow younger.

"Careful!" the young voice from before warned, gently taking his hand. "You should go to the nurse."

Miles looked up, and just about startled seeing a much younger Sammie, sandy-blond frizz of hair, the lenses of his glasses smudged and too big for his tiny, freckled face. His face was also streaked with tears, but he was smiling gently at Miles all the same. "Sammie?"

Sammie beamed much bigger then. "Yeah! That's my name. You're a really good guesser." He giggled, then tugged Miles up to his feet. "Here, I'll walk you to the nurse." Miles followed in a mild daze. "Do you like movies? I wanna be in a movie when I grow up. What about you?"

"Uh... I dunno," Miles mumbled, letting himself be tugged along and sucked in to Sammie as he started babbling, so bright and lively like he was before this entire nightmare. It made Miles start crying again, little hiccupping things that had Sammie hugging Miles to his side as they walked to calm him.

They came to a stop at an office—in their old grade school,

he realized—and Sammie turned to him then, looking at him like he was much older than he actually was. "Miles? You're going to be okay. Things will be hard, and time will pass, but you'll be all right at the end," Sammie whispered, cupping Miles's face in his little hands. Miles jolted with the touch slightly, feeling an extra finger on Sammie's hand skimming his cheek. "You just have to be patient with me, and patient with yourself. I will do everything I can to bring you back." Young Sammie brushed gently along his cheeks as he stared at him like it'd been years since they'd seen each other. "Look for your proof—you'll know you're back then. I just have to improve and look for the way to lead you back to me."

Little Sammie leaned forward and pecked the scrape on his cheek before he pulled back, and as suddenly as the playground came into view, all of Miles's surroundings disappeared. Miles gasped, feeling lost and cold, squeezing his eyes shut against the sudden nausea that slammed into him.

Warmth washed over him, and Miles opened his eyes slowly, barely holding back a curse as he found himself in his old bedroom, Sammie sprawled over the bed, blearily staring at a textbook. "Sammie, what...what's going on?"

Sammie glanced up, his gaze shifting to one much more awake. He had his braces still, so...this must've been when they were sophomores. He huffed at Miles, spinning his pencil effortlessly between his fingers, again showcasing the extra digit. His proof he was still not there; Sammie still needed more time.

"We're studying, doofus. Finals week, remember?" Sammie

flopped over so he was dramatically draped over the edge of the bed. "Ah, to be as carefree as you. Alas, I was cursed with a hamster instead of a brain, and if I don't provide some structure, it will run off and I shall then be brainless."

Miles scoffed, falling back into the easy back and forth between them. "You're such a drama queen." He leaned up from his elbows on the floor and smacked a kiss to Sammie's cheek, wiping the overdramatically sorrowful look from his face. "I miss you like this, you know."

Sammie flipped back, pillowing his head on his arms as his expression shifted, again to something that felt too old for how his body looked. "I know. We've been through a lot, though. Maybe someday I can be like this again... You don't like me better like this, though, do you?"

"I just miss you being happy..." Miles hummed, shifting closer to him, wanting so badly to just take Sammie in his arms and never let go.

Sammie pulled back, his expression softening. "I'm plenty happy. Despite everything, you've been the best damn thing that's ever happened to me, and as much as I'd want all of that nightmare to be different, I couldn't be happier with who I ended up with."

Tears stung Miles's eyes, and as soon as he sniffled Sammie reached forward, gently cradling his face and bringing their foreheads together. Miles hiccupped, bringing his own shaking hands up to Sammie's shoulders. "I...I want to be back there, Sammie...

I miss you, and I miss Naomi and Eddie…"

"I know…" Sammie leaned forward to press a gentle kiss to the tip of his nose. "I'm trying. It's taking longer than I thought it would. They're trying to help as much as they can, but things are busy over here." To Miles's dismay, Sammie started to pull back, and Miles cried, trying to hold on. "I'm still working, I promise. Just give me a bit more time, Miles. I swear, we'll see each other soon. In person. Just a little more time."

The cold swept back in, and Miles felt himself yanked back into that weird in between, cold and forgotten. He sobbed, holding himself as he waited, hoping.

It was hard to tell how much time had passed; the blackness around him was suffocating and unforgiving. Miles waited, and waited, curling up as tight as he could and waiting, and waiting.

The first other thing he felt was a touch to his scalp, warm familiar fingers combing into his hair. Six digits again. Miles shuddered, lifting his head to find himself at the hospital.

His stomach swooped—the morbidly familiar building was the last place he wanted to see. It was just the same as it had been months ago: the same droning pages, the same chemical smells, and the same sense of dread and death permeating the halls. The chair he was crunched up in felt exactly like the one where he'd sat waiting for the doctor to come back after his mom's last surgery.

"I'm sorry I wasn't there for you, then." Sammie's voice washed over him, and Miles glanced up, following the hand coiling into his hair to the current Sammie, maybe a touch older than the last time Miles saw him. He was tired, dark puffy bags under his eyes, his glasses changed to newer, golden-rimmed ones that fit his face a bit better, and his hair had grown out a few inches, curls starting to show through. "I tried to find something happier, but it's been hard to direct your consciousness, especially since I've been trying to tie you back to your body."

The words were confusing, he could piece them together, what exactly they meant, but Sammie couldn't do anything like that, could he?

"I've been practicing," Sammie answered, as if he could read Miles's thoughts. "Things have changed a lot since you've been gone. Naomi and Eddie have been helping me in between their work, either by wrangling your body or helping me work with people way more experienced than I am."

"How..." Miles shook his head, sitting up, the setting around them almost faded to the background. "Sam, how much time has passed since then?"

Sammie grimaced, tucking a strand of hair behind Miles's ear. "It's almost up to two years."

Miles sagged, his jaw dropping, a tear trailing down his cheek as the words hit him. *Two years. Two years I've been in this limbo. I've missed out on two years of my life with Sammie.*

"I know..." Sammie whispered, dropping down to a crouch to catch Miles's eyes, his thumb swiping away another tear as he skimmed his fingers along Miles's jaw. "I'm sorry it's taken so long."

"Why are you still trying?" Miles mumbled, staring into Sammie's sad blue eyes. "Why not just give up? Sammie, that's too long for you to waste your time on me."

"Never a waste." Sammie shook his head before he moved forward and traced a chaste kiss along Miles's jaw. "Miles, I love you. You're it for me; you've always been it. If there's the smallest chance I can bring you back to me, I'm going to take it."

Miles whimpered, barely choking back a sob. "Sammie, I—"

"Wait." Sammie brushed his fingers softly along Miles's jaw. "Tell me in person, when you're back."

An overhead page cut through their little world, his name calling him to the desk to meet with the doctor, and it was as if that one thing pulled him away from Sammie, sucking him back into the darkness. After a split second of hesitation, Sammie spoke again, his voice carrying the slightest glimmer of hope as Miles was dragged back down.

"Just a little while longer, I'm almost done, and you'll be able to tell me then."

*

Time passed in snippets, moments of his life spent with Sammie in secret little moments, time outside passing in unknown increments. It was mostly the same every time; Miles relieving a memory that may or may not have Sammie involved, and Sammie would break through the normal memory to talk with him.

It was the same, until it wasn't.

Miles woke up slowly, feeling sluggish and worn through. He was in a bed he didn't recognize, the room around him completely new. The walls were bare wood, a rich cherry with a few pictures tacked up. The bed was wide, one side made, with a large tome on the nightstand along with a few drink glasses and an ornate iron lamp. The table beside him was bare, only a scrap of paper and a matching lamp there.

The rest of the room was also undone, a single dresser, a wardrobe, and a full body mirror. As Miles sat up, he took stock of himself. His side stretched awkwardly as he moved, and he found a jagged scar cutting across above his hipbone. He'd also found his hair had grown out, now reaching between his shoulders, his stubble evolved to a full-blown beard. He...was he back?

He looked to the nightstand again, grabbed up the scrap of paper, and glanced at it. There it was, Sammie's scrawl, just a few simple words scribbled there.

Back yard your Proof

Miles scrambled up, his heart pounding in his chest. He barely paid any attention to anything else, running out of the bedroom into the main part of the house, looking around briefly through a cozy kitchen, a large bay window showing a wooded backyard, a swing gently swaying with the person in it just out of sight. He threw open the door leading out, barely stopping from stumbling down the stairs as he ran out to the swing, panting as...as Sammie looked up at him, mirth spreading from ear to ear, waving his five-digited hand with a smug little finger wiggle.

Proof. He was back, somehow. Sammie dragged him back.

"Hi." Sammie stopped the gentle motion of the swing to stand and tug Miles into an almost crushing hug. "God...it's been so long..."

Miles let out a simpering whine, pulling Sammie as close as he possibly could. "How...how did you..."

"I told you I wasn't going to give up, didn't I?" Sammie teased, his bright-blue eyes shimmering behind the golden frames.

"Yeah..." Miles laughed wetly, drawing in a choppy sob as he brushed his fingers along Sammie's cheek. He was so beautiful, tiny wisps of grey at his temples, his crow's feet showcasing the age he wore, a little scar on his jaw. "I missed so much..."

Sammie gave a small shrug. "That's why we're starting where we left off now. Which..." He leaned his head to one side, looking just a touch mischievous. "I remember you saying you were going to tell me something when all of this was over."

Miles tucked Sammie's hair behind his ear before tilting his face up. "I love you, Sammie."

The words were practically smothered as Sammie surged up to kiss him. The world felt like it was settling back into place, that hole in Miles's chest filled with all the love and care and effort Sammie put in to bring Miles back.

They parted, slow, like waking up from a dream, and Sammie giggled, tears washing over his face, smelling like relief and home and joy as bright as sunshine. "Guess I got pretty good at that whole decisions thing, huh?"

Little menace.

Miles pulled Sammie back, hitching him into his arms to carry him into the house while they kissed. They had the rest of their lives now, and Miles was going to live this second chance he had to the fullest, starting as soon as he could.

About the Author

Jo M Aring is based in Kansas City, working in mental health by day, plunking away on her many works-in-progress by night. She is a moderately loud but supremely proud lesbian, who dabbles in D&D, video games, and whatever sparks her serotonin.

Email
jmaring_author@outlook.com

Facebook
https://www.facebook.com/share/1AC5kvQT3w

Twitter
www.x.com/rarajoeyanna

Connect with NineStar Press

Website: NineStarPress.com

Facebook: NineStarPress

X: @NineStarPress

Instagram: NineStarPress

BlueSky: NineStarPress

Threads: @NineStarPress